MW00736635

The Changing Tide

Laura,
Thanks for all
the support! ♡

The Changing Tide

Book One of Rogue Elegance

K A Dowling

Copyright © 2016 K A Dowling
All rights reserved.

ISBN-13: 9780692773314
ISBN-10: 0692773312
Library of Congress Control Number: 2016914375
Kelly Dowling, Sharon, MA

For Sam, who has been besting me in epic swordfights since we were old enough to walk.

Acknowledgements

WHEN I FIRST published Rogue Elegance in the fall of 2015, it came out in what could rightly be called a tome. I put the story together the way I wanted it to be put together, with Emerala and Nerani's story as one, cohesive unit.

Spending a year immersed in the heavily saturated, high-paced literary world has led me to decide a Second Edition publication is good and ready for its moment in the sun. The newest edition has allowed me to make some tweaks and right some wrongs that have been plaguing me for a while (Yes, that means James Byron no longer defies science and fills his air with lungs, a typo that several people including myself managed to miss, and one has unfortunately become a popular anecdote around the dinner table at holidays).

With a shiny new Second Edition copy comes another round of people to thank, some old and some new. Thanks to my mom and dad for endless phone conversations listening to me spout off theories and edits and harebrained schemes. As always, they've been my loudest cheerleaders from the very first day, and I probably would have given up a long time ago if it wasn't for them. I want to thank my dad for being my date to writer's conferences, and for dutifully helping me learn everything I can about the world of publishing. He's got a brain for business, whereas there seems to be little space in my brain for anything reality-based, and I couldn't have accomplished the things I've accomplished this past year without he and my mom keeping me firmly rooted.

I also want to thank my husband for graciously accepting his role as a permanent sounding board. He is always ready and willing to listen. I'm grateful to him for continuing to tolerate me in spite of the fact that our evening walks are often comprised of me alternating between yammering about my characters and stopping in the middle of the road to catch Pokémon.

Thanks to Liz, the real-life Nerani the Elegant, for always being willing to read, reread, and read again when I am neck deep in edits and on the verge of pulling out my hair. She is probably one of the few people that understands the psyche of my characters as deeply and as thoroughly as I do, and I couldn't have accomplished any of this without her.

Amanda, Kat, and Catherine, you ladies rock, and you've been fantastic support systems when it comes to getting the word out there. Thank you also to Danielle, Elizabeth, Bekah, Emily, Nicole, Hilary, Amber, Rebekah and Allison for tolerating my endless social media spam and always being willing to share my book related posts. Aunt Peggy and Auntie Rachel, thank you for being fans of the story, and for always making me feel like it's worth it to keep writing, even when I'm not so readily convinced. Hilary, thank you again for kick starting this whole process with your feedback and copyediting. You have a fantastic eye for picking up all the things I've missed, and you somehow always know exactly what it is I'm trying to say—even when I don't. Vikki, thanks for the stunning visual on the cover, you knew exactly what I was looking for and how to execute it.

Last but not least, thanks to you, the reader, for picking up this little book and giving it a chance. I really hope you fall in love with the world of Chancey as deeply as I have fallen in love with it over the years.

This story is Emerala's story. It's Nerani's story. But most of all, it's my story. I hope you enjoy every minute.

Kelly

The Mame's Portent
Delivered to King Lionus Wolham
In the sixteenth year of his reign
Harvest Cycle 1402

Who are you,
The seer asked,
That knows his fate is set?
Your day will come
Your line will fall
Your people will abet.
But in the babe
So soft and pure
Your bloodline will be spared
She'll fall to dust
And dust she'll be,
Forgotten by the erred.
And when the years,
They roll away
Knowing what's to come
Her blood with blood
Will mingle true—
A queen she will become.

"…And on the fifth day of the feast, in the fourteen hundredth and third Harvest Cycle, Lord Stoward rose up and struck the Wolham king from his throne. His sons were slain upon the steps of the palace. Their blood stained the streets of Chancey. The queen was stripped of her fineries and tied to the stake in the marketplace. She burned before the people as her crimes were read. Witch, she was called. Conjurer of the old magics.

The infant, the child, was never found. The Stoward usurper searched to no avail, but she was gone. Her memory faded to dust, whispers of her name were stolen away by passing years. Her father's armor was left to rot in the hall of kings.

But the prophecy remained.

When the heir of Saynti joins the blood of Cairans and the blood of royalty, then shall the Wolham line be restored to the Chancian throne."

Excerpt from Chancey: A Written History
By Scribner Littleton

Harvest Cycle 1511
Chancey

Alarana,
Read this letter once and let it burn.

    I am setting sail today. I know you are angry with me. You must trust me when I tell you there is no other choice. I did this for you. I did this for our children.

    Through my sins I have evoked something older and darker than either of us can possibly comprehend. My mistakes have led to this, and only mine. I am deeply apologetic for any suffering they have caused you.

    You asked me, once, how far I would be willing to go to keep our children safe. I told you I would go to the ends of the world. I meant that.

    I do not know what fate awaits me at the end of this journey, but I take solace in knowing that you and the children will be unharmed in my absence.

Alarana, it is the only way.

Roberts and Emerala are only children. They will forget me quickly. And you—you, too, will forget. Your heart will heal, in time.

Please know that my deepest regret is causing you pain.

Destroy this letter. In the wrong hands, it can be deadly.

Be safe, and know that I did love you, once.

Eliot Roberts

Chancey Harvest Cycle 1525 Midnight

THE GUARDIANS COME quietly that night. Their footsteps go unheard against the din that fills the walls of Toyler's Tavern and spills out onto the murky street. For a moment, they linger before the entrance, bright and clean and out of place. They shuffle their feet against the cobblestone, their mouths settling into deep frowns. Their noses wrinkle at the putrid stench that leaches out from the sewers.

Their golden cloaks catch upon a gust of brackish wind as they shove through the squealing doorway. The inebriated occupants of the room fall into stillness at the sight of them. A jangling tambourine shudders to a stop. In the corner, a silk-clad woman shrinks into the shadows. Her instrument falls to her side with a tinny clatter. All about the room, dark eyes glitter in the dancing torchlight. These soldiers are not expected. They are not welcome. Silence nestles sluggishly into the air, dense with smoke.

Behind the bar, Manfred Toyler watches with bated breath. His beady eyes follow the soldiers as they make their way towards him. He places the glass he is cleaning down upon the bar, startling at the sound it makes. It is too loud against the formidable silence of the room—too crisp against the climate of dread that strings among the rafters. A cold sweat forms upon his brow. He moves to mop it up with his kerchief and pauses, his hand freezing before his nose as the guardians take their seats at the bar. Their faces—newly shaven—sneer at him through the tendrils of smoke that dissipate around them.

Toyler clears his throat. He tilts his chin in a show of respect.

"General Byron." His voice ekes out in a throaty croak. "Corporal Anderson."

"Mr. Toyler." Corporal Anderson's acknowledgement is nonchalant. His slick silver hair catches the light as he glances idly at the room about him. His face, long and narrow, looks as though it could have been carved from stone. His long, crooked lips curl downward into a sneer.

Toyler's tongue feels as though it is coated with sand. "What can I get you gentlemen?" He knows they will not ask for anything. He already knows why they are here.

Before him, General Byron's deep brown eyes are cold. "We're on duty. We've come to visit you strictly on business." His fingers flick at an invisible speck atop the bar. His close-cropped brown hair appears black and oily in the shadows.

Toyler thinks of Thomas of the Wandering Lady and how all that the guardians left was the faded, splintering sign. He thinks of how the fire had spiraled up towards the muddy clouds overhead, and how he had never seen so much smoke. He frowns, fighting to keep his gaze even. He will continue to play the fool.

"What possible business can you have in my humble establishment?"

Corporal Anderson laughs. The echo knocks into Toyler with crippling force. He presses his toes deeper into the soles of his worn leather boots. Steady.

"I hardly think you need to ask." The corporal's sneer widens, but it does not quite spread to his eyes. "You all but keeled over when we stepped inside your bar. A sure sign of a guilty man, don't you think?"

"Guilty?" Toyler repeats. His laugh chokes off in his throat before it can reach his lips. "Guilty of what?"

"Of harboring criminals." The volume behind General Byron's voice is intentional. His words project across the room. His gaze is impassive as he studies Toyler's reaction. The swift shuffling of many garments follows his words. Toyler does not dare to glance over their shoulders. He can feel the dark, sobering gazes scrutinizing the soldiers' golden cloaks. He can hear the treacherous whispers roll across the tavern like a swollen wave.

The guardians before him act as though they are oblivious to the sudden, muffled clamor that overtakes the room. They remain resolutely still upon their stools, their faces blank. Toyler feels his brow deepen across his forehead. Angry heat seeps through his veins.

"How much has Rowland Stoward promised you, General?" Toyler's hands shake as he speaks. He places them beneath the bar and hopes that the soldiers will not notice. General Byron's dark eyes disappear and reappear as he blinks slowly.

When the soldier speaks, it is as though he is speaking to a child. "His Majesty does not bribe his Golden Guard, Mr. Toyler. And he certainly does not deal in the dirty gambles of common men. He is merely attempting to clean up the trash that litters his city."

Toyler sputters angrily. His fist comes down unbidden upon the surface of the bar. "Cleaning up my customers is more like it! You're raking away all my income in one attack after another!" He leans forward, lowering his voice to a murmur as he looks General Byron dead in the eyes. "Your father never would have stood for this, James, not if he was alive."

General Bryon remains silent. The square line of his jaw is locked as he surveys Toyler coldly, but Toyler swears he can see a flash of pain in the young soldier's eyes. Toyler feels a palm press into his chest. He glances up to see that Corporal Anderson has stood from his stool.

"Stand down, you fool," he commands. His brown eyes glimmer with naked disdain. "You will address your superiors with the respect they are owed."

Toyler's mouth snaps shut. He rolls back onto his heels. His breathing comes in ragged pulls as he attempts to settle his nerves. Behind the guardians, the room has gone still.

"What's next, General?" he asks. Sweat has broken out in glistening beads upon the bald curve of his scalp. "Have you come to shackle me and make an example of me before all of the good people of Chancey?"

"Not just yet."

"What about them? Are you to round them up like swine and throw them in prison?" Toyler can hardly keep the poison from lacing his words.

General Byron's voice is detached as he speaks. "No one blames the king for wanting to rid his realm of gypsy scum."

There is the abrasive scrape of chairs across the floor as a few customers rise from where they sit. The pellet bells of a tambourine clink together as a woman gasps. Toyler thinks he sees the candlelight catching on a dagger or two, but he dares not look away from the guardians before him.

"Quiet," he hisses. His beady eyes have narrowed into slits. He is through with respect. There are more frightening men than the guardians lurking in the shadows of the tavern. "Do you wish to start a brawl? You will not win, James, against the wrath of Cairans."

At his words, General Byron rises from his stool to join the standing corporal. A cold smile settles across his jaw. His eyes flash dangerously in the candlelight.

"I will not play games with you or your customers, Mr. Toyler. I came here tonight to deliver a warning. Stop serving the Cairans."

"And if I don't?"

A smirk teases at the corners of the corporal's lips. Next to him, General James Byron draws himself up to his full height. He appears malicious beneath the wavering shadows. "I am not a patient man. Have them cleared out by tomorrow or I'll burn this place to the ground."

With that, the two guardians turn on their heels and head out the door as quickly and quietly as they came.

CHAPTER 1

Emerala the Rogue

THE SKY ABOVE the sea is red this morning. Red, the color of blood. Red, the symbol of death. Red, the harbinger of doom. Red skies in the morning are an omen, everyone who knows anything about anything knows as much. Emerala the Rogue, of course, knows a great deal about a lot of things. More than most people know, and she would bet good coppers on that—if she ever had any coppers to spare. She stands with her back to the sheer cliffs of Chancey and studies the deep crimson reflection that cuts through the black surface of the sea. It looks, to her, like the ocean is bleeding.

Gooseflesh blooms like buds upon the exposed skin of her arms. She shivers, catching her elbows in her fingertips. A cloak would have been fair protection against the crisp morning, but it is not her nature to think of such things. She takes a step forward, pressing her weight down upon her heels. Dull grooves appear in the sand beneath her pleated forest green gown.

The surf at her toes is deepest black, untouched by the fingers of gold that have begun to seep into the sky at her back. The spring storm that passed over the island the night before had raged with a terrible vengeance. The waves are still brimming with vigor; their crests are cut with shadows as deep and as dark as an onyx. Overhead, muffled daylight is streaking across the bloody sky like a whisper.

Emerala watches the morning unfold before her through narrowed green eyes. The wind tugs at her locks, black as night and coiled like a cat waiting to spring. She revels in this time of day—when the citizens of Chancey are only beginning to stir in their cots. She imagines them warm beneath their itching wool blankets, scowling at the frost that clings to their windowpanes. They do not know what they are missing beyond the crumbling walls of their reeking, stacked homes. They do not know what it is to watch the rise and fall of the sea—to shield their eyes against the glittering sun as it tickles the dark edges of the waves at her feet. Chancians do not venture beyond the shaded cliff walls that loom heavy at her backside. They remain tucked away within their fortress. Protected. Ignorant.

She feels a pull in her chest as she stares out at the empty horizon. The merchants arrived with the turn of the seasons. Their white sails were full of wind and their holds teeming with goods from lands that Emerala is certain she will never see. Her lips turn downward into a frown. It is all well and good to bicker and barter over prices with the aggressive, feathered men of trade, but it is not merchandise that her heart desires.

She stares at the space where the sea meets the sky until tears prick at her lower lids. She blinks and her thick black lashes sweep against her olive skin. She remembers the previous spring and the longing she felt within her gut as the season gave way to the orange heat of summer. The merchants, plump and sweating beneath their doublets, had packed up their tents and loaded the ships with whatever goods they had not managed to sell in the marketplace.

She had been in a fit that summer, and the heat made her restless. She forced her way down to the royal ports, her bare feet slapping upon the splintering gilded wood of the docks. Shouting up to the men onboard the nearest ship, she had all but demanded that she be allowed to stow away below deck. *I'll clean*, she promised, her green eyes glittering in earnest. *You won't even know I'm there.*

The crew laughed in her face. *Women en't allowed on board,* they called down at her. Their black eyes were lost in the grooves of their sun-baked skin. *Bad luck.*

The memory of their mockery is as stark as though it happened yesterday. She is doomed; it seems, to rot away on the same island for the remainder of her existence.

The sun finally begins to peek its cylindrical yellow head over the cliffs. The golden warmth of spring prickles against the exposed flesh of her shoulders. The tide is coming in faster than she expected. The sea growls hungrily. It tears at the sand before her with white, foaming claws. It reminds Emerala of the feral dogs from the tangled green forest that borders the outskirts of Chancey. She gathers the fabric of her gown in her fists and places a toe into the lapping waves. A shiver runs down her spine. The water is like ice.

She is faintly aware of the time that passes as she stands idle before the rumbling sea. Her cousin will be awake and seeking her in the marketplace. She sighs. Her green eyes sweep the horizon once again. The sea before her is empty.

"Cairan."

The voice that reaches her ears over the subdued roar of the waves startles her out of her reverie. She spins about on her heels. Her black coils bounce against her taut cheekbones. A few yards down the beach stands a man. He stands tense and coiled like a snake ready to spring, watching her carefully through unreadable brown eyes. His golden cloak is slung uselessly over his right shoulder. It encompasses his silhouette as it becomes ensnared in the brutish wind that rolls in off of the ocean.

A grin spreads across Emerala's face as she recognizes the man immediately.

"General Byron." The voice that leaks out from between her lips overflows with practiced courtesy. "Good morning."

"Rogue." The young guardian nods brusquely in greeting. She bristles at the sound of her pseudo-name upon his tongue. He squares his jaw and continues. "It isn't proper for a woman to wander the beach without an escort."

She keeps her voice light. "Is it not proper for a woman to wander alone, or for a gypsy to be out in the open for all to see?"

He ignores her, taking several steps closer across the sand. His boots leave shallow indentations in his wake. "You're out of the protection of the city. The Golden Guard cannot guarantee your safety beyond the walls of Chancey."

"I'm quite satisfied that you and your men care nothing for my well-being."

"You would be wise to head back into the city." His voice is tight. His brown eyes stare at an invisible entity directly above her head.

"Why?" she inquires. She closes the gap between them, swinging her hips as she walks. "Do you suspect that I am up to no good?"

Before her, the general remains silent. She detects the first twinkle of impatience in his dark gaze.

"If you do, then you're quite right." The sea swallows the echo of her laugh. "I'm never up to anything good."

Again, the general holds his tongue. His eyes snap back down towards her face. Emerala expels a deep sigh. "You're boring today, General. And here I was hoping for some excitement to add to my morning."

One corner of the guardian's mouth twitches. If Emerala did not know better, she would have thought him to be biting back a smile.

"I know by now that it's not wise to get tangled up in your games, Rogue."

"Fine." She proffers an indiscernible shrug. "I was heading back anyhow. The tide will be at the cliff walls within the hour."

She pushes her way past the guardian; ignoring the dark look he shoots her as she walks by. He says nothing else as she makes her way down the narrowing stretch of sand.

The way back to the city is closed to commoners. The royal ports, golden and glittering in the morning sun, are the easiest way by which to access the steep gilded staircase that winds its way up to the top of the cliffs. Emerala knows without a doubt that the general took the staircase in order to access the beach that morning. After all, it is his men that stand guard at the top.

They will not permit her to pass in and out by way of the king's docks. It is only the noble men and women of Chancey that are authorized to access the staircase. Even then they must provide sound reasoning for their visit to the docks. Only in the spring do the guardians grow more lenient, allowing merchants and the like to drag their carts of foreign goods into the marketplace.

Emerala lives for the spring. In the decaying autumn and frost bitten winter she hungers for the flurry of sights and smells and strangers that clog the narrow streets of Chancey. It is a reprieve from the rest of her boring, pitiful year, when she is required to make up her own fun and unjustly expected to stay out of trouble. She thinks, too, that it is the only time that pirates are likely to slip unnoticed into their midst, swaggering with drink and disguised as merchants.

She pauses to watch the golden docks glisten in the sun. The ships that are anchored in port are all far too well maintained to belong to the barbaric men of the high seas. It is just as well. Her elder brother has been keeping a closer eye on her this year after he discovered her failed attempt at stowing away upon the merchant ships the previous summer. If pirates have managed to manipulate their way into Chancey, she is sure her brother will not allow her within a mile of the taverns where they set up shop. While the merchants would not permit her to board their ships, pirates most certainly will. They are a fearless sort of men, and she is certain that men who kill you as soon as look at you are not frightened of anything as intangible as luck.

Emerala can feel the general's eyes upon her back as she dithers upon the sand. She fights the urge to roll her eyes. *He worries too much*, she thinks. As though she can get into any sort of trouble out in the open, surrounded by nothing but sand and sea.

To her right, the sheer wall of the cliff splits into a broken partition. It is here that she and the other Cairans of Chancey are able to descend and ascend without being interrogated by the Golden Guard. Years and years of erosion have worn away at the surface of the cliff. The corrosion, coupled with the man-made path cut by centuries of feet plodding up and down, have created a natural stairwell of sorts. She heads towards the stairwell, careless of General Byron's watchful gaze. She is certain that the guardian is already aware of the stairwell's existence. No one really cares what her people do to occupy themselves, as long as they stay out of underfoot and do not garner any negative attention. She is certain, in fact, that the general would have been perfectly content had she lingered on the beachfront for too long and washed away in a riptide.

One less Cairan for the Stoward king to worry himself sick over, she thinks ruefully as she begins her ascent.

She thinks as she walks that it was rather odd, looking back, to run into the general alone on the beach. It is unlike the guardians to spend any of their time beyond the cliffs of Chancey. The island is a fortress, protected on all sides by the nearly impenetrable precipice. History has proven the golden naval ships unnecessary for the protection of the small island, and the guardians even less so. These days, the men of the Golden Guard are more brute force than anything. They are responsible for keeping the lower class Chancians from embarrassing his royal majesty, the rotten king whose name the young woman can never seem to remember. Her nose wrinkles in consideration. She wishes she had thought to interrogate the general further. He despises when she asks him questions.

She reaches the top of the staircase, panting only slightly. Up ahead looms the grimy edge of the city. It is nothing more than crumbling brick and perpendiculars, stacked in heaps and staining the sky with soot. Emerala's eyes narrow into slits at the sight of it. The wind that whistles through the constricted alleyways before her threatens to bowl her over as it careens over the edge of the cliff. The roar of the sea that she so loves has grown muted with her climb. As she presses her bare feet downward into the loam she allows her ears to readjust to the clatter of carts and the bickering of businessmen that cascade towards her, carried out of the city upon the breeze. The smell of baking bread reaches her nose and her stomach growls. She follows the scent hungrily.

She enters a narrow roadway, shivering against the shadows that stain her flesh. The cobblestones are pressed tightly between the mildew eaten sides of two stone buildings. Before her, the alley empties out into a bustling pedestrian street. A horse drawn cart rolls by and she listens to the slow, lazy clip-clop of the animal's hooves upon the cobblestone. It sounds discordant paired with the squeaky complaining of the worn down wheels.

Apart from a reeking drunkard and his cat, she is the only occupant of the alley. Alone. That is exactly how she prefers to spend her time. She ambles along, watching shards of hazy golden light spill down through the lines of dank and moldering laundry that someone has strung from window to window.

"What are you doing?" The voice that snaps at her from beneath the hood of the drunkard is startlingly familiar and decidedly feminine. Emerala starts, whirling about on her heels.

"Nerani?" she asks, astonished. "What are *you* doing?"

A sigh; exasperated. Emerala watches as the drunkard, now revealed to be her cousin, rises to her feet. Folds of the young woman's indigo gown fall out from beneath the patched and putrid cloak she wears about her shoulders. With a screech, the ragged cat leaps to the cobblestones. It hisses up at Nerani, arching its back and baring its sharp, white teeth.

"Oh, be gone with you," Nerani cries. Her toes protrude from beneath the gown to shoo the creature away. "Go, you smelly thing!"

Emerala watches the feline slink off into the shadows. "I don't think it's the cat that smells." She fights the urge to cover her nose with her fingers.

Nerani removes her hood, revealing a pair of stark blue eyes. Her dark brown hair falls about her face and cascades down her backside. Even donned in a tattered and ugly garment, she is uncommonly beautiful. Golden sunlight plays upon her fair skin as she leans down and scoops a chipped mug off of the stones at her feet. Emerala hears the clatter of coins in the bottom of the cup.

"You were gone when we woke up this morning," Nerani accuses, her eyes upon the mug. "I had to invent some absurd story to appease Roberts. You know how he worries." Her lips move silently as she counts her earnings. Emerala thinks of her brother and wonders just how irate he had been to find her absent upon awaking.

"I went for a walk," she explains with a shrug. "You know, you would make more dancing in the marketplace than pretending to be some ugly, old drunk in the corner."

The tinny sliding of the coins stops. Nerani's eyes snap up from her counting. "Roberts made me promise I would keep a low profile today. He wishes you would as well." Her shapely eyebrows drop in suspicion. "Where did you go walking? I've been all over the marketplace and not seen you once."

Emerala ignores the inquiry. "Why is Rob so concerned with always spoiling all our fun?"

"Answer my question."

"Sorry." Emerala fusses with a stray coil of hair that has fallen into her eyes, thinking absently. "What was it?"

"Emerala—" Nerani chides, impatient. The coins rattle in the mug as she drops her slender arm down by her side in agitation.

Stifling a groan, Emerala relents. "I went for a walk on the beach. Just to watch the sunrise, nothing more."

Pink heat flushes across Nerani's cheekbones. "Are you mad?" she whispers. "If Roberts finds out—"

Emerala cuts her off before she can finish. "He won't. You won't breathe a word, and neither will I."

Nerani's full lips drop into a sullen frown. She surveys Emerala in silence for a moment before speaking. "Fine. But please don't go back down there again. Word is that the guardians have spotted a brigand ship off to the north."

Pirates. Emerala fights to keep her gaze even as her chest swells with excitement. She places her hand in the small of her back and crosses her fingers. *Don't let them pass by the island without docking,* she wishes silently. There are plenty of small, secluded islands that rise out of the water a few miles off of the western shore of Chancey. If they want to visit Chancey, they will find a way. Her mind wanders to the general, and how his presence on the beach that morning was unusual.

He was watching for the ship, she concludes, although it still does not feel like a satisfying answer.

Nerani has gone back to counting her coins.

"Is that why Rob wants us to stay out of trouble today?" Emerala asks.

"What?" Nerani murmurs, distracted by her counting. She glances up at Emerala, taking several moments to realize what has been asked of her. "Oh. No. According to Tayland the Con, the guardians threatened to burn Toyler's tavern last night."

Emerala thinks of the Wandering Lady and how it had been set aflame only weeks before. The streets were suffocated with smoke the entire afternoon. No one knew whether or not the owner was inside when the fire was started. His charred corpse was not discovered among the ruins, and yet no one has seen him since. The guardians posted a sign outside the wreckage the very next day.

Burned for condoning the practice of witchcraft and for abetting the antics of the lawless Cairans, the slanted writing read. It was a scare tactic, and it worked. For days afterwards the taverns across the outer portions of Chancey were empty of the usual drunken revelers.

Yet it had only lasted for just that—days. The taverns were full again before the week was up, and the guardians had said not a word.

Emerala reflects upon the incident as she rolls back and forth upon the balls of her feet. She has snuck into the Wandering Lady many a time to steal a dram of ale and listen to the local chatter. Never once did she see anyone practicing anything that could resemble witchcraft. She scrunches her face in thought, wondering if the guardians would be so bold as to burn down another tavern. Clearly it had not been successful the first time around. Emerala decides that Nerani's sources must be false. Tayland the Con is a drunk and a liar.

"How does Tayland know anything?" she demands.

Nerani takes a moment before answering, sorting her coins into a pouch that she keeps tucked away in her black-laced corset.

"He was there," she says at last. "According to him, General Byron himself paid Manfred Toyler a visit to deliver the message. Roberts went by the tavern today to talk to Manny. The king's tolerance for our people is growing shorter every day, it seems."

"I saw the general on the beach," Emerala says. The words slip out from between her lips before she can call them back.

Nerani's eyes enlarge into perfect circles of blue. "This morning? Saynti, Emerala," she curses. "What did you say to him?"

"Nothing exciting. We exchanged pleasantries. I went on my way, and he on his."

Nerani shakes her head, baffled. "How is it that everything is a game to you? Cairans have been disappearing left and right, and General Byron is behind the arrests. Roberts asks us to lay low and you spend your morning ruffling the feathers of the golden elite."

"I didn't ruffle any feathers."

"Maybe not today, but there's a reason the general knows your name, Emerala the Rogue." She shakes one slender finger in Emerala's direction, scolding her. "If you keep getting into trouble in the market the way you have been you'll be the next Cairan to go missing."

"I know that," Emerala huffs. "I'm not dense."

"Sometimes I wonder," Nerani mutters under her breath. Emerala sulks, jutting out her lower lip. If Nerani sees, she feigns ignorance. "I didn't make nearly as much as I'd hoped," she remarks, squinting into her pouch before tucking it back into her corset. "And I've been out here all morning."

"I keep telling you—you should be dancing. The merchants and their crews would have showered you with coins. They're always entranced by gypsies."

"And be run off by the guardians?" Nerani asks. "I'm not you, Emerala."

"You know, you used to be much more entertaining."

Nerani opens her mouth to offer a retort but is cut off by the jolting sound of a gun being fired. The cousins jump at the noise. The sound ricochets off of the narrow walls of the alleyway. The echo is trailed almost immediately by the wild barking of dogs. From the street beyond come the discordant shouts of men and women alike. A horse lets out a shrill whinny.

"Look!" Nerani exclaims, pointing. Beyond the rooftop of one of the buildings plumes of heavy black smoke are billowing upwards. They drift apart among the clouds, dirtying the bottoms of the engorged masses with ugly grey residue.

"Do you think—" Emerala lets her question die upon her tongue. It has to be Toyler's. She thinks of Rob and feels her heart drop to the pit of her stomach. She grabs hold of her cousin's arm. Nerani's mouth has fallen open. Emerala drags her down the alleyway, heading straight for the street outside the alleyway. Instinct tells her to head away from the smoke—to double back and make for the cliffs and the fresh air. Already, the heat is blazing in her throat.

She cannot turn around—she has to see for herself.

Her eyes fill with stinging tears. The cinders carried in by the ashen wind feel as though they are tearing at her face. She emerges into the street, tugging Nerani behind her. They are met by such pandemonium that they at once fall back into the entrance of the alley. Screams and shouts split through the rancid air. The smoke is so thick that Emerala can only make out the vague outlines of people running past. A child is crying somewhere nearby. Its plaintive wail pervades the air about them. A black, rider-less stallion gallops across their paths. Emerala listens to the uneven clatter of the horse's hooves upon the cobblestones as they swell to a steady thunder and then fade upon the wind.

"Come on," she says. She tugs at Nerani's arm. Her mouth fills with tendrils of searing smoke and she coughs.

"Where are you going?" Nerani has found her voice. She withdraws her arm from Emerala's grasp. Panic is pooling in her dark blue eyes.

"I want to see the tavern."

"Why?" Nerani snaps, annoyed. She shakes her head. "I'm not going to parade further into this disaster to satisfy your galling curiosity."

"Someone was shot, Nerani. Killed."

"We don't know that for sure."

The cinders are alighting on Emerala's exposed shoulders, singing her flesh. "What if it was Rob?"

Nerani hesitates, swallowing thickly. "It wasn't."

"How can you know? He went to speak with Toyler today. You said so yourself."

"That was early this morning," Nerani says. "I'm sure he's long gone by now."

The look that Emerala flashes her cousin is mutinous. Nerani sighs; coughing as she swallows the stinging smoke. "We can't, Toyler's will be crawling with guardians. It's not safe. We'll go home. Roberts will be there waiting."

"What if he isn't?" A thin film of soot covers Emerala's arms. Her skin itches.

Nerani frowns. Her blue eyes are bright against the streaks of smut upon her face. "He will be," she promises. Her voice is firm but her lower lip trembles all the same. Emerala thinks that she does not look as certain as she sounds.

All the same, she allows her cousin to take her arm and lead her down the smoke filled alleyway towards home. Her heart thuds heavily against her rib cage, keeping in time with her footfalls against the street. Overhead, the mid-morning sun is a muddled white circle of light. It fights to burn its way through the angry screen of smoke that is stretching across the sky. Emerala thinks of the sunrise that morning—of how the sky had been as red as blood, as violent as death. She thinks of Roberts, and of the creases that splinter around his emerald green eyes whenever she does something that causes him grief.

All thoughts of pirates and of guardians and of the open sea dissolve from her mind as she runs.

Please be at home, she begs her brother silently. *Please.*

CHAPTER 2

Seranai the Fair

THE GREY-EYED WOMAN'S memories of her childhood are not pleasant ones. Her father, a butcher and a drunkard, belonged to the commonwealth of Chancey. He wed and bed her Cairan mother on a drunken whim and then spent the next ten years of his life regretting his decision with the back of his hand and the smooth leather of his belt.

Cairans are worthless, he would say to her when she was just a toddler, still bouncing upon her mother's lap. *You are worthless.*

And so she grew, surrounded by the smells of fermented ale and spoiling meat, hating her mother and her people for poisoning her blood with worthlessness. When her father finally died—drank himself to death they said—she did not cry. She stood beside her mother and watched while they buried him in the dirt.

Spoiled meat, that was all she thought. The bruise upon her cheek had by then faded to yellow. No one ever bought the spoiled meat when they came to see the butcher. It was good for nothing but pig slop. It was worthless.

Standing at her father's grave, her thoughts ran wild. He may have been gone, but she was still alive, and she did not belong anywhere. He made certain she knew her place before he went.

Her mother's people adored her. They fussed over her white blonde shock of hair, her startling grey eyes. Seranai the Fair, the Mames called her when she was of age. They admired her flaxen features and her quiet reserve. *Such a prim little girl*, they said. It was laughable, their praise. Who was to know that she was only submissive because he had beaten her into it? The bruises had long since faded—the feelings had not. Cairan blood was worthless blood.

And so she had grown in silence, biding her time and waiting for her chance to rise into worth.

Now, she stands against the backdrop of a swirling inferno, listening to the rush of screams that hurry towards her through the narrow, empty alleyway in which she stands. The roadway is choked with smoke. Tendrils of blistering orange heat snap restlessly against a soiled grey sky. The Chancian people, drawn like moths to a candle, flock together at the far end of the roadway in order to watch Manfred Toyler's tavern burn.

Burn it all, Seranai thinks wryly. *Burn it to the Dark Below.*

The tavern is nothing but a place for thieves and commoners to gather and commiserate against the crown. It is a breeding ground for sedition and everyone knows as much. The Cairan people—her mother's people—fill the reeking corners with their grime, whispering treason against the Chancian king.

She will not allow herself to be affiliated with such filth, will not allow herself to be aligned with those of the tainted, gypsy bloodlines. Her halfblood heritage is all she can cling to these days—her grey eyes and hair as pale as homespun gold are the only features that set her apart from the olive skinned and blue eyed people on her mother's side. She is lucky, she supposes, that she took after her father. He never gave her much, but her gave her that. He gave her a chance at slipping through the cracks, at wearing a mask of pale gold to hide her muddled bloodlines.

She turns her back on the burning sights up ahead, her throat burning as she inhales the ashen air. Smoldering flecks of ash swirl past her, alighting upon the exposed skin of her arms with a fiery kiss.

She recognizes the golden figure in the street up ahead the moment she lays eyes upon him. Stalwart and still, General James Byron stands with his back to the rushing sea. He is as silent and as unmoving as a statue, his jaw locked and his expression grim. Only the orange glow of the fire flickering through his impassive brown eyes give any hint that he is a living, breathing man and not merely a golden effigy.

Seranai's heart constricts tightly in her chest. The air chokes off in her lungs, leaving her throat stinging and raw from the clawing heat of the burning ash.

"James." His name flies from her lips before she can stop herself—before she can call it back to her. It hangs heavily—damningly—in the air between them. It tastes foreign upon her tongue, his name, so long has it been since she has dared to speak it aloud, even to herself.

At the sound, his eyes snap down towards her. The light from the inferno at her back casts deep shadows in the pits of his face, causing him to look gaunt and pale. Even burning, she thinks, he is uncommonly handsome. A muscle twitches in his jaw and she sees the impassivity of his gaze give way to immediate dislike. She resists the sudden urge to recoil from his glare.

"James," she repeats, inching carefully closer. The hem of her deep scarlet petticoat drags across the cobblestone like a whisper. "Are you alright?"

At this newest proximity, Seranai can just make out the glistening sheen of sweat upon his skin. His fingers twitch at his sides. The square line of his shoulder, usually tall and formidable beneath his heavy golden cloak, slouches forward ever so slightly. All traces of his usual decorum are gone—burned away, perhaps, by the heat of the growing flames up ahead.

"The city is burning," he murmurs, although not to her—not to anyone. His brown eyes drift upwards as he studies the smoldering grey of the skies, listens to the shouts of the soldiers and commoners in the streets. "I never gave the orders."

Encouraged by the doubt in his eyes, Seranai inches still closer. She is starkly conscious of the plunging neckline of her décolletage—the supple roundness of her porcelain breasts above her cinched, hourglass waist. He had not been able to resist her beauty, once, she remembers. James Byron had not always been a soldier. He had been a boy, once, easy to charm and even easier to please. She had fallen for him hard—fallen for him in a way that she had never fallen for the elder, stringent men of aristocracy and politics. They filled her pockets and kept her dressed in fineries, to be sure, but they were nothing to her—only a means to an end.

James Byron had been a beginning.

He loved her, once, she is almost certain of it.

"James," she says a third time, drawing close enough to touch. There are new lines upon his face—harder lines—but the cool, aloof gaze is as familiar to her as an old dream. The square, clean-shaven jaw and shallow, permanent dimples are the very same that she has traced time and time again in the night.

"James, please," she whispers, pleading now. "Talk to me."

She plants her hand gingerly upon the sleeve of his left arm. Her touch causes him to jump as though he has been branded. His eyes snap down toward her face. His lips curl into a grimace and he steps away from her.

"You will refer to me as general, gypsy," he barks. His voice is cold.

Seranai finds herself suddenly fighting back an uncharacteristic onslaught of tears. The smoking ash tears at her eyes. "Don't do that," she whispers. "Don't talk to me as if I'm a stranger to you."

The dislike on James's face deepens still further. "I don't have time for this," he growls, pushing past her in the street. Overhead, the soiled clouds break open as it begins to rain. Tepid fingers of water slither down Seranai's face. She turns with James as he storms away, grasping desperately at his cloak. The sleek, golden fabric slips through her fingers like water, rippling out of her reach.

"James," she calls out, desperate.

He ignores her, heading briskly towards the sputtering smoke that wheezes beneath the cool reprieve of the rain. The golden line of his shoulders is mottled with dark spots of moisture. He does not look back, not once.

Rage, hot and unbridled, boils deep within Seranai at the sight of his departure. She storms after him, her white locks plastered against her face as she shouts his name into the thundering rain. Her words are drowned out by the shrieking coastal wind, blown in sideways by the sea. Her foot catches upon a loose stone and she loses her balance, plummeting ungracefully to the ground.

There is a sharp pain in her backside and the sound of something snapping—the fragile whalebone of her bustle, she is certain of it. She pulls herself to her feet, her cheeks burning. Up ahead, James has rounded the corner and disappeared. The flames that licked at the skies for hours have sputtered and died, beaten back by the rain.

Seranai stands in the middle of the street and tries not to scream.

Moving off to the side of the road, she takes meager shelter beneath a faded yellow awning. The smell of stale bread reaches her nose from inside the door of the shop. Pressing her back up against the cool brick, she allows herself to cry freely. The stinging salt of her tears mingle with the rainwater that saturates her skin. A feeble whimper is lodged in her throat. She is ruined. James Byron has ruined her—destroyed everything she ever worked for with a look and a smile.

Seranai remembers when she first saw him, sword fighting in the palace courtyard with the young Prince Frederick. She had loved him at once—had loved the slope of his nose, the permanent dimples that bordered his unsmiling lips. Even back then he had been a serious boy—too serious, she would tell him later when he was hers—but that day his mood had been jovial and light. That day, he laughed beneath the sun as his sword sang against the blade of the Chancian heir.

She had never been to the palace before that day, and she has never been since. Her father, still alive, had been commissioned to craft a sword for the eldest prince for his sixteenth harvest day celebration. It was a great honor, and Seranai had been permitted to come along as long as she promised to keep quiet and keep her hands to herself. She had spent hours that afternoon hiding behind her father's cart and watching James Byron thrust and parry with his sword, his limber muscles dancing beneath the summer sun.

She has loved him since—loved him from afar in the years after her father's death, loved him when he took a knee before Rowland Stoward and pledged his allegiance as a soldier. She loved him even as she encouraged the love of other men—as she accepted their gifts and their baubles, as she used their standing to claw her way into worth.

When finally she revealed herself to him, young and innocent as he was, he had loved her too. At least for a time. How stupid she had been, to fail to see the end coming before it arrived and slapped her across the face.

James was promoted to general three harvests ago. The elevation came as a surprise to everyone in Chancey. He was young—too young, they said—and not born of nobility. And yet Rowland Stoward favored him. James had become like a son to the king in the wake of Frederick's untimely death. Rowland wanted to give him everything, but he could not give him a place in his court—not James, the son of a fisher and a maid. Even Rowland's hands were tied when it came to the laws of royal inheritance. Instead, he bid James kneel before him as he raised him up to a position of power.

Seranai should have seen it coming.

This can't go on, James said to her one night. His golden regalia glittered in the moonlight as he thrust her hands from his. *What will people say?*

None of the desperate pleas that rose to his lips were able to convince him to stay. He walked on without a word, his shoulders squared against the sound of her sobs.

Months rolled into years. If James saw her on the streets, he acted as though she did not exist. His cold eyes were void of any recognition. Her heart broken, Seranai gathered up her resolve and forced herself to move on. She had spent years using her looks and her charm to claw her way to the top of society and suddenly she was back at the bottom rung of the ladder.

James Byron was a disappointment, to be sure, but she will not allow one little bump in the road to deter her from pursuing what is rightfully hers—a place in the Chancian commonwealth.

Seranai sighs, feeling tired. Beyond the tented overhang the rain is slowing. It feels, to her, like the calm before the storm. When did it become night? She did not notice the darkness creeping across her skin like a blanket. She fidgets against the shattered whalebone netting of her gown, feeling annoyance rooting within her as her backside throbs.

"Roberts!"

The disembodied voice that is carried down the road by a gust of stinging wind draws her back into the shadows. Her cautious grey eyes study the street in the darkness. Up ahead, she can just make out the lean figure of a man hesitating upon the drenched stones. His curly black hair hangs down into his eyes. Seranai wonders when he turned the corner, and how long he has been standing there. She ought to have been paying better attention. It is not wise for a woman to be out alone this close to the slums of Chancey once night has fallen.

A second figure emerges from a nearby door. The man with the unruly dark hair tenses visibly at his appearance. Seranai strains her ears to hear the conversation that passes between them. The second man in the street is a full head taller than the first. His rounded shoulders are slightly bowed as he leans in the black-haired man's direction.

"Are you Roberts the Valiant?"

The black-haired man is silent for several moments. Seranai frowns at the mention of his Cairan title, quickly losing interest in the interaction. She has never cared for the matters of her people, and even this proximity to them, now, makes her skin itch with impatience.

"I am," the man called Roberts answers at last. Suspicious, he adds, "Who wants to know?"

"Nobody," the second man says. Seranai glances up at the implication in his tone, feeling her breathing catch in her throat. Even from where she stands, Seranai can see the man flash Roberts a knowing grin.

A memory springs to the forefront of Seranai's mind with startling clarity. She sees herself as a child, clinging to her mother's hand in the marketplace. Her father had just died. It was the custom of Cairans to offer gifts to grieving widows, and so for days after his death men and women arrived at the door with baskets full of all sorts of food and goods. That morning, however, as they stood in the marketplace, a dark man approached them. He handed Seranai's mother a glittering golden band set with blood red rubies. Her mother gasped at the sight.

Who is this from? Her trembling voice barely rose above a whisper.

Nobody. The word was swaddled in the man's sugared laugh. And then he was gone.

Later that night, as Seranai watched the light of the candles dance in the faceted surface of the gems, she asked her mother the question that had haunted her all afternoon.

How can something so beautiful come from nobody at all?

Not nobody, darling. Her mother smoothed back her white locks of hair. Her eyes were red and raw from crying. *The Cairan king.*

But why wouldn't he just say that?

We don't speak our leader's name out in the streets.

Why not? Seranai was intrigued, but only mildly. She yawned, and the red light of the rubies stretched and glimmered between her fluttering lashes. Her mother smiled down at her with sadness in her eyes.

It wouldn't be safe to acknowledge his existence. Not within hearing of the Chancians and their loyalties.

Seranai thought of the lavish king that resided within the great, grey palace walls. He had just recently heralded the coming of his second son, sending a parade of courtiers and jesters alike dancing wildly through the narrow streets of Chancey—flanked as always by an army of golden guardians. She had been mesmerized by the grandeur of it all—the untouchable opulence.

I thought King Rowland was our king.

At that, her mother's gaze went dark. She stared off into the shadows, her lips pressed together in a thin line. When she spoke, her voice was careful.

Rowland Stoward was your father's king. He is not my liege, and he is not yours.

Her mother would offer her no more explanation. She kissed her on the forehead and sent her off to bed. Seranai had not thought of the conversation again. Until now.

Before her, the man called Roberts has closed the distance between himself and the mysterious figure. Seranai presses clinging locks of hair out of her eyes and leans forward to listen over the pattering of the rain.

"You have my attention," she hears Roberts say.

"Were you present at the burning of Manfred Toyler's tavern this afternoon?"

A pause. "I was."

"You will bear witness to everything that happened?"

Another pause, longer this time. Roberts clears his throat before continuing. His words are measured—careful. "I never said that I would."

"But will you, if asked?" muses the towering shadow of a man.

"I suppose. It depends who asks it of me."

The stranger laughs. "Nobody will."

This time, Roberts returns the grin with a cautious smile of his own. "Then yes."

"Noon tomorrow. At the cathedral," the man explains. "Wait for a sign." He melts back into the darkness. Somewhere beyond the crumbling brick, a door slams shut. For a long time, Roberts stands frozen in the street. He watches the spot where the man stood. The rain is picking up again, slathering the road in puddles. At long last, Roberts begins to whistle.

Seranai watches as he put his hands in his pockets and heads slowly down the street. She studies his figure in the gloom as he turns the corner and disappears. The echo of his whistle cuts through the rain. In her mind's eye she sees the red sheen of the rubies upon the priceless golden band. The Carian king is an elusive man, nothing more than a shadow and a ghost—a whisper in the streets. Still, whispers are a wonderful thing. The Cairan king is a wealthy man. Everyone knows that he alone holds the location to the incalculable Carian fortune.

She is a woman in desperate need of fortune.

Her pink tongue flickers across her lower lip as she considers her options. Roberts the Valiant. Under normal circumstances, she would never lower herself so far as to seduce a gypsy. Such a feat is below her. The thought of it makes her stomach ill. And yet Roberts the Valiant is about to be granted access to the Cairan king himself. She has heard the Mames swear that the leader of the gypsies has more wealth than the Chancian king could ever hope to get his fingers on.

She smiles bitterly and thinks of James Byron—ashamed to be with her, ashamed to love her for what she is.

She thinks, then, of her father, gutted like a fish and breathing his last.

I won't be worthless anymore, father.

She thinks again of his body as they lowered it into the dirt. Drank himself to death, the neighbors said. She knew better. She had watched his blood run across the floor of the shop. It had mingled with the stinking blood of pigs and cows—had warmed the pallid palms of her trembling hands.

Murderer, her mother accused upon her deathbed when Seranai finally garnered enough courage to confess her secret. She thought the woman would be grateful. Seranai had freed them both.

Roberts the Valiant, she muses, and she smiles. Her grey eyes glimmer hungrily in the darkness. She has always been the type of woman prepared to sacrifice anything if it means advancing her status. Immediately, she knows what it is she has to do.

Tomorrow at noon.

She will be at the cathedral when Roberts the Valiant arrives. It won't take long to make a man like him fall in love with a woman like her.

CHAPTER 3

Captain Alexander Mathew

RAIN IS COMING down in torrents upon the shallow seas, encompassing the darkened hulk of a wildly rocking ship in ferocious, howling winds. The sound of the half frozen droplets splintering against the wooden deck causes the men onboard to cringe beneath the frigid sea air. Squaring their shoulders against the downpour, the harried crew slides from starboard to port and back again in a frenzied attempt to douse the black sails that whip to and fro in the brutish tempest. With a jarring collision, the keel of the ship meets the full force of a hammering wave. A few men that have not taken steady grips upon the shrouds fly unexpectedly forward. Stinging, salty fingers of water clutch maliciously at the ship's chains, threatening to capsize the entire vessel.

Amid the chaos, his feet planted firmly on the quarterdeck, stands Alexander Mathew. His fingers grip tightly at the wheel as he fights to keep the ship on track. His untamed hair, weighted down by the rain, falls into bright hazel eyes that study the horizon with steadfast resolve.

"BLEED THE SAILS," he cries aloud, his words coming in vain. "QUICKLY!" His hoarse shout is lost immediately; carried away in an icy gust of wind as soon as it leaves his chapped and stinging lips.

His gaze, burning with tenacity, is trained to the east. That afternoon, just before the cover of clouds had choked out the sun and brought with it the inevitable frustration of spirited spring squalls, he caught sight of the small island looming in the distance.

"Chancey," he whispers again, tasting the salt on his lips.

He reminds his aching bones the importance of pressing onward. He cannot drop anchor now, not in this storm. Already, he has managed to maneuver through the nearly impossible miniature islands of stone that stretch out of the western waters offshore the cliff-like fortress of Chancey. His success was much to the amazement of his crew, who had only the night before told him the countless stories of ships that had been run aground attempting to traverse the maze of rocks in even the most favorable of conditions.

Alexander has no time to allow himself even a moment of satisfaction. They may be free of the ship-rending terrors below, but they still have a great deal against them, both from above and ahead. He gazes upward. The mizzen above him creaks dangerously in the wind. It teeters back and forth against a black sky that is being slowly suffocated by skeletal, purple clouds.

The ship is once again jostled upon the ocean as an unrelenting wave pounds fitfully against the hull. The pirate hardly looks away from the island, concealed now by a veil of vertical silver slits, even as he hears the maddened shouts of his crew sliding into the starboard side.

A voice close to his ear startles him.

"We be gettin' righ' close ter the cliffs, en't ye think, Cap'n Mathew? Thinkin' we ought to come about starboard a bit, mayhap."

Alexander recognizes the booming voice of his first mate, Thom. He glances out of the corner of his eyes and sees the burly man staring back at him with quiet grit. His straggled red beard is tangled with droplets of ice as gestures forward into the rain. Alexander struggles to peer through the heavy onslaught of the storm. Sure enough, he can just make out the vague outline of the steep cliffs of Chancey looming in the distance.

"Hawk!" The hoarse bellow that flies from Alexander's lips is barely audible over the discordant tumult of the storm. The shrieking wind carries a salty spray of ice water against his numbed cheeks. He leans forward over the wheel.

"Hawk!"

A figure materializes at his side and he hears a dry grumble in his ear. "I told you these wretched spring seasons are cursed even more on this edge of the world, aye?"

Alexander wrenches his eyes away from the storm before him, turning briefly to face the newcomer to the quarterdeck. Lanky and nearly invisible beneath his tattered black cloak, Evander the Hawk's sharp golden eyes gleam wickedly at his captain through the downpour.

Alexander flashes the pirate a wry smirk. "We're headed too far northeast," he shouts over the hammering rain. "We need to maneuver back southward or we'll end up past the ports and straight into the cliffs."

"The wind will be against us if we turn to the south," the Hawk retorts, squinting up into the tempest.

"The wind is against us whatever way we turn in this storm. We can't bring the ship into port in this madness; the weather is too unpredictable to swap out the colors. I won't risk Rowland's Golden Guard seeing the black sails." He shakes his head, allowing stray, stinging droplets to fling from his hair and fly into his hazel eyes. "We'll find a place to dock offshore."

"And drop anchor in this storm?" The Hawk's golden eyes are wide. "Are you mad?"

"It'll die down soon. Storms like this always do. We'll circle around until its quiet."

The Hawk shrugs his shoulders against the rain. "Aye, what orders do you want me to give the crew, then?" His voice cracks over the fluttering snap of the black banner overhead. Alexander stares at the flapping flag, his eyes trained upon the blood red skull stitched into the coarse fabric. It was his father's insignia, once. It stood for persistence—for fighting until the last, bloody breath. It his crest now, and he'll go out the way his father did.

He briefly considers his options. None of them are ideal. Luckily for him, he's a resilient man. He's never shirked back from a little rain.

A grin spreads across his face and he feels determination warming his saturated bones. "Tell the men to help me bring her south. We'll circle around and tether her to one of the rocky outcroppings offshore. This is your homeland, Hawk, you know better than I how to bring us in in one piece." Alexander's voice is swallowed whole upon the air. He wonders for a moment if the lanky pirate has heard him. Finally, blinking his golden eyes clear of rain, the Hawk nods. He slips off into the dark without another word.

Setting his eyes ahead, Alexander grins in the unrelenting rain. Deep inside his gut he feels the excited twinge that comes with the approach of new and unknown territory. Before him, he can see the massive cliffs of Chancey rising out of the water like a stronghold against the storm.

He thinks of the tip he received in the Westerlies—of the rumor that the man he has hunted across the wide, endless sea has finally set up shop in the small, overlooked port of Chancey. It was only that—a rumor—and yet his heart swells with promise all the same.

I'm coming for you, Jameson, he thinks. *And this time, there's nowhere to run.*

Wrenching the wheel heavily to the right, he lets out a bellow as the ship veers dangerously south and into the heart of the storm.

CHAPTER 4

Nerani the Elegant

NERANI THE ELEGANT was presented her Cairan title at the annual naming ceremony during her tenth year of age. She had waited her turn in line, silvery sweat pooling within the lines of her palms, and watched as the revered Mames of the clan made their slow way towards where she stood. Her white cotton dress, which her mother had labored over for days, was stained with soot at the sleeve. Emerala's cursed fingerprints. She had shouted at her younger cousin to leave her alone that morning—she was not dressed for playing—and yet the wearisome girl had continued to give chase.

She shuffled her feet upon the splintering wood floor beneath her and tried to ignore the cloudy black stain that clawed at her peripherals. She hoped that her mother, watching from the crowd of onlookers, could not see the marks. She would surely be scolded.

Nerani. The sound of her name being called made her jump. She glances up to see Mame Galyria standing just before her. Quivering, she stepped forward. She reached out her arm, allowing Mame Galyria to grab hold of her wrist. Her hand was flipped over unceremoniously. The Mame dragged her index finger along the clammy lines of her palm. She cringed at the texture of the woman's tough skin against her hand.

Nerani was starkly aware of everyone's gaze upon her. Her breathing grew shallow as the room around her faded out of focus. She held her breath and trained her deep blue eyes upon the face of the Mame before her. The woman's skin was riddled with deep, shaded grooves. Her heavy lids were lined with a thick smudge of black, the creases smeared with violet paint. So many lines—so many stories.

She glanced down at her own palm, upturned for all to see. She was unlined—an empty canvas. She wondered what story the Mame would read upon her flesh.

The woman was muttering beneath her breath. Her heavy violet lids fluttered closed. A dreamy smile inched its way across her face, causing several deeper, darker grooves to stretch like clay upon her skin.

Nerani heard an audible whisper escape the Mame's blood red lips. She leaned in to hear. *She will grow into a beautiful young woman*, Mame Galyria said. *Gracious, kind.*

Nerani leaned back. Relieved. It would be nothing horrible. Harrane before her had been granted the title of the Hostile. It was true enough, and yet his cheeks had flooded with red heat all the same. She held her breath and waited for the Mame to announce her title to the waiting crowd.

Nothing happened. Mame Galyria continued to grip tightly at her hand. Over the woman's shoulder, Nerani saw the figure of her mother rise to get a better view.

Look at me. The Mame's command seeped out through clenched teeth. Nerani let her gaze snap back to the woman's heavily painted face. Her heart pounded against her chest. The Mame's eyes were open. The blacks of her pupils had devoured the color of her irises.

Gold blood bleeds red. The woman's ragged whisper trembled. *You will do well to remember that, Nerani the Elegant.*

Next to her, Nerani could feel Harrane the Hostile's eyes planted upon her face. She swallowed. The Mame dropped her hand. The room around them was as still as death. Nerani wondered if anyone else had heard the cryptic words the Mame had uttered.

Mame Minera, one of the younger Mames, bustled forward.

Nerani the Elegant, she announced to the crowd. The smile plastered across her face did not quite manage to eradicate the worry from her eyes. The room was filled with applause. Nerani the Elegant allowed herself to smile. Her eyes searched the room for her mother and father. They were applauding with the rest of the group, their expressions ecstatic.

And so she was named.

Nerani sits shivering upon her cot, reminiscing. The rain patters ruthlessly against the soiled glass of the windowpanes. It has been many years since she recounted that day. It is not like her to summon the memories of ghosts. She prefers happier things. She prefers the present. The past and those that reside there are beyond her control.

The coarse blanket that she has drawn about her shoulders scratches at her skin. It does little to keep her warm. Across the room, Emerala is staring at her through pointed green eyes. Her long, narrow nose twitches in consternation. Nerani sighs.

"Yes?"

"Rob hasn't come home yet," Emerala states. Her tone is accusatory. Her gaze is dark. They have been sitting vigil in the quarters for hours. They watched in silence as the rain broke through the spirals of smoke and the hazy colors of day melted back into night, and still he did not arrive. It is growing dark outside. It is not like Roberts to be out so late.

"He'll come." Nerani does not know what else to say. There is not much that they can do besides wait. It is dark, and the streets will be prowling with guardians.

There is a knock at the door. They both jump, their eyes meeting across the darkness. Their expressions mirror one another as they fade first from hope to disappointment and then to alarm. Roberts would not knock.

"Come in," Nerani calls, her voice tinged with diffidence. The door is not locked. She thinks that perhaps it should be, given the events of the past few months. Tensions have been rising—guardians have been violently accosting Cairans in the street with no justification for their actions. One can never be too safe these days. Still, the latch upon the door has been broken for years. Nerani is certain that they will never get around to fixing it.

The hinges squeal as the door is pushed open. The figure in the entryway is drenched with rainwater. Her long black tresses are slicked to the side of her ebony face. Her dark blue eyes survey them from shaded lids as her lips pull back against a line of straight white teeth. A lantern has been lit in the hallway outside. The orange flame burns Nerani's field of vision. She had not realized how long she had been sitting in the dark. The door slams shut and the light is extinguished. Traces of blue residue creep across Nerani's retinas.

"Orianna." Emerala sounds as surprised to see her as Nerani feels. "We weren't expecting any visitors tonight."

"Obviously not," the young woman called Orianna remarks. She sashays through the doorway, her dark gown swaying with her hips as she walks. The staccato black and violet hem sweeps ceremoniously against the rotting wooden floor.

Orianna the Raven, Nerani thinks, watching her friend make her way across the small expanse. She has never appeared more like her title than now, with her glossy black hair as slick as feathers and her gown rippling as though the wind sits beneath her wings. Her mother once told her that ravens were the bearers of bad news. She blinks. Another ghost. Her fingers dance idly upon her lap as she struggles to refocus.

"Why have you come all this way in the rain?" It has been a while since Orianna paid them a visit. She has recently been called upon to complete the rigorous training of the Mames. They believe her to have the natural born skills of a healer. Nerani is proud of her—very few women are ever given the honor and the preparation is no easy task. Even so, Nerani notes that her generally carefree friend looks tired—older, perhaps.

Orianna draws to a stop at the center of the room. "I saw Rob." The implication in her tone does not go unnoticed by either cousin. Orianna's eyes flicker back and forth between them as she adds, "He was at the burning of Toyler's."

Emerala leans away from the window. Her green eyes glitter like emeralds in the dark. "You were there?"

A bead of rain makes its way down Orianna's forehead as she nods. She reaches up and flicks it away with a finger. "Mame Minera had me go with her to tend to the wounds of those who were locked inside."

"Was anyone killed?" The question sounds hollow in Nerani's ears. She realizes that she is petrified to know the answer. Instant relief floods through her as she sees Orianna shake her head.

"No. We were lucky. A few of our people charged the guardians that stood outside the inferno after they first realized what had happened. One of the guardians fired his gun, but only into the air." Orianna sighs and adds, "It could have been much worse."

Nerani remembers the echo of the gunshot—how it had seemed to reverberate through her bones. Her knees feel weak beneath her gown. *At least no one was shot*, she reminds herself. Her chest feels unusually tight.

"Did Rob say anything to you?" Emerala demands. "We've been waiting all afternoon for him to get back."

Orianna nods. "I spoke with him, but only briefly. He asked me to stop by and check on the two of you. I came as soon as Mame Minera permitted me to go."

"Where is he?" Emerala's face has settled into a deep scowl in the darkness. She hates to be left on the outside—hates to be left behind. Roberts once told Nerani that his sister had an insatiable need to be the center of attention. Nerani does not doubt that this is true.

"He's gone to Mamere Lenora's," Orianna says

Emerala scoffs, her gaze incredulous. "The brothel?"

Nerani feels a small pull at her heart, like the tearing of stitches. The words escape from her before Orianna can continue speaking. "Don't say it like that, Emerala."

Emerala's green eyes glide across her face. Her thick black brows have disappeared beneath her curls. "How did I say it?"

"You know—with such disdain."

"Disdain?" Emerala spits the word out like poison. "It's a whorehouse. How would you like me to react to my brother visiting a home for prostitutes?"

"It was our home too, for a time," Nerani snaps, feeling herself growing tense. "Or don't you remember?"

Orianna cuts in, her cheeks flushed with embarrassment. Nerani knows that her friend has always loved Roberts, ever since they were children. He is blind to her affection, as young men are like to be. Emerala's suggestion makes Orianna visibly uncomfortable. Her next words fall too quickly from her lips. "Anyway, he obviously hasn't gone to seek companionship." She clears her throat. "He's seeking out Mame Galyria."

The seer. Nerani thinks again of the older Mame that read her palm all those years ago. She wonders if it is any coincidence that she called upon that memory on such a day as this. The knot in her chest pulls tighter, robbing her of her breath.

"Rob doesn't buy into that prophetic nonsense," Emerala rejoins. "Everyone knows Mame Galyria resides there because it is only drunk commoners that are willing to eat up the drivel she feeds them."

Orianna shrugs. She drops down onto the cot next to Nerani, rubbing at her still flaming cheek with her left palm. "That's where he went. I didn't ask him why."

"You should have."

Orianna rolls her eyes, shooting a sidelong glance at Nerani. "I won't make the same mistake again," she says dryly. Her words are punctuated by a yawn. "Can I sleep here tonight? My place is too crowded, and I'm exhausted."

"Of course," Nerani says. She thinks of Orianna's four younger brothers rolling about their mother's tight quarters. She is glad for the quiet of the rain against the window. "It's much too late for you to go anywhere alone, anyway. The streets aren't safe."

Nerani can feel her eyes growing heavier even as she speaks. She tries and fails to blink away her fatigue as she lies back upon her cot. The mattress is cold and she shivers. Shifting to the side, she allows room for Orianna to curl up next to her. The flame of the lantern is burning low, growing close to sputtering out completely.

"Emerala?" Nerani's voice echoes out into the looming darkness of their quarters. She is met with silence. She is being ignored.

"Emerala, are you going to sleep?"

Again, there is nothing.

Orianna is already snoring lightly. Her chest rises and falls heavily. Poor girl, Nerani can only imagine what she felt earlier this afternoon as she watched people—her people—be pulled from the smoldering tavern.

Moments roll into hours. Sleep does not come. Nerani blinks heavily, staring up at the dark beams of the ceiling above her head until her vision blurs. Colorful dots do pirouettes across her vision. Emerala is still quiet. Unusual.

Nerani can make out her silhouette pressed against the glass. She has fallen asleep in the windowsill, lulled into unconsciousness by the sound of the rain. Nerani smiles.

She thinks of Roberts, and of Mame Galyria.

She recalls again the day of her naming, and how later that afternoon she had confided in Roberts what the Mame had whispered to her. Roberts had only laughed and ruffled her hair. *It's a bundle of rot, Ani. It's meaningless. Think about it, what does that even mean? Gold blood bleeds red?*

Nothing. Nerani felt immediately embarrassed for having allowed it to trouble her on such an important day.

Roberts grin had widened as he scooped her up. *Exactly. Those seers know nothing about the future. It's all for entertainment. The present is the only thing that matters. Now. Today. Everything else is out of your control.* She thinks of how his olive skin had been burnt from the sun. It was a characteristic of his mother's. His green eyes, however—his firm belief in everything tangible and logical—those were his father's. It was the nobility in his blood—the Chancian ancestry that ran deep within him. He was half-blooded, as was his sister. Their Cairan mother had always insisted that their father's blood was what made them so terribly hot-headed, so consistently willful.

Ghosts, again. Nerani chides herself silently. The night is full of them tonight. She cannot shake them. She rolls over and tucks her palms beneath her cool pillow. Across the room she can just make out Robert's empty cot.

What are you looking for, Rob?

She hopes he will come home soon.

CHAPTER 5

Roberts the Valiant

DEATH IS NO stranger to Roberts the Valiant. He has been surrounded by it—saturated in it—from the moment he entered the world, red and screaming and cringing in the light. What is another death to him but a notch on his belt?

Standing outside the brothel and listening to the lively music that drifts out from the open windows, he thinks of his childhood. Those days—days that should have been filled with the wide-eyed innocence of boyhood—were redolent with the ever-present promise of death.

He thinks back to the day his father had taken his hand and led him to the market square. There was an execution that afternoon—a former kitchen boy accused of being half Cairan. The king did not like tainted blood working within the walls of his palace. He did not like the thought of gypsies putting their hands on his food. Roberts, then too young to understand the darker implications of the boy's crime, thought that perhaps the boy was being punished for not washing his hands. His own mother had always boxed his ears when he failed to scrub behind them.

The boy was to be hung in the gallows. Roberts can remember how he climbed atop his father's shoulders to get a better view.

Always watch, his father instructed. *Never look away. Never flinch. It will make you less of a man, and you will need to be a man once I am gone.*

Staring at the boy's tiny feet as they hung limp beneath the scaffold, Roberts never thought that day would come so soon. He had not been ready. He would never be ready. But if life has taught him anything, it is that death waits for no man.

The tinny sound of clattering cans echoes out from a nearby alleyway, calling Roberts out of his memories and back into the present. Roberts draws back into the narrow side street at his back, relishing in the cool shadows that drape across his face. He watches as two guardians stroll out from the darkness, the golden regalia of their uniform catching ablaze beneath the slanted light that falls from the brothel windows. They murmur quietly to one another as their eyes scan the street before them. Their faces are masks of barely stifled distaste as they listen to the raucous sounds that spill out from the second floor. Someone laughs too loudly, her cackle cutting through the splintering wooden paneling of the outer wall and dissipating against the crisp night.

One guardian murmurs something to the other, his voice rising in the familiar lilt of a question. The other guardian shakes his head in response.

"Not tonight. You heard General Byron—we lay low tonight."

"If you say so, sir." The first guardian, the taller of the two, has a voice like gravel. Roberts watches as they begin to retreat back into the alleyway, clearly determined to carry on their evening patrol far from the reaches of Mamere Lenora's brothel.

Good, he thinks. *Leave her alone.*

He thinks of Mamere Lenora, the brothel's self-appointed den mother, and of the way she had cradled Emerala the day their mother died.

No. Roberts catches himself, correcting his wording. *She didn't die, she was murdered.*

Rumor has always spread like wildfire through the narrow streets of Chancey, and the day of their mother's murder had been no exception. Mamere Lenora came running the moment she heard—had found Emerala and Nerani playing in the streets and told them not to go home. When she came to the apartment for Roberts, he was lying beneath the couch, his fingers curled in a pool of blood that was not his.

He remembers the sound of Mamere Lenora's husky voice as she sang softly into Emerala's head of curls. Her lullaby had mingled with the ceaseless sobs that expelled from his sister's chest. Nerani stood silently next to them, her wild eyes a sea of blue against a pinched face as white as snow. He had not been a man, then. He had thrown up in the powder room, trying in vain to purge the memories of the way his mother and aunt had lain, white and lifeless upon the blood-stained sofa. The echo of the gunshots rattled about his brain.

Mamere brought the three of them to the brothel—had let them live among the whores.

Orphans, they were called. Their parents had succumbed to martyr-dom. *Selfish, really*, it was whispered by the concubines, *what with children so young.*

Roberts had been cowardly. He should have been able to take care of the girls on his own. He should have grown up faster. His father never would have let his daughter and niece be raised in a house of women that sold themselves. But by that time, Eliot Roberts had already been long gone. The man had relinquished his right to make decisions for Emerala and Roberts the moment he had sailed west and left them behind.

Roberts lets out a deep exhale, the sound of his breathing cutting short as a subsequent shattering follows his sigh. He trips and his heart seizes within his chest. Beneath his feet, several abandoned milk cartons have shattered into shivering glass fragments.

He does not need to look up to know that the guardians have turned back around.

"Who's there?" snaps one of the soldiers. "Show yourself."

Fantastic. Roberts groans internally. This is the last thing he needs tonight. He moves out of the alleyway, cringing as the moonlight drapes over him in a pale wash of muted white. The two guardians are drawing nearer, their golden cloaks billowing behind them as they approach. Their gloved hands hover just above the barrel of their pistols. As they come to a standstill before him, he can see the caution in their eyes replaced with mirth.

"What have we here?" The gravel voice of the taller guardian reaches Roberts from across the narrow street. His lips curl upward in a smile. His short-cropped hair and cleanly shaven face make him look identical to the smirking man at his right. If it were not for the extra stripe upon his uniform signifying him as an officer of higher rank, Roberts would not be able to tell one man from the other.

The guardian continues speaking, nudging Roberts in the chest with his gloved knuckles. "What a surprise—a gypsy pawing at the doors of the whorehouse. Fitting, don't you think, Johnson?"

The guardian called Johnson gives a low chuckle. "Do you think he has the money for one of these girls? I hear Mamere asks a hefty price for her ladies of leisure."

You would know firsthand, I'm sure, Roberts thinks darkly. He bites his tongue, keeping his eyes trained forward. Now is not the time to stir up trouble. He did not come here for that.

The guardians before him are laughing. "If he does have the money, I'm certain it was stolen," the higher-ranking guardian asserts. "Did you steal money, scum?" He presses his knuckles forcefully into Roberts's chest, sending him stumbling back a step or two.

"It doesn't matter whether or not the king himself financed him," Johnson remarks to his partner, still laughing. He turns his attention to Roberts before continuing. His dark, brown eyes blaze with mirth. "Even a whore wouldn't condescend to sleep with the likes of you."

At that, Roberts's temper snaps. He spits, rejoicing as his shot lands directly into Johnson's eye. The guardian cries out in rage, wiping at his eyes with the back of his glove. Quick as a shot, the higher-ranking guardian charges him. Roberts bites down hard upon his tongue as his back slams into the wall. The cool weight of a pistol presses against his forehead. He exhales sharply, his breath blowing the wild black curls out of his emerald eyes.

"You wouldn't shoot me," Roberts asserts. He fights to put out the temper that still smolders red hot beneath his skin. "I've done nothing wrong."

"Is that so?" The guardian's voice slips out from behind his crooked sneer in a hiss. "It looks to me like you've assaulted a member of King Stoward's Golden Guard. That's a misdemeanor in my book."

"I didn't know the guardians were in the practice of killing citizens over a little bit of saliva," Roberts remarks boldly. He immediately regrets his comment as the barrel of the pistol presses more firmly against his skin. The guardian's dark eyes narrow dangerously.

"State your name, Cairan."

"They call me the Valiant."

"I don't care for your quirky little customs, scum," snarls the soldier. "I want your name. Your real name."

Roberts swallows hard, considering his options. Anything but honesty at this point will get him badly beaten, if not killed. Acts of blatant hate are no longer rare occurrences. These days, it's normal to hear stories of Cairan men beaten close to death for the simple crime of being in the wrong place at the wrong time.

He thinks again of those tiny feet hanging in the gallows—blowing softly in the quiet seaside wind. The boy had not been killed because he forgot to clean his hands before touching Rowland Stoward's food. He was killed for being a gypsy—for having Cairan blood running through his veins. It is hatred that fuels the king, and it is hatred that sits in the barrel of the pistol against his head—cold, unmerited hatred.

"My name is Roberts the Valiant," he says quietly.

He watches as the guardian before him contemplates this new information. His brown eyes widen and he allows the pistol to fall away from Roberts's head. Behind him, Johnson swallows a laugh. Roberts can already feel his blood beginning to boil. The feelings are old and the roots of his anger grow deep into his spirit. He thinks of his father's winking green eyes, of the sorry sight of him the day he left his family behind.

It is the legacy he bears, as Eliot Roberts's only son.

"Roberts?" The guardian repeats him in a voice dripping with mockery. Humor glistens in his eyes—dances upon the corners of his lips. "Roberts, did you say?"

"Yes," whispers Roberts, scowling. He is suddenly all too conscious of his own deep green eyes, so very different from the vivid blue eyes that mark the Cairan people—his people.

Johnson hoots loudly, his eyes creasing shut as he laughs. "A bastard boy," he exclaims. "I didn't realize we'd stumbled on a half-blood."

The higher-ranking guardian frowns down at him. "That takes the fun out of this, then." He holsters his pistol at his waist. "I'm not in the market for half-bloods tonight."

"Lucky you, bastard." Johnson sneers at him from behind his superior officer.

Roberts scowls back at him, feeling the tension seeping out of his shoulders all the same. He watches as the guardians draw away from him, their eyes still gleaming with mirth.

I'm glad someone finds the humor in this, he thinks darkly.

"Until next time, Roberts the Valiant," comes the stony voice of the superior guardian. His figure is already swallowed by the dark of the street. The sound of their boots grows quieter against the cobblestone. Roberts listens to the pattering footfalls until they fade to silence, knowing that there will not be a next time. They will forget his name, the guardians, as they always do. They cannot be bothered with remembering. He is nothing to them, and he is content to remain that way if it is what keeps him alive.

Glancing up at the low moon overhead, he groans. The night is getting old. The interaction with the guardians has cost him a great deal of time. He thinks of his sister. He is sure Emerala is livid that he has not yet returned to their quarters.

He draws closer to the brothel, his nerves singing beneath his skin. He is here for the seer, and nothing more. There are questions to be asked tonight—questions that only she can answer. He will make his visit as quick as he can.

Drawing to the open door, he steps inside. The foyer to Mamere's is crowded. He thinks it is the lingering adrenaline from the spectacle at Toyler's that draws solicitors to the whorehouse. All of the common men of Chancey seem to have found their way to the outskirts of the city that evening. He supposes everyone wants to share a piece of the excitement.

He shoulders his way through the crowd, frowning at the shaded and stinking figures that linger in the smoky common room. His hands are shoved deep into his pockets. His eyes scan the faces of those before him.

"Roberts!" An all too familiar voice in his ear causes him to cringe. He thinks that perhaps if he keeps walking he will manage to lose the prostitute in the dimly lit room.

"Rob!" The grating voice is louder this time—closer. A hand rests upon his shoulder, pulling him backwards through the throng of people. He pauses, agitated. The powdered woman that appears before him is wearing a tattered top hat. Golden curls peek out from beneath the rim. She smiles coyly, tilting her exposed shoulders in his direction as she does a dramatic curtsy. The soiled fabric of her dress is too large for her frame. It is held in place upon her body by a ripped black corset.

"Hello, Whinny." Roberts inclines his head respectfully. His green eyes scan the crowd above the flat top of her black hat. Discouraged, he realizes that he cannot make out a single familiar face in the gloom.

"Didn't expect to see you 'round these parts," Whinny croons. She pushes herself upward on her toes in an attempt to try and draw his gaze back down towards her. He relents, realizing that he is never going to find his way successfully through the tangle of dark and crowded corridors on his own.

"I'm looking for Lenora," he admits to her. Her wide eyes are circled with streaks of black charcoal. She bats her lashes, smiling shyly.

There's nothing shy about her, he thinks dourly. He questions whether or not she's understood him. It does not appear as though she has. She sidles closer to him, flashing him a bit of pale, porcelain leg beneath the slit in her ruffled gown.

"Would you like to go find someplace more quiet to talk?" She plants a firm hand upon his chest, pushing him a step or two towards the staircase behind him. "Upstairs, 'haps?"

"No." He cannot think of anything he would like less.

"We can stay here, if you like." She is still smiling, and he notices that she has a bit of something stuck in her crooked teeth. "I'm flexible."

Roberts clears his throat, uncomfortable. "I'm looking for Lenora." This time, when he speaks, he is careful to enunciate.

"I heard you," Whinny assures him.

Roberts is about to turn and walk away when he hears another voice call out his name. The familiar sound is a welcome escape. By some stroke of luck, Mamere Lenora has managed to catch sight of him through the crowd. He can see the plump, older woman making her way across the room. She sweeps boisterously through the pressing throng, bumping carelessly into velvet sofas and splintering coffee tables as she attempts to avoid the chattering cluster of customers.

"Never mind," he says wryly. "Thank you for your help."

"Of course." The sour response from the young prostitute next to him perfectly matches the look of annoyance on her face. Her nose crinkles glumly as she watches Lenora's approach. Shoving Whinny aside, the stout woman draws Roberts into a bear hug. He returns it gladly, breathing in the familiar smell of her perfume. Lenora releases him after a moment, her gaze sliding towards Whinny.

"What are you doing, standing about, girl?" Lenora glares at the girl over her tightly cinched bosoms that protrude from her mauve, laced bodice. Her lips settle into a fearsome scowl.

Whinny shrugs. She fingers a golden coil of hair as she moves closer to Roberts, placing a palm in the crook of his elbow. "I was just making conversation."

"He's not a customer, fool."

"I know that." The girl does not move.

Mamere Lenora rolls her eyes, shifting her attention to Roberts. "What brings you here tonight, darling?" She steps closer, lowering her voice to a ghost of a whisper. "I've heard the news. Awful. Absolutely awful." She shakes her head and lets a low sigh escape from between her lips.

"What news?" Whinny inquires.

Mamere Lenora fixes the girl with a frightening stare. "Go embarrass yourself somewhere else," she snaps. She shoos the girl away with an exasperated wave of her hand. "There are plenty of men here."

Roberts and Lenora watch as the young woman disappears grudgingly into the crowd. Only once he is sure she will not return does Roberts speak again, leaning in close to ensure that Mamere Lenora will hear him over the din.

"I'm looking for Mame Galyria."

Mamere Lenora nods. "I guessed as much. She's not taking visitors tonight, dear."

"She'll see me," Roberts promises. "She needs to."

Mamere Lenora considers this, studying him closely. "Are you all right?"

"Yes." It is mostly true.

"And the girls?"

"Just as horrendous as always."

Lenora smiles, taking his hand within hers and giving his fingers a squeeze. "You know that they love you dearly."

He returns the smile. "Lenora, listen, I know it's late. I need to speak with the Mame."

She purses her lips for a moment before responding. "Fine," she assents. "Only do not keep her long, she is not as young as she used to be."

They take the back staircase to the top floor. The winding steps are uneven—treacherous. Roberts fights to stay within the reach of Mamere Lenoras's candle. His shadow dances upon the peeling floral wallpaper. His feet whisper against the dusty velvet carpet underfoot. As they reach the top landing the smell of burning incense reaches his nose. Lavender, and something else he cannot place. The rafters lean inward and meet at a point. It is hot up here. Stuffy. The air tastes stale upon his tongue.

There is only one door in the narrow hallway. Mamere Lenora knocks lightly upon the wooden frame.

"Mame? Are you awake?"

Roberts can hear the sound of someone stirring in the room beyond. A muffled croak, like a frog, reaches them from the other side of the wall. "I am now, aren't I?"

"A man is here to see you, dearest." Mamere Lenora's typically gruff demeanor has grown soft—polite. The Mames command respect, even outside the circle of Cairans.

"I told you, I am too ill for visitors tonight."

Roberts catches Mamere Lenora's gaze. She shakes her head, leaning towards Roberts in the stuffy foyer.

"She is nothing of the sort. Only old."

Roberts suppresses a smile as Mamere Lenora leans back into the door.

"He is Cairan," she calls, speaking directly into the wood. "Roberts the Valiant."

There is a brief period of silence, followed by the sound of shuffling footfalls upon the creaking floor. The door is wrenched open. Violet fumes billow out into the hallway. Roberts fights the urge to cough. Before them perches a bent old woman. Her long grey hair is piled into a haphazard bun at the top of her head. Her dark eyes are lost within a sea of wrinkles. Her heavy golden earrings pull at her skin, stretching her lobes nearly to her shoulders. Her bony fingers clasp restlessly at one another as she blinks in Roberts's direction.

"I knew you would come," she rasps at him.

Roberts doubts that she did. And yet here he is. There is no other response for him to give than to smile and nod. "I needed to see you."

"You have questions, ah? You want to know why their golden hearts are filled with such hate."

Roberts hesitates before responding, his brows furrowing over his eyes. "Yes."

"I don't have answers."

Her reply takes him by surprise. He stands uselessly before her—waiting—not knowing what to say.

"Lenora. Leave us," the elderly woman commands.

"Of course, dear," Mamere complies. Smiling, she turns to face Roberts. The light of the candle catches beneath the shadows of her eyes. "Leave the way you came, when you are done. Take the door through the kitchens. No use being hassled by that dreadful Whinny on your way out as well."

"Thank you Lenora," Roberts says. "Really."

She flashes him a grin. "No trouble at all, it's always good to see you, boy. Give my love to the girls." She saunters off into the darkness without another word. He listens to her steps receding down the stairs. And then he is alone with the old woman.

From her perch in the doorway, Mame Galyria stares at Roberts through wizened black eyes. He stares back at her. The quiet is uncomfortable.

"May I come in?" he asks, after his ears begin to ring.

"No."

Silence. "Oh."

She teeters in the doorway. She is so frail that Roberts is concerned she will fall over if she does not sit down. He contemplates offering to fetch her a chair before thinking better of it, instead standing uselessly before her and waiting for her to speak. When at last she does, her voice is reedy—ancient.

"Do you know why I make Mamere's my home, ah?"

Roberts says nothing, certain that she means to continue whether or not he offers a response. She takes a breath, validating his suspicions.

"Commoners are like to believe anything one reads upon their palms or sees in their tea leaves." She chuckles, and the sound that crinkles out of her reminds Roberts of leaves rustling in the wind. "It doesn't take much to be a seer, boy. Just a little bit of insight and a lot of ambiguity, and one's customers will do the rest of the work, ah?"

Roberts blinks, surprised. He thinks again of his father, and how Eliot had reacted once upon a time when Roberts's mother had attempted to talk him into visiting a seer. She proposed that it would be fun, but his father was unconvinced.

Seers are nothing but clever little entertainers for the weak-minded, he argued. *All it takes is a little bit of insight and a lot of ambiguity, and the customer will do the rest of the work.*

Mame Galyria is rocking upon her heels before him. Crow's feet crease around her eyes as she smiles. Her mouth is riddled with black gaps where her teeth have fallen out.

"But I don't need to tell you that, do I, child? You aren't a believer."

Roberts realizes there is no use in lying. Not to her. "I'm not."

"Prophecies are vastly different than fortune telling." Mame Galyria's shriveled face grows somber. One withering hand shoots out and grabs his wrist. Her flesh feels like sandpaper. "Are you listening?"

"Yes."

"If one has visions of a prophetic nature one cannot control them. One cannot call them up at will. Most often, one is not even aware that the revelation is occurring."

Roberts says nothing. He is suddenly eight years in the past, watching Nerani pace back and forth with urgency. It was hours after her naming ceremony and she had been distressed all afternoon. Accustomed to the young girl's tendency to fret, he had teased her relentlessly.

What's wrong with you, Nerani the Elegant? Don't like your new name?

Do you believe Mame Galyria can truly predict the future?

What? Her question threw him off-guard. *Why?*

She told me something today, at the ceremony. Her eyes got all funny.

What did she say?

Nerani swallowed. She leaned in closer. *Gold blood bleeds red.*

Before him, Mame Galyria is nodding at him through slotted eyelids. Her expression seems to suggest she has somehow managed to read his thoughts. The idea rattles him slightly—more than it should. "You know what it is I mean," she croaks. "You understand."

"I think I might."

"Then you know why I cannot answer your questions. The things you are going to ask me do not yet have an answer. They must run their course. You have work to do, boy. The blood of Saynti runs deep within your bones. Fate has long foretold your destiny. It is a precarious path that lies before you, and it is not I who is meant to send you off on your journey."

Roberts hesitates in the dark hallway. He feels a sudden chill in the air that has nothing to do with the cold rain pattering against the roof overhead. He opens his mouth to speak, but she holds up a hand to silence him.

"No questions. You will understand everything in due time."

"But—"

She cuts him off again, her eyes narrowing. "I can tell you this much—you must visit Mame Noveli."

"The storyteller?" Roberts had thought the old woman to be dead and gone. She was older, still, than Mame Galyria, if such a feat were possible.

"Yes. You see, child, sometimes our past tells us more about our future than a seer ever can. She will help you."

Roberts nods, unconvinced. He chews at his lower lip, thoughtful.

"Now," declares the Mame, rubbing at her brittle knuckles. "I am going back to sleep. I am not young anymore, and time does not take pity on an old woman's bones. I trust you will see yourself out, ah?"

She is backing into the room, closing the door. A thousand questions dance upon his tongue. Only one reaches his lips.

"Mame—wait. Where can I find Mame Noveli? There is no one alive who has seen her in years."

At this Mame Galyria laughs. The sound leaks out through her pores. It swallows the air whole. Her black eyes glitter with a sourceless light.

"You are quite right, my boy. Nobody has seen her. Nobody knows."

The door is slammed shut.

CHAPTER 6

General James Bryon

CORPORAL THOMAS ANDERSON is asleep when James Byron enters the barracks. He has not even bothered to turn down the itching grey wool sheets. His golden cloak is draped over him like a blanket. It rises and falls along with his breathing.

"Get up," Byron barks. He kicks the base of the cot with the toe of his leather boot. The corporal is up in an instant. His cloak falls away from his uniform as he leaps to his feet. His silver hair, normally carefully maintained, is mussed from the lumpy pillow at the head of the mattress.

"Sir?" There is no trace of sleep in his voice. Byron wonders if he was even slumbering at all, or if he was merely pretending. He thinks, *do snakes sleep?* A frown deepens upon his face as he stares into the bright eyes across from him.

"You know exactly why I'm here, Corporal."

A smile. "But I'm afraid that I don't."

"You were to await my orders regarding torching Toyler's tavern."

"Ah." Anderson yawns, but the general is sure that he is faking. "You were nowhere to be found yesterday morning."

Byron ignores the annoyance that bristles beneath his skin. He does not immediately respond. He should not have lingered so long on the beach that morning. It is hard for him to stay away on mornings such as that—when the sky is red as blood and the electricity of an incoming storm clings to the air. It is nostalgic for him—soothing. He has been in a terrible need of some sort of escape. Tensions in the city have been high—the people have been prone to riots and looting.

Before him, Anderson stretches his arms wide over his head. "His Majesty did not want us to waste any more time." Reaching down, he pulls at a fraying bit of golden thread that has unraveled from the rectangular sigma upon his grey sleeve. The number of golden stripes a guardian has upon his arm signifies his status within the golden guard. Byron himself has four. He has risen quickly in the ranks for a young man his age. Corporal Anderson resents that, he is certain. The guardian is older than he, though not by much. His father is the Viscount of Rowland's court. He feels it is his due.

That is his first mistake.

"I know what the king wants," Byron snaps. "He and I spoke face-to-face regarding Toyler's."

"Then you were well aware that he wanted you to take immediate action should Mr. Toyler refuse to clear out his tavern."

Byron swallows. He fights the heat that is curling through his veins like wildfire. He thinks of the tavern, and of the flames that tickled the sky. He blinks, slowly, and tries in vain to clear from his head the memory of the screams that pervaded the street.

We were told to burn it down, he thinks, *we were never ordered to kill.*

"Those Cairans were sent to a slaughter."

"Indeed," Anderson agrees. Grooves splinter across his skin as his smile widens. "As they very well should be."

"There are crimes punishable by death, Corporal. This was not one of them."

"My men tell me there were no casualties."

"My men," Byron corrects. "And there easily could have been. If that had happened, the Cairans would have rebelled. It would have been a mess. Our responsibility is to keep the peace, not to disturb it."

Anderson sniffs. "They were given every chance to remove their slobbering, drunk carcasses from the premises before we lit the tavern on fire."

"Then they should have been manually cleared prior to the tavern being lit."

Anderson's lips curl into an uneven smile and he meets Byron's gaze head on. The lack of respect in his eyes is palpable. "Is that so?"

Byron swallows thickly, biting back his rage. He allows his hard gaze to remain trained upon Anderson for a long moment before responding.

"Next time, you wait for my orders, is that understood?"

"Of course, sir. You're in charge."

There is a clamor from the other side of the room. A throat clears. A plump woman with a mess of graying hair stands perched in the doorway. Her apron is stained with flour. She smiles politely at the two guardians, but it is clear that she does not have the time to spare. Her chest rises and falls as though she has been running.

"Adeline." Byron inclines his head respectfully towards the kitchen matron, recognizing her at once. He has known the woman all his life, since he was a young boy getting underfoot in the kitchens as his mother kneaded bread. "How may we be of service to you?"

"His Majesty has requested your presence in his quarters."

Anderson sniffs again, louder this time. "His valet was not sent for us."

Adeline's smile wanes upon her face. Her shoulders straighten in a statement of pride. Her stance says, *I am somebody.* Byron wonders if he, too, fights as hard to matter within the crowded walls of the king's thriving palace.

"No, sir, he was not," she assents evenly. "But I was. His Majesty has asked that you come immediately." She pauses and adds, "He is not in the most pleasant of moods."

Byron flashes her a genial smile. "Well, then we had better hurry. Thank you, Adeline."

She nods, backing out of the barracks as quickly as she came. She does not wait for a dismissal. Byron watches her go—watches the fraying hem of her soiled gown sweep against the wooden door frame. At his back, he hears Anderson scoff.

"Rotten kitchen wench. What business has she telling us what's expected of us?"

Byron glances over his shoulder at the corporal, feeling a grimace settling in upon his lips. "You should show more respect to the palace staff, Corporal."

Anderson pats at his blonde hair with the palm of his hand, choking back a quiet scoff. "Adeline may have been your mother's friend, but she cleans my mother's bedpans. The woman will respect me, as is her place. Nothing more."

Byron's grimace deepens, darkening the shadows about his lips. He feels a burning annoyance flicker deep within his chest. Anderson never misses an opportunity to point out Byron's impoverished upbringing—his unimpressive bloodlines. As the son of a lord and lady, he fancies himself superior to everyone save for the king himself. Shouldering his pride, Byron heads for the door without another word. He has no desire to engage Anderson in a pissing contest—not now, when Rowland waits for them in the throne room.

He hears Anderson's boots fall into step with his own as they head out of the barracks and towards the main building of the palace. Scowling—trying in vain to push the memory of screaming, the knowledge of his inferior officer's insolence, out of his head—he quickens his pace and looks to the day ahead.

CHAPTER 7

King Rowland Stoward

"Your Highness?"

Rowland Stoward startles. The folds of his chin double over his fist. His elbow slides off of the gilded armrest of his throne and he sputters, sitting up straighter in his chair. He has fallen asleep again. With a lazy wave of a heavily ringed hand, he gestures for the harpist on the far side of the room to cease his playing. There is a strum, strum, twang and the man's fingers settle into stillness against the strings. The courtiers that line the walls stretch inconspicuously. They peer sleepily around the room, blinking, surprised—pulled back to the present from their respective daydreams.

"What?" His voice is heavy with sleep. His valet perches humbly before him. His arms are folded behind his back and his eyes are trained respectfully toward the ground. His perfect posture reflects back up at him from the polished marble floors.

"If his Majesty will excuse me interrupting his music, your son is here to see you."

"Frederick?" Rowland's eyes narrow into slits. The wrinkled folds encompassing his eyelids deepen across his face. "Frederick is dead." He glares down at the valet in contempt.

The valet gulps. Discomfort creeps across his features.

"No, your Highness." He clears his throat. "Prince Peterson, your youngest, has requested an audience."

"Ah. Yes." Rowland closes his eyes and his mouth tumbles open in a yawn. His tongue falls across his lower lip. The folds of skin beneath his jowl increase and then decrease as his mouth snaps closed. The valet waits. His eyes remain trained upon the floor beneath his feet. "What does it want?"

"I am not sure, your Grace, I only know that he wishes to gain an audience with your Majesty."

"I have things to do." The answer is absolute. Final. It echoes languidly across the room.

The valet nods, his chin bobbing frantically above his chest. "Of course. Of course, your Highness. Shall I pass the message along?"

An air of annoyance seizes the king's portly features. He leans forward upon his throne. Locks of auburn hair fall across his forehead.

"Shall you pass the message along?" He is met with silence from the valet. "Did you think I was explaining myself to you for your own benefit?"

The valet shakes his head.

"I asked you a question."

"No, your Highness."

"No?"

"I will pass the message right along to your son."

"Excellent." Rowland sits back. He shifts his weight upon the cushion beneath him. He will need to call someone soon to plump it. It has grown lumpy and uncomfortable. He smiles down at the valet. His exposed teeth, yellowed and crooked within the deep lines around his lips cause him to appear wolfish. "I am a busy man. I have important matters with which to deal. Tell the boy he may seek me out later if he still wishes. If he has any immediate qualms, send him to his nurse. That's why he has the woman in the first place."

"Yes, your Majesty." The valet bows low to the floor, extending his waist so far that it seems for an instant as if he will tip over. He remains frozen there in silence.

"You may go," Rowland snaps, growing thoroughly agitated with the whole affair.

"Thank you, your Grace."

"Get out."

Rowland watches as the valet absconds eagerly from his sight. The door slams shut. He continues to stare at it for a few tacit moments. He is suddenly all too aware of the unnerving silence that has overtaken the room.

He hates silence. It makes the room feel far too empty. He lifts his hand into the air and snaps his fingers together. With a start, the harpist resumes his playing.

He is in a rotten mood. His temper is short. He can feel it boiling just under the surface of his skin, waiting to erupt. He frowns. Victoria was in his dreams again the previous night. Victoria, his wife—stone cold Victoria with her bitter, dead eyes. Victoria the effigy, hidden away in his dying labyrinth.

Victoria the corpse.

He hates dreaming of her. She is never with a heartbeat—thump, thump—in his dreams. She is always cold. Cold and dead. Like a fish.

He shudders involuntarily—hopes his courtiers do not see. He glares at them sideways from where he slumps in his throne. They are all making a rather extravagant show of examining the floor. Fools. He should have them all thrown out.

There is a sour plunk of the harp. It is immediately followed by silence.

"Your Majesty?" It is his valet again, peeking his deplorable face around the grand golden double doors at the opposite end of the room.

"What?" His reply is terse. His thick fingers drum against his armrest.

"General Byron is here, sir. As you requested. Corporal Anderson as well."

"What took them so long?"

The valet stammers—he does not know. The heat beneath his skin grows hotter. It singes his flesh.

"Send them in and go away." Rowland steeples his fingers in an attempt to center himself. Calm. He has been waiting for the guardians to come. Now he can have a bit of fun.

"Of course, your Highness," the valet is saying. As though he would say anything else. His head disappears behind the door. An instant later, both doors are thrust open.

General Byron sweeps formally into the court. His regalia gleams in the golden sunlight that streams in through the yawning, narrow windows. His golden cloak is draped over his right shoulder. He bows low, his brown eyes trained upon the king's polished hunting boots. Rowland is pleased, as always, to see the young soldier before him. James Byron has been like a son to him—has been loyal and unswerving in his devotion all his life. He stood by Frederick until the day he died, as faithful and as reliable as a dog. There are precious few he trusts as much as the young man. Too many have betrayed him. Too many will betray him, still.

Just behind James is the corporal. He, too, drops into a bow. His brows are raised upon his forehead as though he has stumbled upon something amusing. Rowland notes this with annoyance.

He is laughing at me, he thinks. *He thinks it comical that I dream of Victoria, dead. He knows.*

The notion is unreasonable, he knows, but it clings to him all the same—unflappable and tinged with the cold prick of unease. All around the room, the courtiers are waiting for him to speak. The guardians remain in a position of subservience. Rowland tries to remind himself why he called them to his throne room. It will do him good, he imagines, to focus on something else for just a while.

"Rise," he barks. They comply, straightening. They study him respectfully, but they do not make eye contact. It makes him uncomfortable. *Will no one look at me?* He fidgets upon his cushion. It is lumpy beneath his rear. Why has no one come to plump it for him?

"I received word that Toyler's tavern is nothing more than a charred ruin in the square. Is this true?"

"Yes, your Majesty," General Byron says.

A giggle rises in his throat like bile. He coughs. "Excellent. And did they squeal?"

A pause. "Your Majesty?"

"The Cairans inside, James. Did they squeal like the pigs they are while they burned?"

Before him, General Byron is silent. His brown eyes are like stone.

Corporal Anderson steps forward, falling in line with General Byron. "They were rescued, your Majesty. We tried to contain them, but a small uprising in the square impeded us. It was chaotic."

Rowland's lower lip protrudes from his face. He considers this. He heard as much from his valet when he awoke this morning. The grey dawn leaked in through his windowpane as he lay sweating beneath his golden sheets, trying in vain to shake the dregs of his dreams.

"I heard such rumors. I wanted it to be verified by my top men."

It is treason to encumber a guardian in his line of duty. He has already made the necessary arrangements. Retribution will be swift. His lips curl into a crooked smile. This is what he has been waiting for all day. This will right what was made wrong in the night.

"I spoke to your men early this morning. Every insurrection has a leader. Once we did some sniffing about the slums, we were able to discover your man." He claps his hands together, feeling excitement ripple through him. "Bring him in!"

To his left, a smaller golden door slams open. Two guardians drag in a protesting figure. A bag has been pulled down over his head and tied about his neck. Rowland watches the men before him to gauge their reactions. Corporal Anderson is fighting a smile that tugs at his lips. His fingers itch at the hilt of his gun. General Byron remains silent, still. His gaze is unreadable. He stares back at the king.

"Who is this man?"

Rowland snaps his fingers. One of the guardians removes his hood. The captive blinks in the light, staring around the room. His feet struggle aimlessly against the polished floor. At the other side of the room, the courtiers have clumped together like a drooling pack of dogs to watch.

"State your name, Cairan," Rowland barks, delighted.

The Cairan shakes his head. His voice quakes. "No."

Rowland clicks his tongue against the roof of his mouth. "It could save your life."

"You'll kill me anyway." The captive is breathless from struggling. His chest rises and falls heavily beneath the cotton of his undershirt.

"I most likely will," Rowland avows cheerily. "Tell me, Cairan, did you lead your people in a surge against the good general and his men yesterday afternoon in the square?"

The captive swallows hard. His larynx bounces beneath his skin. "I did not."

"Hmm," Rowland breathes. Adrenaline is coursing through his veins. He is hungry for death. "I am afraid that I do not believe you. Several of my men have placed you at the scene."

"I was there, yes, but I did not lead the attack against the guardians. I give you my word."

"Your word?" A laugh tickles the back of Rowland's throat. It spills forth from his lips—distends upwards towards the painted cherubs that float in frozen bliss amid the garlanded clouds upon the ceiling.

The room around him is frozen—watching. They cannot look away. He collects himself. His mouth settles back into its usual frown.

"What good is your word to me, Cairan? You are nothing but a liar."

"I swear to you," the captive Cairan pleads. "I did not instigate the uprising."

"Tell me who did," Rowland hisses, sneering down at him. "Give me a name and perhaps I will let you go free."

The Cairan is silent before him. The color has drained from his skin. Defeat floods his watery eyes.

"Who staged the revolt in the square?" Rowland demands again. Spittle gathers at the corner of his lips.

The Cairan scoffs. "Nobody did," he says. His voice is quiet. His eyes flutter closed.

Rowland feels the temper creeping back into his skin. He can feel himself turning as red as his doublet. "James," he seethes. He can sense General Byron's stony brown eyes upon him. He thinks again of Victoria—dead, sapped of her life, and he realizes he wants this Cairan before him dead, too. *Kill them all*, he thinks. *Every last one*. Kill until it is made right.

"Shoot him," he commands.

The general draws his pistol from his holster.

"Please," the Cairan whispers. There is a sharp bang—the pungent smell of gunpowder—and the man is dead. Rowland stares down at the corpse, watching the pink life seep from his cheeks. A crimson puddle is gathering beneath the Cairan's body. It pools between the tiles upon the floor. Useless. The gypsy was utterly useless.

The puddle of blood is pressing outward. How can any one body have so much of that inside them? He can smell the blood from here, or does he just imagine that? There had been no red when his Victoria died. Only her skin, cold and white. She had gone like the wind, extinguished as though she were a candle.

He leans back upon his throne—rubs at his temples with two heavily ringed fingers. What to do? He should have questioned the Cairan further. Perhaps the man would have buckled with more pressure.

The death, without any new information to spare, has not quite lifted his spirits as he hoped it would.

"Clean this up," he barks to no one in particular. He feels suddenly exhausted. "When you are done, take the body and hang it in the square. Let the Cairans see what happens to those who rebel against the crown."

"Yes, your Majesty." General Byron's voice sounds as though it reaches him from miles away. He lets his eyes drift closed. He will go back to bed. It is better—in dreams—to see his dead wife, than to roam the corridors awake and remember that she will never again be among the living.

He will feel better once he is rested. He thinks of the corpse, and how it will hang like a lifeless flag in full view for the remainder of the day. Crows will come—black scavengers from the forest. They will take his eyes and peck at his flesh. The Cairan's body will be desecrated before his people. He can take comfort, at least, in knowing that his message will be clear.

The Cairans will see that he is not a man to be trifled with. He will not tolerate insolence. He will not be made a fool.

CHAPTER 8

Emerala the Rogue

ROBERTS DID NOT return home until the early hours of the morning.

Emerala is sure of this because she woke with the dawn, her backside aching against the hard surface of the window ledge and her limbs frozen stiff. She glanced around the room, illuminated in sleepy gray hues, and tried to shake away the icy remnants of sleep that clung to her insides like frost. It was then that her eyes fell upon the bulge beneath the sheets of Roberts's cot. Relief flooded through her veins, warming her as thoroughly as a piping hot cup of tea. It was immediately followed by annoyance.

What had he been doing at Mamere Lenora's? He had no business going there, she was sure of it. Nothing from the fire at Toyler's could have led him to the brothel so late at night. She fell asleep the night before wracking her brain for possibilities, and found that she was able to come up with exactly none. This, of course, led her to the only possible conclusion she could fathom.

Roberts was keeping secrets.

If there is one thing Emerala hates more than secrets, it is being left on the outside of a particularly juicy one.

"Are you going to purchase that?"

The merchant's voice is rough in Emerala's ear. One askew plume of his feathered hat brushes against her cheek. She startles—places down the dagger she has been admiring. The sunlight that trickles down through the latticed tent overhead catches upon the iridescent hilt. She has lost herself in a daydream, replaying the quiet grey morning over in her mind.

"Right." She takes a step back. "No."

The merchant crosses his arms over his violet clad chest. He stares contemptuously down at her over the bridge of his hooked nose. "That's what

I thought. Now clear out—other customers are waiting. Customers with money."

Emerala feels a scowl deepening upon her face. She turns away from the merchant without another word. Staring around the tent, she sulks as she fusses with the olive cotton of her gown. Her wild black hair is a tousled mess of uncombed curls upon her head. One golden earring hangs in a hoop from her left earlobe. Her right earlobe is bare, the remaining earring left forgotten upon her cot at home. She glares at the idling parasol wielding ladies milling about her—studies their fitted jackets and their tight, lace collars—and sighs.

Today has been terrible. From the moment she awoke, it seems, those around her have been nothing but infuriating. First Roberts with his secret keeping, and now the merchant, feathered like a hen ready for plucking.

The tent is crowded. It was set up only the day before to house the newest arrival of goods. These are no ordinary goods, however. Unlike the rest of the shops that line the marketplace, this one has not been brought to Chancey from the Westerlies. The merchant has had his men prowling the street all morning spreading the word—these goods have been delivered from the island of Caira.

Caira. There is something enchanting about it. Emerala thinks of the stories that she heard as a child—stories of the Cairans of Chancey and the island from whence they hailed. The legends are resplendent in nature—magical in a way that Chancey will never be. Yet the stories are old, passed down from generation to generation. There is not a Cairan alive who can claim to have been there. Her people are so far removed from their homeland—their blood so tainted with the blood of Chancian commoners—that they might as well have severed all historical ties to the mysterious island of Caira.

It is a world that, now, only exists in the kind of stories children whisper to one another in the dark.

She is so deep in thought that she hardly notices the dark stranger watching her from one shaded corner of the tent. It is not until she hesitates before the opening to stare around at the chattering customers in contempt that she feels his eyes upon her face. Her gaze snaps towards the shaded figure. He is leaning against a splintering post, his brown moth bitten coat draping his lanky silhouette. From beneath a tilted black tricorn hat, two stark golden eyes stare pointedly at her. He realizes that she has seen him and he winks, one eye disappearing and reappearing like the flip of a coin.

Strange. The man is watching her with such familiarity, and yet she is sure that she has never before laid eyes on him. Ensnared by her curiosity, she moves back into the tent. There is a loud clamor at her back—the sound of glass shattering upon stone. The merchant is shouting at a customer, berating him for breaking a piece of his collection. Emerala glances over her shoulder, distracted, and turns back towards the post.

The dark stranger is gone.

Emerala frowns at the crowd mulling about her. Nowhere among them does she see a man wearing that same black hat. How could he have exited without her seeing? She only looked away for a moment. Her shoulders droop. Slowly, keeping her eyes peeled for any sign of the man, she exits the tent and heads out into the street.

The marketplace outside is far too crowded for Emerala's liking. She shoves her way through the throng of Chancians that have fallen to meandering aimlessly from tent to tent, studying each face as she passes. None of the men she sees appear to have those same bright golden eyes. She curses silently and allows herself to be swallowed by the mass of shopping Cairans.

The sound of a familiar voice calling her name pulls her out of her foul mood. Glancing over her shoulder, she spots Orianna is running towards her through the horde of Chancians. Nerani is at her heels, her long brown locks streaming in the sunlight. The draped fabric of her ivory gown is bunched within her fists. The women are breathless—their chests rise and fall beneath their tightly laced bodices.

"There you are," Nerani exclaims. "We've been searching for you all morning."

"Why?" Emerala asks, growing immediately defensive. She wracks her brain, retracing her steps that morning as she searches the banks of her memory for any condemning actions she might have undertaken. Coming up empty, she crosses her arms across the tightly laced brown fabric of her whalebone corset. "What have I done?"

Orianna ignores her, tugging roughly at her locked arms. "You have to come! Quickly!"

They are, each of them, far too excited for Emerala to bother playing at being disinterested. Her curiosity aroused, Emerala allows herself to be led back through the crowd. As she walks she scans the faces around her one last time. There is no trace of those golden eyes—that dark, beckoning face. She tries to closet her disappointment. She focuses her attention instead on the girls before her. "What is it? Where are we going?"

"Pirates are in the square." Orianna shouts to her over the rising volume of the crowd. Emerala catches Nerani's gaze. Her cousin shrugs; smiles. Sure enough, as the girls make their way closer to the square, the crowd grows more condensed. Several people are shouting heatedly. Their voices overlap one another in a raucous roar that climbs towards the sky. Emerala strains her ears to listen. She cannot make out anything intelligible. The mass is pushing forward relentlessly, each onlooker more eager than the last. It is no use trying to shove their way to the front of the crowd. The girls keep to the outskirts, their backs pressed against the cool brick of the surrounding shops.

"Damn you! Stand still!"

Emerala hears the incensed roar cut through the commotion like a knife. A gunshot ricochets through the square. At the sound, a collective gasp ripples through the crowd. Everyone falls silent at once.

"Stand still, I say!"

The women have managed to make their way around the crowd and into a more sparse collection of stragglers. Before them stands an elderly man donned in an oversized red coat. On his head sits a black tricorn hat laced with gold. In one hand he holds a half empty pint of ale. In the other, a pistol. He stumbles forward, clearly heavily inebriated. Spittle flies from his lips as he bellows indistinctly, waving his gun in a haphazard, jerking motion. The crowd draws back, frightened. The sight of a weapon, carelessly wielded, has robbed them of their bravado.

Emerala cranes her neck to see past the slobbering drunkard. There, perched upon the back of a fruit-laden cart, stands a smirking young man. His tricorn hat has been swept from his head in a grand gesture as he addresses the crowd nearest to him. Wild brown hair falls down into bright hazel eyes. His face is burnt from the sun, and even from here Emerala can make out the spattering of freckles that coat the bridge of his crooked nose. He hops down from the pushcart as the drunkard's gun goes off again.

"Stop movin', you bilge rat," spits the man.

"If you weren't three sheets to the wind, likely you would have shot me by now, mate," the young man shouts back. He laughs at his own words, his hazel eyes twinkling. A few in the crowd laugh along with him. He has captivated his audience with a smile and a bow, this grinning visitor.

A shout from beyond the crowd sends a section of the watchers scattering. Another voice, authoritative and clear, calls out, "Make way!"

"Clear on out," calls another voice. Emerala watches as a section of the crowd parts in nervous obedience. Silence has once again settled over the square and its inhabitants. At the far end of the gathering, General Byron is making his way towards the center of the commotion. His dark eyes scan the crowd. His jaw is set in an angry line. Behind him march five more guardians. Their weapons are drawn. Their expressions are hardened into stone. Their golden cloaks gleam in the morning sun as they surge forward towards the brawling pirates.

"Emerala, it's time to go," Nerani hisses in her ear. She feels her cousin's nails dig into her wrist. She ignores her, shaking her arm free from Nerani's vise-like grip. Her green eyes are glued to the scene.

"Emerala, we're going." Orianna's voice slips out from the shadows at Emerala's back. They are already leaving. Neither of them is eager to stick around and risk exposure with the guardians so close. It's understandable, but Emerala knows that she can take care of herself. She is far too captivated to walk away now. She needs to see how this ends.

"Go on, then. I'm staying."

"Suit yourself," Orianna murmurs darkly.

Nerani's voice barely climbs above a whisper. "Be careful." And they are gone.

Emerala studies the scene before her. The drunkard drops his pint of ale to the ground as he catches sight of the approaching Golden Guard. Several onlookers jump at the sound of shattering glass upon the street. His gun droops limply at his side. He watches in silence as the guardians approach him, his eyes opening and closing as though he cannot quite believe what he sees. His lower jaw has gone slack against his face. General Byron slows to a standstill directly before the old man. He raises one gloved palm above his shoulder. The guardians behind him draw to an immediate stop. It seems to Emerala as though everyone in the square is holding their breath. Watching. Waiting. They have transformed from an unruly mob to a captive audience.

"State your name, foreigner."

"J-jameson," stammers the man. He clears his throat. "Jameson."

"He's a pirate!" The accusation comes from somewhere behind Emerala's back.

One eyebrow rises upon the general's forehead. "Is that so?"

Jameson the drunkard is shaking his head wildly. His lower lip trembles like the drooping jowl of a hound. One stubby finger jabs at his chest. "Me? En't got a clue what that bloke be on about."

General Byron appears unconvinced. "What is your business in Chancey, Mr. Jameson?" His dark, unblinking gaze is trained upon the man. He is the picture of propriety in his golden uniform, standing tall beneath the mid-morning sun.

"Sellin' goods," Jameson says, before hiccoughing violently.

"Ah." General Byron smiles wanly. "So you're a merchant?"

"Aye, that I am. A merchant." Jameson flashes the general a toothy grin.

"I suppose, then, you wouldn't happen to be the similarly named Captain Jameson of the brigand ship *Red Skull* that my men and I took into custody earlier this morning?"

The grin is rapidly fading from Jameson's face. He is silent. A silver haired guardian steps forward, a polite smile imprinted upon his face. In his free hand he dangles a pair of golden shackles. The sound of the cuffs clattering against one another resounds loudly throughout the square.

"You see, Jameson, the captain was not present with his crew when we boarded the ship," the guardian with the silver hair explains. "The crew was surprisingly amiable towards the good general and I. They were not feeling well—they'd fallen ill to a bout of scurvy at sea. They needed supplies—food and water. Said that the captain gambled away their goods and they had nothing left to trade. It's a sad story, truly. They gave quite the description of their fearless captain—a description that I'd say you fit rather nicely."

He snaps his gloved fingers together, grinning. "Private Provence, wouldn't you say this man looks just like the Captain Jameson they described?"

"Yes, sir," barks a young guardian that has positioned himself at General Byron's left shoulder.

"Really, the resemblance is uncanny," General Byron marvels. "Could it be there are two Captain Jamesons wandering around our island?"

Before him, Jameson sputters wordlessly. His gun trembles within his fist.

"I'd wager not," Corporal Anderson offers.

"If you're lookin' to arrest anyone, arrest him—the thievin' bastard!" Jameson shouts, gesturing his free hand wildly in the direction of the pushcart. General Byron glances over his shoulder. Emerala follows his gaze. The young pirate that stood there only moments before is gone.

Another disappearing act, Emerala considers, intrigued. He had been in full view the entire time, and yet she had not seen him depart from the square.

"I'm afraid there's no one there, Mr. Jameson," General Byron points out.

Jameson's mouth is agape. "He were there only moments ago!"

The silver-haired guardian—Corporal Anderson—makes a mock show of looking concerned. "And you claim that this mystery man was a thief?"

"Aye."

"What did he steal?"

Jameson hesitates. Winces. "Well, I en't able to tell you that."

At this, General Byron smiles. "I thought that might be the case. Men, arrest him."

The guardians surge forward, ignoring the wild protests of the pirate as they clap him in irons. Emerala watches in silence with the rest of the crowd as the guardians drag a protesting Captain Jameson around the corner and out of sight.

General Byron is the only guardian that remains behind. He stares wordlessly at the throng of people before him. They stare back.

"Well?" he snaps at last. His voice projects through the crowd. "The show is over. Go about your business."

It is as though the onlookers have been set free from a spell. All at once, everyone is moving and chatting as though nothing out of the ordinary has happened. Emerala falls back against the brick buildings, watching. From the shadows, she studies the general. He is standing in the midst of the commotion, his cold gaze trained upon the shattered pint glass upon the street. His fists are clasped in a tight ball at the small of his back. She tries to imagine what it is he is thinking, standing there alone, and if it is the same thought that led him down to the waterfront the day before.

He looks up, then, and she wonders if he has somehow heard her thoughts. His dark eyes scan the crowd—he is watching for someone—waiting. His gaze alights upon her face. His lips deepen into a frown.

Time to go, she thinks. She veers to her left, ducking sharply into a narrow alleyway between the shops. The air within the cramped lane is thicker somehow—heavier. Speckles of dust drift down in broken shafts of sunlight. The crumbling brick swallows the commotion of the crowd in the square. She surges forward into the shadows, eager to avoid a run-in with the general. Her frame collides hard into a figure that lurks beyond the reach of sunlight.

"Watch where you're going," she snaps, startled.

"I see the Cairan hospitality hasn't changed a bit since I've gone." A laugh slips out from between the stranger's lips—tickles the curls at the top of her head. She backs away, uncomfortable.

"Who are you?"

"A friend." The response is given pleasantly enough, but Emerala feels a shiver of unease run through her all the same.

"Come into the light where I can see you," she demands of the shaded figure.

Obliging her, the man steps into a shaft of sunlight that spills down onto the hay-ridden dirt path beneath their feet. Two golden eyes twinkle merrily out from a handsome face as he grins down at her.

You again. With all of the commotion in the square, she had nearly forgotten about her brief interaction with the golden-eyed stranger in the tent earlier that morning. The nervous excitement that winds through her veins curls her toes upon the earthen street.

"Who are you?"

"The Hawk, at your service." He sweeps his tricorn hat from his head and dips into a theatrical bow. Unwashed black hair tumbles down into his face. Emerala scowls at his use of a title. He is not a Cairan—she would know him if he was. The bronzed skin of his face suggests that he is a foreigner. He should have no understanding of the way the gypsy titles work. Even so, she finds that she is afraid to ask for his true name. Cairan custom requires her to offer her true name in exchange for his. She does not know how much he knows. She is not willing to risk such personal information to find out.

"Why are you following me?" she demands, narrowing her eyes.

He shrugs. "I'm not."

"You are."

"How entirely arrogant of you to think so. I suppose I should expect as much."

"What does that mean?"

A smile dances in the Hawk's golden eyes. "I've brought you something," he says, ignoring her question. He holds out one dirty hand. His long fingers are wrapped around a familiar looking object. The sunlight catches on the rounded, iridescent surface. It is the dagger she had admired earlier that morning beneath the merchant's tent.

"What is this?" It is not one of the hundred questions that bubble within her chest, and yet it is the only one that manages to find a voice.

"Well, it's a dagger, of course."

"I can see that," she snaps tersely. "Why?"

A crooked smile teases at corner of his lips, dimpling his cheek. "It's a gift."

"I can't take that."

"Aye, you can. It'd be rude not to."

She hesitates, her eyes traveling hungrily along the glistening silver blade. It is thinner than paper—as fragile-looking as the trilling rim of a wine glass.

Yet she is certain that, if wielded correctly, the blade could be deadly. Rob would never approve of her having such a weapon.

That is exactly why she covets it.

"What do you want for it?"

Another laugh. "If I wanted something in return, it'd hardly be a gift now, aye?"

"Nothing comes for free," she retorts.

"Indeed," the Hawk agrees, grinning. He replaces his tricorn hat, his golden eyes drifting down towards the knife in his hands. One idle finger runs along the blade. It makes Emerala uncomfortable to see the ease with which he handles the weapon. She feels suddenly helpless—trapped before the stranger in the narrow shade of the alleyway.

"Tell me," the Hawk says, "where is it you get those lovely green eyes?"

"Sorry?" She is caught-off guard by the question.

"Your eyes—it's not common to see eyes that color in a Cairan."

Emerala is silent. He is right, of course—most Cairans have blue eyes. It is the color, the Mames always said, that the gypsies brought with them on the long journey from Caira. Those that are half-blood—the offspring of both Chancians and Cairans—will often sport brown eyes, maybe even hazel, but not green. Emerala has never before seen anyone with eyes quite like hers and her brother's. It's a distinguishing feature, and one that she is proud of. It is what sets her apart.

But how can he know that—this stranger to the island?

"I just couldn't help wondering if those eyes came from your mother or your father?" he asks again, trying to elicit a response. He has moved closer to her without her even noticing. She keeps her attention trained upon the blade of the dagger. The tip rests dangerously close to her bodice. She can see the warped reflection of her faded olive gown within the surface.

"What does it matter?" Emerala asks, suddenly suspicious.

"It doesn't matter a lick, I'm just curious is all."

"Well it's none of your business."

"I suppose it's not." His smile widens, and she can see one golden tooth rooted within his bottom jaw. "Do you want the dagger or not?"

She hesitates, chewing at her lip.

"It'd be wise, I think, to have some protection. Keep yourself safe."

She crosses her arms protectively over her chest. "What do I need to be kept safe from?"

"Guardians," he says and shrugs. "Pirates." The crooked grin upon his face stretches impossible wider, crinkling his golden eyes. "Times are changing—getting dangerous. See for yourself." He nods towards the square at her back. She watches him, unmoving, reluctant to turn her back to him in order to look into the square.

"Look," he says again, gesturing this time with the point of the dagger.

Her curiosity getting the better of her, she turns. Her green eyes seek out the object of his gesticulation. There, in plain view, his body bound by rope to the rotting wood of a post, is the corpse of a familiar looking young man.

Harrane the Hostile.

So that's why General Byron was so close to the square with all of his men that morning, she realizes. She feels as though she is going to be sick. His blood has dried upon his flesh in the sun. It is cracked like red mud baked by the summer heat. A crow perches idly upon his exposed shoulder, pecking hungrily at his ear lobe. Tears prick in Emerala's lower lids at the sight of him.

"It's good to be armed in times like these." She can feel the Hawk's breath warm against her neck. He presses the dagger firmly into her hand and closes her fingers around the hilt. Her heart seizes up within her chest.

Releasing her hand, he moves away from her. She turns, wrenching her eyes from Harrane's hanging carcass, but the Hawk is gone. The alleyway around her is empty. She is alone. She stares down at the dagger in her fist. She thinks again of the body in the square and her blood surges with the heat of rebellion.

She will wait for General Byron to go, and then she will have to act fast.

CHAPTER 9

Captain Alexander Mathew

So far, the island of Chancey has given Alexander anything but a warm welcome. He grimaces about him as he wanders through the bustling streets of the marketplace. He does not have to push and cajole his way through the crowd. In fact, the throng of Chancians that swarm about him, reeking of sweating powders and putrid perfumes, are more than content to offer him a wide berth as he passes. Their eyes remain glued to their carts. Their whispered mutterings are riddled with treachery.

Is it the hat that gives me away, he wants to ask, *or the sword at my belt?*

It is not as though he expects anything more. In fact, it seems as though the inhabitants of most of the islands that he and his crew have visited lately end up chasing them back onto their ships before the week is up. He can hardly blame them. The men of his crew are not the neatest of houseguests, or the most polite. And most of them are terrible at keeping their hands to themselves.

And yet he has specifically instructed his men to lay low during this visit to Chancey. They did not drop anchor to pick up supplies or to gamble away useless goods or to find easy women. This time, Alexander came ashore because he had an actual agenda, and one that he couldn't afford to miss out on because another one of his men was caught in bed with a local lord's daughter.

He had received word that Captain Jameson had holed himself up in a tavern on the island of Chancey about a month back. They had been stocking up on gunpowder at the eschewed port of Caros after a nasty shootout with the Westerly navy at sea. He had been in the middle of telling his woes to a particularly earnest young woman and her breasts when the Hawk had appeared with an old man that he introduced simply as Smith.

What's Smith to me? he snapped, frustrated from his fruitless search for Jameson and beginning to feel a little bit inebriated.

Smith is Jameson to you, that's who, the Hawk responded. *He's got word of him, anyhow.*

Alexander has been tirelessly searching for the old mercenary for nearly a year. Before that, the mission had been his father's fruitless, lifelong quest.

He thinks of Captain Samuel Mathew, and how his father and commander had passed his life's mission to his son from his deathbed.

Find Jameson, Samuel had whispered, *find the map wot he stole from me.*

His father had been royalty in his own right—had been one of the seven appointed pirate lords of the Western seas. He had been sure in his dying moments that his command would be followed. Alexander was bound to his oath—both by blood and by loyalty to his captain. Alexander could not, for the life of him, fathom what could be so important about a map. And yet his father had taken his last breath before Alexander could dare to ask.

So there he was, left in the dark and sworn to solve a mystery for which he had not a single clue. Weeks passed. Then months. Finally, as the year drew to a close and he was no closer to finding Jameson than before, he was about ready to give up.

He was not so sure that would have been a terrible ending to the story. His men were sick of trekking aimlessly about the seas. And so, too, was he.

Smith and his information had either been a godsend or a curse.

Docked in the port of Chancey, 'e did, Smith said, holding out one adamant palm for coins. *Picked up a nasty bit of scurvy in the Agran Circle ov'r the wint'r seasons. Came 'ere first but we en't even got enough t' feed ourselves.*

Alexander had not wanted to set sail for Chancey—had not wanted to risk tearing his ship to pieces in the wild spring storms that raged offshore the island—and yet he could hardly pass up the first glimmer of an opportunity he had received. The news Smith gave him was sound enough. More so, anyway, than any of the cryptic tips they had received in the past. As soon as he was sober he had gathered up his crew and lifted anchor.

He was determined to do his father proud—as though that would somehow make up for the time that was lost. Stolen from them, really. Captain

Jameson had managed to successfully evade his father for years. For reasons unbeknownst to the captain and the crew of the *Rebellion*, the mercenary had been extraordinarily adept at knowing the exact whereabouts of the *Rebellion*'s location at any time.

But Alexander has finally done it—he, the green captain's son that nobody believed in. He has done what even his father, the famed pirate lord, could not. He smiles to himself as he thinks of his luck upon arriving to the bar where Captain Jameson was said to have hunkered down. The mercenary had been asleep face down against the bar, his cheek resting in a puddle of his own drool. The item in question—a map—was peeking visibly out of the pocket of the man's tattered coat.

It was too easy.

Alexander thinks of his mother, safe within her ward back in Senada, and wonders if she would be proud of him. He wonders, too, if she even thinks of him at all, now he is gone. She is consumed by the thought of his father, he is sure, just as she has always been.

Alexander frowns at the unwelcome thoughts of his mother. He pushes them away and glances upwards. The brick buildings that line the marketplace press inward over his head. Curling puffs of white are pushed by the wind across a mild blue sky. He fills his chest with air, nostrils flaring. He feels trapped between the silent red edifices. He is never comfortable when he cannot smell the sea.

The great bells of the cathedral are chiming the hour. The very foundations of the buildings around him seem to shake with each resounding clang of the imposing brass instruments that dwell in the towers overhead. He counts the hours silently. It is noon. When did it reach midday? The hours slipped by so quickly this morning. Slowly, the bells fall back into silence. The echoes ring in his ears.

Alexander is called back to the streets by the sharp braying of an animal and a loud, unfortunate yelp. Glancing around in surprise, he searches for the source of the clamor. Upon finding it, he nearly laughs aloud. An agitated looking donkey perches firmly upon the cobblestone, his long ears flattened against his scalp. His broad hoofed feet are splayed obstinately over a young, fair-haired woman that perches helplessly in a puddle of mud.

Alexander ambles over towards her, fighting hard to choke down the laughter that bubbles within him. The woman's skin tone matches the cherry color of her full lips, the bottom one of which trembles slightly.

"Here." He reaches his arms down and takes hold of her slender wrists. "Let me help you." With a slight tug he is able to drag her back upright. Her soft carnation gown is covered in splashes of mud. She pulls her wrists from his grasp, crossing her arms protectively across her tightly laced corset. Her striking grey eyes are damp with tears.

"I'm Alexander," he offers, choosing not to identify himself by his rank among his crew, but instead by the name his mother gave him. It is safer that way, he thinks. He keeps a friendly smile etched across his sun-kissed face. "You look like you could use some help with your animal, here."

The young woman sniffs, shuffling one bare foot against the ground. With an idle hand she flips her white-blonde hair over her shoulder. He notices how waiflike her figure appears, quickly realizing that she is far too slender and too fair to be dragging a donkey through the streets. He wonders, now, if the animal even belongs to her at all.

"I don't need your help," she snaps, her lip still trembling. "You've gone and done enough damage already, thank you."

Alexander hesitates, thrown off-guard by her response. The young woman is staring pointedly over his shoulder. Her brow is creased in frustration as she scans the crowd at his back.

Odd.

"You have a nice day, miss." He smiles, touching his finger to his hat as he turns to leave, suddenly wishing to be as far away from the strange woman as possible. Those grey eyes snap back towards him as he speaks.

"Actually," she croons, her demeanor changing drastically. "Now that you've mentioned it, I suppose I could use some help getting this animal to the square."

Alexander chews his lip, feeling thoroughly vexed by the young woman's abnormal behavior. The square is in the opposite direction from where she had been previously heading. He thinks of the stories Evander the Hawk told him about the Cairan women of Chancey.

Mysteries, all of them. It's why I never bothered. Saints, it's why I left.

He shrugs. "Sure." He supposes he has nothing but time now that he's secured the map from Jameson. He thinks of it sitting in his pocket and smiles. Taking hold of the donkey's fraying lead rope, he pats the tormented animal reassuringly upon the head before leading it down the street. He is certain that the Golden Guard will have cleared Captain Jameson out of the square by now. It should be safe enough to return.

The grey-eyed woman falls into step at his side as they walk. He can feel her eyes upon him as they make their way through the crowd. Her white-blonde hair sways against her exposed shoulder blades. As the stinging red seeps out of her cheeks, her pallid skin begins to appear translucent beneath the warm rays of sunlight.

It is a short venture back to the square. The donkey walks easily enough when the woman is not tugging relentlessly at his face. Its hooves clatter against the uneven stones of the street. It expels air outward through its wide nostrils. The skin flaps noisily against the force of its breath.

"I didn't manage to catch your name," Alexander says after the silence between them becomes uncomfortable.

"I didn't offer it."

"Oh."

The woman sighs, flipping her hair over her shoulder. "They call me the Fair." Glancing up at him suspiciously she says, "I don't speak with pirates, as a rule. I only needed help getting this ridiculous animal to move."

"I see," Alexander says, finding himself beginning to regret ever helping the ungrateful young woman out of the mud at all. Finally, after what seems like far too long, they round the corner and enter the square.

"HALT," bellows a voice. Both Alexander and the young woman freeze. The donkey harrumphs in agitation as he is pulled to a sudden stop. Alexander wonders for a panicked moment if perhaps the Golden Guard has not quite gotten around to arresting Captain Jameson, and if the drunken mercenary has managed to identify him as the man that stole his precious map. He glances around the square. Not a single person is looking in his direction.

"Cease and desist, in the name of His Majesty!"

Alexander's gaze settles upon a young guardian. The soldier's face is white; his dark eyes are wide with apprehension. In his nervousness, he has drawn his ceremonial sword rather than his pistol. Curious, Alexander leads the donkey further into the square. He keeps to the shadows that linger at the edge of the open expanse, eager to remain invisible. His eyes scan the scene before him.

There, on a post that Alexander is quite sure was bare when he was here not long before, someone has strung a bloodied corpse. It is not the sight of the corpse that captures his attention, however, but what lies just beneath. Positioned under the body, her hands waving madly at the shrieking crows that swarm about her head, is a woman with wild black hair. She has shimmied up the length of the wooden post, her legs wrapped tightly about the wood for support. Her gown drapes down beneath her in waves of heavy olive fabric. Between her clenched teeth sits a gleaming dagger. She is making a terrific show of being deaf to the guardian's commands.

"Come down or I'll shoot," he bellows.

Alexander wonders if he's given any thought to how he plans to shoot her with his sword.

"What is going on here?" A second guardian has entered the square. Alexander recognizes him immediately as the lead officer from his squabble with Jameson. His golden cloak ripples in the wind as he surges into the opening. At Alexander's side, the flaxen woman shrinks back behind the donkey. Her eyes are wild with fear. The guardian takes no notice of her. Instead, his dark brown eyes are glued to the woman on the post. She has removed the dagger from her mouth and has set to sawing through the rope that binds the corpse.

"Rogue," barks the guardian. She pauses long enough to glance down over her shoulder before continuing.

"I'm cutting him down, General."

"I can see that," he replies calmly. "You're committing treason."

The woman called the Rogue continues to saw away at the rope. Her brow is furrowed. She pants from the exertion of holding herself steady upon the post. Alexander wonders how she plans to get the body down after she has untied him. Certainly, the cadaver is too heavy for a girl of her stature. Furthermore, once she is down, he wonders where she plans to run.

The general seems to have come to the same conclusion. Clasping his hands behind his back, he remains a safe distance out of reach of falling corpses.

"Rogue, if you continue to disobey orders, you will be placed under arrest."

"Whatever he did, he deserves a proper burial," the Rogue shouts down to the general. "And I'm sure he did nothing at all," Alexander hears her snap to herself.

The rope is almost cut all the way through. The body has begun to pull away from the post. Alexander watches the general for a response. The guardian stands as though frozen to the street. He swallows hard, his brows pulling together above his dark gaze. He says nothing else, but waits. What else is there to be said? The Rogue is brimming with determination. She cannot be physically apprehended until she reaches the ground.

She has managed to cut the entirety of the rope away. It falls to the ground, coiling upon the stones like a snake. Alexander watches her struggle with the leaning weight of the corpse. She grunts, sliding a few inches down the pole before completely losing her grip. With a gasp and a thud she hits the ground hard. The corpse lands besides her; silent.

Alexander is surprised at the ease with which she jumps to her feet. Surely, she is hurting after taking such a spill. If she is, she shows no sign of pain. As she rights herself, she whips around to face the waiting pair of guardians. Alexander is caught off-guard by the steely challenge etched across her sharp, olive features—captivated by the way the sunlight catches in her striking green eyes. It is as though she is filled to the brim with the wild sea.

She glances around the square. Her eyes alight briefly upon Alexander and the flaxen haired woman.

"A little help?" She pants lightly, flashing them a smile. Her black curls are suctioned to her glistening cheeks.

The general turns to see whom it is she has addressed. Next to Alexander, the young woman's plump, heart shaped lips have fallen open into a small, distressed "o". The general's eyes widen momentarily in what Alexander is sure is a flicker of recognition. The look is gone in an instant, however, overtaken by such severe composure that he immediately doubts what he has seen.

"Are you involved in this?" The general sounds annoyed. Alexander is not sure whom he is asking—him or the young woman at his side.

It is the woman who responds. "No," she squeaks. Her wide, grey eyes are unblinking. Her next words are a barely subdued plea. "I don't even know her."

"Clear out of here," the general barks.

She runs.

You forgot your donkey, Alexander thinks. The lead rope is still planted within his fists. The animal gives an indifferent snort and continues chewing at a bit of hay.

The general does not wait to see if Alexander leaves as well. He turns his attention back towards the Rogue. She is attempting to move the corpse from where it has crumpled at her feet.

"This didn't have to end this way, Rogue," the general says.

"Yes, it did," strains the Rogue.

"You could have walked away."

She is silent. She tugs uselessly at the arm of the cadaver. Her left hand wields her dagger as though it is a sword.

"Arrest her," the general barks at the young guardian. Alexander watches as the two guardians slowly corner the girl. She glares back at them. He can see the wheels in her head turning; does she abandon the body and run or continue trying to move it?

Run, you fool, he thinks. *He's already dead.*

She stays where she is, defiance written across her taut cheekbones. Alexander groans inwardly, knowing already the dangers in doing what it is he is about to do. He glances down at the donkey, giving the animal a wry smile.

"And here I told my crew how important it is to lay low while in Chancey," he mutters. The donkey studies him with disinterest, its teeth clicking together in a chewing motion.

"Sorry about this."

Alexander draws his cutlass from its scabbard and whacks the donkey hard on the backside with the flat edge of the blade. The animal shrieks, rearing up in agitation. It kicks its back legs out once, bolting forward at full speed. Hot, angry air comes snorting from its nostrils as it charges straight at the two guardians. Sheathing his sword, Alexander races along directly behind the animal. The golden soldiers dive out of the way. He grabs the Rogue around the waist and pulls her away from the corpse.

"Let go!" she shrieks. Her legs kick wildly. He groans as her knee comes into contact with his ribs. Drawing his pistol, he ducks his head as the blade of her dagger sweeps right by his ear. As he does so, he catches a glimpse of the low overhang above the door of one of the shops. A large roost of crows has settled to ogle the corpse through hungry, black eyes. They ruffle their feathers, chattering impatiently. A few of them land upon the ground near the body as he drags the woman away.

Nearby, the general has gathered himself. He, too, has drawn his pistol. Alexander can see him leveling the weapon, aiming it at his head. He aims his gun at the door to the shop, shooting in the direction of the birds. They take off in a flurry of screams and feathers, obscuring the general from his view.

Taking his chance, Alexander ducks down into the nearest alleyway. The Rogue is still struggling within his grasp. He sets her down hard upon the ground, keeping his hand tight about her wrist.

"Let me go," she snarls.

"If I do, will you run with me?" He is dragging her along the alleyway, ignoring her muttered protests. There is no time to stop—the general will be hot on their heels. He curses himself silently.

What have I done? It was none of my business.

"Fine," the young woman snaps. "You're hurting me."

He releases her arm. She moves in step with him, her breathing falling erratically from between her lips.

"Where next? They'll find us down here in minutes."

"In here!" whispers a disembodied voice. To their left, a heavy wooden side door swings ajar. The smell of day old meat leeches out into the alley. "Quickly!"

The young woman catches Alexander's eye and he proffers a small shrug. They slip through the door into the darkness. It slams shut behind them. They are swallowed in shadow. Panting, they linger before the door while they try to catch their breath. Alexander can hear boots on the street outside—the general. He races by the door, his muffled footfalls fading into silence.

"Wait a few moments, catch your breath," urges the voice. Alexander keeps his pistol trained upon the darkness as he stares into the shadows. The voice, undeniably male, seems to emanate from all around them. He cannot locate the source.

"The good general's shift is almost over for the day. He will not continue to give chase once he is off duty, you can count on that."

"Who are you?" the Rogue demands.

A languid chuckle echoes through the expanse. "I think the question you should be asking is not, who am I, but who is the mysterious savior that plucked you from the square?"

Through the shadows, Alexander can feel those green eyes alight upon his face. He grimaces and says nothing.

"Put your pistol away, Captain. I mean you no harm."

"Who are you?" the Rogue repeats, more nervously this time.

"I am Nobody," replies the voice.

CHAPTER 10

Roberts the Valiant

ROBERTS WENT TO the cathedral at noon, as instructed. He waited upon the steps—his suspicious green gaze scanning the crowd around him—and tried to be patient. Shuffling his feet upon the grey stone of the great staircase, he counted the bells as they chimed the hour. He could feel the reverberations deep within the ground beneath his feet.

And then he heard a voice.

Roberts the Valiant?

It came from behind him, nearly blending into the chatter of the oblivious crowd that mingled upon the steps. He nodded to indicate that he had heard and contined to peer out into the street. Across the way, a donkey was braying loudly. A young woman, her gown stained the color of mud, was perched upon the street beneath the animal. He watched the scene unfold, trying his best to look unremarkable. No one was looking at him.

Follow, came the command.

He turned obediently and found himself walking up the steps after a very ordinary looking man in a brown tunic. The man did not glance back at him. He did not say a word. Roberts followed him through the grand double doors of the building and into the marble foyer.

Now, only moments later, he stands alone—abandoned, it would seem, among a flurry of melting candles. Clumps of hot wax pool upon the floor at his feet. He stares around at shadows. The muttered prayers of Chancians are stifled by the lingering darkness.

He lost the man as soon as they were deep enough inside the cathedral. A cluster of scarlet-robed Elders passed them by, their voices joined in a humble tenor tune.

Confess, the stranger whispered into his ear. And then he was gone. Roberts never even saw his face. The Elders rounded the corner and disappeared out of sight. The echo of their somber hymn trailed eerily behind them.

The multitude of flickering candles makes it hard for him to see. The flames prick at his vision. Beyond the golden aura of light he can only make out indistinct shadows. He moves deeper into the cathedral. His bare feet are silent upon the floor. The Chancians do not take any notice of him as he passes. They kneel upon the checkered stone tiles, their heads bowed and their eyes closed. Lifeless grey statues loom heavily over the praying figures that kneel at their stone feet. Their dead eyes and austere faces appear inhospitable to Roberts. They are holy saints, he knows, and yet he cannot name a single one.

What did the stranger mean, confess?

He wonders if perhaps the man meant for him to kneel at a statue as well. If so, which one? He glances around. All of the saints seem to be taken. He wanders further through the cathedral, trying his best to remain invisible. It is not that he and his kind are not permitted within the walls of the church—far from it, in fact. Rather, it is not common to see a gypsy wandering through a place of prayer. His people do not practice the monotheistic religion of the Westerlies as men of Chancey do. His mere presence beneath the ribbed vaults of the towering arched ceiling will certainly draw unwanted attention. There has been so much secrecy around his meeting with the elusive Cairan king. He is sure he is not meant to cause a scene. Not here—not now.

As he nears the far end of the church's main building he spots two enclosed booths along the wall. They are constructed from a dark oak, but the latticed panels upon the doorways are gilded. One door has been left open and Roberts notices that it is empty inside. He is thrust, suddenly, back to his childhood, when his Chancian father would come to the church in order to confess his sins to the religious Elder. Roberts would sit in the booth upon his father's lap and wonder how long it would be until he could go back outside and play.

Forgive me Elder, for I have sinned, his father would begin.

Roberts feels suddenly confident.

Confess, the man said to him. He is sure, now, that this is what was meant. Roberts heads over to the abandoned booth, taking care to stick to the shadows that hover in the cool shade of the low, wooden pews. Taking a seat inside, he pulls the door shut.

He is enveloped in instant darkness. The stippled light that seeps through the gilded panel does not manage to illuminate the rest of the booth. The golden pane glitters peculiarly as the wavering flames outside dance across its uneven surface. Roberts sits in silence and waits.

Nothing happens.

"Hello?" He feels unreasonably foolish, sitting there, whispering at shadows.

There is, as he expected, no response. Agitated, he begins to think that he must have done something wrong. He does not understand why the stranger on the steps could not have been more direct with his orders. No one was paying the slightest bit of attention to the covert exchange that passed between them. He feels sure, in fact, that this whole theatrical show of mystery is entirely superfluous.

He is about to stand up to go when he hears the muted squealing of hinges at his back. There is a rush of air—an icy puff of wind upon the back of his neck. He glances over his shoulder and is instantly surprised by what he sees. There, behind the stiff wooden chair in which he had been seated, is a narrow opening. A flickering torch sits in a sconce upon the wall. Roberts can just make out the outline of a steep staircase winding into the darkness and out of sight.

He glances in front of him at the glittering golden panel upon the door before turning his attention back towards the looming darkness.

Here goes nothing, he thinks wryly. Stepping carefully into the shadows, he begins his descent. The air is cold, here—the steps are steep. As he descends the narrow stars, he realizes that he is heading deep into the catacombs beneath the church. A shiver creeps unbidden down his spine. The lambent aura of the torch at the top of the steps does not reach very far. Before long, he is encapsulated by the pitch-black night that lurks beyond the warm, orange glow.

He uses his toes to feel forward, seeking out the definitive edge of each step before moving forward. Slowly but surely, he makes his cautious way down the stairs. He can feel the darkness tearing at his skin—or does he just imagine that?

He is not sure how long he has been walking in the dark before he sees a thin strip of flickering light in the inky blackness. As he draws nearer he can see that it is the flicker of a candle spilling out from the bottom of a doorway. He feels the last step with his big toe—steps with relief onto flat ground. His nose is nearly pressed into the wood of the door. He knocks—waits.

A panel is pried open with a squeal. Golden light spills across his face. He blinks rapidly in the sudden radiance, his eyes narrowing. Two blue eyes study him from behind the slot in the door.

"State your name."

"Roberts the Valiant." Surely the man behind the door already knows who he is. He doesn't imagine the Cairan king entertains many social visitors down here in this damp, dark hole.

"What is your purpose here?"

Roberts hesitates, considering the question. "I was invited," he mutters after a moment. He does not know what else to say. He is not entirely sure what the purpose of this visit is, after all. The panel before his face is pulled shut with a thump. He hears the brassy click of several bolts on the other side of the wood. The door is wrenched open.

"Come inside." The man that stands before him is portly in size. His doublet—a faded red color—is several sizes too tight. Numerous bronze buttons look as though they might pop free of their grommet at any moment. The man stares down at Roberts from the top of his hooked nose.

"Er, are you the king?" Roberts asks when the man remains silent. This question causes the well-built man to burst into laughter.

"That's funny," he says at last, pawing his eye with the back of his hand. "He'll like that, he will."

Roberts frowns, his answer received. He glances behind the man to survey the room in which he finds himself. It is small and unassuming, hardly the type of quarters he would expect a king to own. There is but one seat in the room—a beaten green divan over which someone has arbitrarily tossed a violet satin blanket. The rest of the room consists of a number of tables of various shapes and sizes. Upon each of these tables sits curled and crinkling maps. He cannot make out the details from where he stands, cornered before the entrance. His curiosity aroused by the peculiarity of his circumstance, he longs to move about the room and study the maps more closely.

He glances towards the man before him and decides better of it. The guard—if that is indeed what the man is—is still staring him down in unreadable silence, his bulging arms crossed tightly over his chest.

"Will he be returning soon then, the king?" Roberts asks.

"Yes."

He had hoped to receive a more fulfilling answer than the one he is given. He clears his throat and thinks of another question.

"Where has he gone? If you don't mind me asking."

One bushy eyebrow rises upon the man's head. "I do mind."

"Oh. Sorry."

They fall back into silence. Roberts is saved from having to ask any more unwarranted questions when a small door is wrenched open at the far side of the room. A lean, violet clad figure springs into the quarters. His sleek black hair is pulled loosely from a widow's peak at the center of his forehead. High cheekbones cut across his face, causing sharp shadows to paint the lower half of his face. A golden hoop dangles from one earlobe. He is panting as though he has recently been running. Seeing Roberts standing uselessly at the center of the room, a wide smile cracks across his lips.

"Roberts," he cries, surging lithely across the space. He takes Roberts's hand roughly in greeting. "I have been waiting hours for your arrival!"

Roberts thinks it an interesting choice of words, considering the man before him was the one who was late. He opts not to voice this thought aloud.

"Yes, hello," he replies, surprised at the firmness of the man's grip.

The Cairan king shoots a sidelong glance at the portly, lopsided man besides Roberts.

"Tophurn, you can go."

Roberts watches as the man called Tophurn turns away without a second glance. He stalks wordlessly across the sparse room and disappears through the narrow doorway at the far end of the expanse.

"I hope Tophurn wasn't too threatening." The Cairan king continues to vigorously shake Roberts's outstretched hand. "He isn't the friendliest of men, but he gets the job done."

"I can see that." Roberts watches the door slide back into place in its frame, lifting his palm out of the man's firm grasp.

"You must be wondering why I've called you here."

Roberts proffers a shrug, venturing a guess. "I assume because of the fire at Toyler's yesterday."

The lanky man laughs at that, and the sound spills easily away from him. His blue eyes, so deep they are almost violet, twinkle in the hazy golden candlelight. "Quite right," he says. "I'm sure I don't have to tell you, friend, that times are changing."

Roberts thinks of the recent arsons in the city—of the occasional unexplained disappearances—all at the hands of the guardians. He thinks also of his family, killed in cold blood all those years ago. Furrowing his brow, he wonders if in fact things have not simply always been this way. He is about to mention this when the man changes topics abruptly.

"Do you know Harrane the Hostile?" He paces away from Roberts, a strand of sleek, black hair draping across his face. His left hand twists a thick golden ring round and round upon the thumb of his right hand. "Or, I should say, did you?"

Roberts pauses, caught off guard by the question. "I do, yes," he admits. "Although not well." He takes silent note of the man's careful word choice. *Did,* he thinks. *Has he died?*

"He kept to himself," the man explains, rounding upon Roberts with glittering eyes. "He was one of mine, you see."

"One of yours?" Roberts repeats, feeling confusion flickering across his brow.

"Yes." One corner of the man's lip twitches slightly as he studies Roberts's perplexed expression. "They call themselves my Listeners. I have recruited a handful of men to help me to infiltrate the city—to be my eyes and my ears upon the streets of Chancey. Tophurn is one of them, in fact."

"Oh." Roberts finds himself suddenly wondering what any of this has to do with him, or his presence at the fire the previous day. The man does not wait for Roberts to add anything valuable to the conversation before continuing on without him. He drops down upon the green divan, a cloud of fluttering dust motes dispersing about his narrow frame.

"My Listeners were at present Toyler's when it burned. We had received word long before General Byron and his men even visited poor Manfred Toyler—rest his soul—that they were planning on torching the place. I called together some of our strongest to spark an insurgence against the guardians. We wanted to create enough of a distraction to allow the Mames and their maidens to clear out the wounded."

Roberts recalls the way that the Cairans had rushed the golden guard as the flames licked at the sky. He had thought it was an act of passion—an angry response to the evil that had been done that morning. Who was to know that it had been premeditated?

"I, of course, was responsible for the act," the man continues. "Harrane was against it from the beginning. He believed that the guardians would simply execute us on the spot for our actions. He went along easily enough, however. He always did. It's his duty to agree with me." He laughs at that, although his indigo gaze is laced with naked grief.

"He is dead—Harrane. My Listeners inform me that he was executed at the usurper's feet before breakfast." He swallows thickly, clearing his throat. "It is tragic and unnecessary. He died for me— protecting my identity from my enemies."

Roberts considers this. "How can you be so sure that he was killed?" Surely the Listeners, as skilled as this man might believe them to be, have not been so adept as to be able to infiltrate the palace walls. It is more likely that Harrane the Hostile was taken into custody in prison. "King Rowland prefers public executions. He likes a show."

The man is nodding his agreement, the movement causing a stray lock of hair to spring out from his sleek pompadour and fall across his brow. His lips have settled into a solemn grimace. "Indeed he does. That is why, earlier this morning, Harrane's corpse was strung up in the square to be picked apart by crows."

Roberts freezes. His hands clench into fists at his side.

"It's a reminder to me," the man says, leaning back against the violet throw. "It's a message from my enemy. The usurper doesn't like to be crossed. He thinks that this will frighten me back into the shadows."

"What do we do?"

A small flicker of a smile teases at the king's lips.

"We?" he asks.

"Yes," Roberts asserts, feeling more than a little annoyed. "I may not be one of your Listeners, but I'm a Cairan. This affects me, too."

"Indeed it does," is all the man says, lapsing into a long silence as he studies Roberts through narrow, glittering eyes. Just when Roberts begins to fidget uneasily beneath his gaze, the man resumes speaking.

"All that can be done for now has already been accomplished. That is why I was late to our little meeting today. I went to the square myself. Harrane didn't deserve such a degrading funeral. He has a mother, and his body should have been with her, the dear old woman. I meant to cut him down myself—I owed him that."

"Meant to? You mean you didn't?"

"No, I didn't. The body had already been cut away by the time I arrived. You may know the young woman responsible for the act. I believe she is your sister."

"Emerala?" Roberts feels his blood run cold. She had been gone when he woke up this morning. He had given little thought to her absence, so distracted had he been by his looming meeting with the Cairan king. "Where is she?"

"Safe, for now. It seems she partnered with a rather clever pirate to help her cut Harrane away from the post where he had been strung. I spoke with them both. He agreed to accompany her to a safe place."

A pirate.

"*Where* is she?" Roberts's pulse is beating rapidly beneath his skin, pounding against the walls of his veins.

The man smiles, his expression compassionate. "Here, of course. I spoke with the lead Elder, and he's offered Emerala sanctuary within the walls of the cathedral."

"Sanctuary? Why? She will be safe enough with me."

The man purses his lips, regarding Roberts through narrowed eyes. "I'm afraid not," he disagrees quietly. "General Byron witnessed her in the act. She will be a wanted woman now, and I would be surprised if the usurper doesn't post a warrant for her arrest. He hates to feel as though someone has gotten the better of him, and your sister most certainly has."

Roberts curses his sister silently. *Why can't she keep her nose in her own business?* He already knows the answer to that question. She never can. He tries to imagine himself in her shoes—tries to imagine himself stumbling upon corpse of one of his people. He does not know if he would have been able to walk away.

But a pirate? He has warned her a thousand times, if he has warned her once. She is not to speak with pirates. They are wild men—unpredictable men—and not to be trusted.

The man is watching him carefully, his indigo gaze unreadable as his eyes flicker back and forth across Roberts's face. His index finger runs thoughtfully across his lower lip. Roberts fights to get a hold on his nerves. He clears his throat, he runs his fingers through the tangle of black curls on his head.

"That happened this morning," Roberts points out, attempting to redirect the conversation. "You requested my presence yesterday."

"True," the man assents, rising to his feet. He wanders across the room, drawing close to one of the curling maps that unfolds across a table in the corner. Running his fingers lightly over the brittle parchment, he glances at Roberts over his shoulder. "I told you, times are changing. The city of Chancey is becoming more and more dangerous for our people. I'm looking to draft more men to my cause."

"You want me to be one of your Listeners?" Roberts lips curl downward into a frown as he tries in vain to study the map over the man's shoulder. *A spy. He wants me to be a spy.*

The man does not answer Roberts immediately, instead turning his attention back to the parchment before him. "My men brought back a number of reports from the fire at Toyler's. Most impressive were the stories of your fortitude in pulling victims from the tavern. You are a brave man, Roberts the Valiant."

Roberts thinks of Harrane, and of his poor, widowed mother. She will have no one left, not now that her son is gone. Roberts has grown into adulthood in trepidation, always tiptoeing through the shadows—always sidestepping unnecessary peril. Without their parents, it fell upon him to care for Emerala and Nerani. He cannot afford to put himself in danger. He cannot make himself vulnerable to the possibility of death. The girls need him— Emerala now more than ever, the foolish girl.

"I have a family," he says, his gaze darkening.

"Most men do," comes the reply. The man continues to study the map, his slender fingers pressing hard against the parchment.

Robert shakes his head, his curls bouncing into his emerald eyes. "That's just it. Only myself, my sister, and my cousin are left. Everyone else is dead."

"Except for you father, I believe." The man's words catch Roberts off guard. He swallows hard, feeling as though his heart has risen into his throat. Realizing he has hit upon a nerve, the man turns to face Roberts. He leans back against the low table, his palms gripping the splintering edge.

"Except for Eliot Roberts, correct?" His gaze is heavy with implication.

"How—" Roberts begins, and stops short. "What—How do you know that?"

The man's lip twitches. He raises his chin, the flickering light of the lanterns upon the wall casting his face in a somber gloom. "I took some liberties of looking into your life. I hope you don't mind."

Roberts does mind. In his memory he sees Eliot Roberts perched uselessly in the doorway, his top hat spinning uncomfortably in his hands. The man stared down upon him through tormented, emerald eyes. He had not uttered so much as a word of goodbye—he had not attempted to console his wailing, infant daughter. He only pressed his hat upon his had and turned his back to his children.

Roberts feels something old and angry brewing within him. "My father left the island of Chancey years ago," he says, his voice growing choked in his throat. "He is nothing to me, and he is a stranger to Emerala. The man is as good as dead."

"Perhaps," the man says, and flashes Roberts an apologetic smile. "Tell me, how did your mother come to pass?"

Roberts recoils, feeling his skin prickle with annoyance beneath his collar. Ghosts from the past—ghost he has spent years fighting to repress—come surging to the forefront of his mind. He glances down towards the stony floor at his feet, inhaling deeply.

"She was gunned to death by a guardian." He cringes as his voice cracks beneath the weight of his words.

"Why?"

Roberts's gaze snaps up towards the man's face as latent anger undulates through his veins. The bluntness of the man's question threatens to bowl him over. He exhales sharply, his nostrils expanding as he fights to get ahold of his simmering temper.

"When Eliot Roberts left my mother, she took my sister and I to live with our aunt and uncle, Anerani and Gerwinge. She told me that she didn't feel safe on her own." He pauses, wincing slightly in remembrance as he scratches at the back of his neck.

"I don't know why she felt safe there, either," he continues quietly. "Gerwinge was a large advocator of the old magics. He had been publically scourged in the past. At first, when the guardians came to the apartment, I thought that that's why they were there."

"And it was not?"

Roberts glowers at the man in silence for a long moment before continuing. "No. It wasn't. They demanded that my mother tell them where my father had gone."

"I take it she didn't?"

"Even if she had wanted to, she couldn't," Roberts says, rubbing his palm furiously across the nape of his neck. His insides feel cold—weighted down by memories. "He left her without so much as an explanation. The guardians shot them all."

"And you were there? You witnessed this?" A deep groove appears between the man's eyes.

"I was hiding behind the couch," Roberts mutters, staring at the shadows over the man's shoulder. He is not proud of this fact—is quite ashamed, in fact—but what else could he have done? He was only a boy. He remembers how he had knelt in the blood that seeped towards him from beneath the dilapidated bit of furniture. He could not cry out—could not move until the men had left. The memory is painful. He can feel it sticking in his heart like a needle.

"I know it's painful, Roberts, but it's ammunition."

The man's words startle him into blinking furiously. He returns his gaze to the hard lines of the man's face. A pair of deep, indigo eyes survey him silently across the dancing shadows. "What?" His voice is hoarse.

"The usurper sent his men to rob you of your family," the man explains, straightening his shoulders as he draws to his full height. His head nearly scrapes against the low hanging ceiling overhead. "As a result of his hate, you grew up alone. And now, he is going to send men to rob you of your sister. I can keep her safe."

"I can keep her safe," Roberts retorts darkly. *I have always kept her safe.*

"No," the man disagrees. "Not by being invisible—not anymore. Your life has more significance than you know, Roberts the Valiant. Your fate bears more weight in this world than you can possibly begin to understand. The time for idling in the shadows is done. You need to fight back. You need to outsmart the enemy in a game of wits."

"You want me to spy for you." It is not a question.

"Yes," the man confirms simply, holding up his palms in a shrug of invitation. "We do not have the strength to bear arms against the Golden Guard— nor do I want to engage my people in a war. We need to stay one step ahead of the usurper. That is the only way we will survive."

Roberts swallows—contemplates the offer that sits before him. Only one coherent thought rises above the jumble of warring memories within his head. "Why does he despise us?"

A crooked smile dances upon the man's lips. "I have some theories," he says lightly. He does not expand upon what those theories are. "The fact of the matter is this—the Stoward reign has poisoned Chancey against us. We need to reclaim the island from under the usurper's feet."

Roberts is silent before the Cairan king—this whispered name in the streets, embodied now by a lithe, towering figure with stormy, violet eyes.

"I'll do it," Roberts says finally, sucking air in lightly through his teeth.

The man smiles wider, exposing a gleaming line of ivory teeth. "A wise choice, Roberts the Valiant. Now, I have kept you long enough. Your sister should be arriving at the cathedral any moment. I'm sure you'll want to speak with her. You and I can speak more later on this evening."

Roberts nods, feeling suddenly eager to go. He is tired of being below the earth—tired of being packed within the dark catacombs, left alone in the company of this mysterious king. Without another word, he heads towards the main entrance. Reaching out for the door, he pauses, pressing the toes of his boots into the ground underfoot.

"Wait," he mutters, more to himself than to the man behind him. He tilts his chin to the side, glancing at the Cairan king out of the corners of his eyes. "Mame Galyria told me to seek out Mame Noveli. She hinted that you might know where she is."

"I do," confirms the man. "She's here—In the catacombs."

Roberts dithers upon the stone, wondering what to do. The man appears to pick up on his hesitancy.

"Go and see your sister," he suggests. "Make sure she's made it here safely. I will send for you both tomorrow evening. Mame Noveli will be eager to meet with our newest Listener, I'm sure."

"Oh," Roberts mumbles. He had not expected it to be so easy. "Thank you."

Without another word, he turns towards the stairs and heads back upwards into the reach of the light. As he ascends the narrow steps, he replays in his mind the strange conversation with the king.

A Listener. He feels a flicker of regret wash over him and he wishes he had thought to ask more questions. He has no idea what will be expected of him as a spy for the Cairan king. It is exciting, in the very least, and Saynti knows he can use a little bit of excitement in his life. Every moment until now, it seems, has been dedicated to trying to keep Emerala out of her own way.

He thinks of his sister locked away within the impenetrable stone walls of the cathedral and he nearly laughs out loud. She will go mad beneath the shadows of the saints—unable to visit her usual haunts and stir up the proper amount of trouble. At least, then, he won't have to constantly agonize over whether or not she has managed to get herself arrested by the golden elite. At least, then, he can worry about himself.

He reflects upon the events of the past two days, his mood souring as he thinks back to the cryptic message the Cairan king had delivered to him only moments ago beneath the pressing stone.

Your life has more significance than you know, Roberts the Valiant, he had said, his eyes glittering violet in the darkness. *Your fate bears more weight in this world than you can possibly begin to understand.*

He mulls over the enigmatic words, wondering what the man could possibly have meant by that. It is not until he reaches the confessional that he realizes that the elusive king never offered him a name.

CHAPTER 11

Seranai the Fair

"Here's your animal."

Seranai the Fair holds out the fraying lead rope with an agitated snap of her wrist.

The blacksmith's apprentice, a young boy not much older than fifteen, stares back at her chest with a dirty face and an impish grin. His hammer, which he had been using to bang out an unwanted bend in a wrought iron pole, has ceased its racket. It hangs suspended in the air between them.

"Hope you got your money's worth, miss." The boy pats his coat pocket with three grimy fingers. Seranai grimaces as though the boy has delivered her a sharp slap to the face. She thinks of the gold coins she gave him in exchange for borrowing his donkey—of the cold, diminishing weight of them as they trickled through her fingers and into his outstretched palm. She has not come close to getting her money's worth, in fact.

She stomps towards the door without another word to the rotten boy.

"Don't be too sorely put out, love," leaks a voice from the shadows. Seranai pauses. Her grey eyes travel curiously towards the far side of the room. Beyond the reach of the light, she can just make out the profile of a lanky man perching lazily against a dust-ridden table. His fingers tap idly against his thigh in a fervid rat-tat-tat.

"Excuse me?" she asks, taking a cautious step in his direction. The muddied hem of her gown disturbs the sawdust that litters the floor and she is suddenly haloed in a ruddy cloud of dust. The man lets out a throaty laugh. From beneath the shadow cast by his tricorn cap she can see the glistening sheen of a golden tooth.

"I'm only saying, you aren't the cap'n's type anyhow. You shouldn't waste time being bitter at him." His fingers fall still against his leg and she notices that the beds of his nails are yellowed from tobacco.

Her reply is terse. "I'm not bitter."

An affected sigh draws her gaze back to his face. A crooked grin teases at one corner of his lips. "Now me, I would have paid good mind to you if you walked my way."

He hops off of the table, flicking his hat upwards upon his head with one dirty finger. The dusty afternoon light that pours in through the soiled windowpanes falls across his features. A full-blown grin cuts across his jaw, shaded with unkempt scruff. A pair of shockingly golden eyes stare her shamelessly up and down from beneath wild, black hair. She fidgets uncomfortably beneath his gaze, becoming suddenly aware of the silence that grips the room. With mild agitation, she realizes that the young apprentice is hanging on to their every word.

Nosy brat.

She raises her chin, glancing down at the gangling man from the tip of her upturned nose. "I don't consort with pirates."

"I'd reckon you don't." He takes a step closer to her, those golden eyes studying her with far too much familiarity for her liking. "I don't know what your game is, love, but I think I'd like to find out."

"I'm not playing a game," she retorts, drawing back a step—determined to keep a safe distance between them.

The crooked grin on his face widens. "We'll see, won't we?" His hand encloses about her elbow, his slender fingers becoming lost in the fragile white lace that borders the hem of her sleeve. His grip is too tight as he draws her in close. Leaning down, he places his lips by her ear. She can smell the pungent reek of ale on his breath as he whispers, "I'm not afraid to get my hands dirty. Remember that, if you ever need something done right."

"I'll keep that in mind," she snaps with insincerity, wrenching her arm from his grasp. Before her, his lingering gaze is making her skin crawl.

"Who are you, anyway?"

He sweeps his tricorn hat from his head in a grand gesture, bowing low. His tangled black hair falls into his face, momentarily obscuring those strange, golden eyes.

"Evander the Hawk. Pleased to make your acquaintance."

She sniffles audibly. "Evander the Hawk? That's a Cairan name."

He straightens, his eyes glimmering with delight. "Insightful, aren't you? I was born and bred upon the good island of Chancey."

"There's nothing good about this place," Seranai retorts in spite of herself.

One eyebrow rises upon his head as laugh lines splinter outward around his eyes.

"Bright girl," he sings. "I left as soon as I was old enough to know better. You would too, if you knew what was good for you, love."

The apprentice drops his hammer, then, and it falls against the wrought iron bar with a bone-shuddering crash. Seranai is suddenly and painfully aware of the pirate's proximity to her in empty expanse of the blacksmith's shop. She pulls away from him with a grimace, pushing a stray lock of hair out of her eyes.

"Good day to you," she says coldly, and adds, "pirate."

He says nothing, only replaces his tricorn hat firmly upon his head with a jovial wink. Her mood soured impossibly further, she heads quickly away from the foul blacksmith's and its lowly occupants. She does not continue onward through the busy main streets of Chancey. She has no desire to run into any of the pedestrians that mill about, bartering with the merchants and running errands. Her dress, a dusky rose-colored gown that she has not worn in years, is covered entirely in mud. She cannot bear for anyone to see her in such low-class attire, let alone garments that look as though she slept with swine the previous evening. She fumes as she stalks along, turning as quickly as possibly down an empty side street.

Her luck as of late has been utterly rotten. She sniffles, trying in vain to pick some of the dried mud out from the folds in the cream colored fabric of her petticoat. She did not intend for that pirate—what had been his name? Alexander?—to stop and offer to help her out from the mud. In fact, she had been counting on being left quite alone.

She set out earlier that morning with a very particular goal—to arrange a chance meeting between her and Roberts the Valiant. She knew that he would be at the cathedral when the clock struck noon. All that she needed to do was be present and vulnerable, and she was sure that he would swoop in to offer her aid. No one else would even give her a second glance. She had made sure to pick clothing that would identify her as a Cairan. There was not a single Chancian upon the street who would look twice at a gypsy girl struggling in the street.

It was easy enough to get the donkey outside of the blacksmith's shop once she had paid the apprentice. In fact, the animal had nearly bolted for the door as soon as she took the lead rope from the hands of the grinning boy. Once they had walked a safe distance away from the square, however, the stubborn beast refused to go either which way she pulled it. At first, this was not a bad thing. Seranai had hoped, in fact, that Roberts would witness all the trouble she was having and offer to help.

The only problem was that the donkey had perched itself contently before a barrel of vegetables just outside the grocer's. It was clear after a few moments of tugging that the rotten animal had no intention of going any further. There was a sea of Chancians milling about between her and Roberts. She was certain he would be unable to see her from the steps of the cathedral.

Seranai was able to get the animal to take just a few steps in the right direction when it stopped again, having discovered an apple core lying in the street. Crying out in aggravation, she leaned all of her weight away from the donkey as she tugged at its lead. This made it difficult for the donkey to reach its target snack, which in turn aggravated the animal. Flattening its ears, the creature had charged at her. It was this unexpected release that sent Seranai flying backwards and into the mud.

She groans internally at the memory. If it were not for that pirate, perhaps Roberts would have seen her in time. Perhaps he would have pushed his way through the crowds in order to help her off of the ground.

It does not matter, now. Her chance is long gone. She will have to find another.

She ambles along through the narrow roadway. There is a chill beneath her skin. The afternoon is growing late. The sun is falling back behind the buildings. *A day wasted*, she thinks irately.

Seranai's afternoon might have been salvaged, she thinks, if it were not for that girl in the square. How depraved of her—Seranai would never in her life put her hands on a dead body. She would never attract that kind of negative attention to herself. It is no wonder that she despises her people. Who can blame her? It is girls like that who bring shame upon the Cairan name.

She thinks of James Byron and the way he addressed the Cairan girl. *Rogue*, he called her. He knew her title. He addressed her with an odd sort of respect, as though they were old friends. Seranai had watched him from behind the donkey, feeling resentment build up within her heart like rust.

Are you involved in this? he asked when the rotten girl unfairly dragged her into it. As though their kinship bound them together. As though the brat expected Seranai to help her drag the reeking dead man away and risk arrest.

No, James, Seranai wanted to shout, *Don't you know me? Don't you remember? I care nothing for these gypsies.*

Instead, she was barely able to squeak out a coherent response, standing there before him in her mud-ridden garments.

Clear out of here, he snapped. She recoiled from his indifference. His voice, filled with underlying disgust, had drilled through her bones. Fighting back tears, she fled from the square.

Now, it dawns upon Seranai that James has never seen her like that before—dressed in the garments of a common vagabond. He has only seen her in her fineries—her costumes. She sniffs bitterly and thinks, *stolen goods.*

Of all the things that have gone wrong today, Seranai resents this the most.

She rounds a corner, feeling the afternoon warmth leaching out of her pallid skin. The cathedral looms before her. The crowds have dissipated with the onset of evening. Heavy orange sunlight is lost within the fragments of the thick stained glass windows. Beneath the long shadow of the church stand two familiar figures.

She frowns, freezing where she stands. She recognizes the man at once—it is Alexander, the handsome young pirate she had run into earlier that afternoon. He is perched before a young woman in an olive green gown. The Rogue. Her black curls cascade down her shoulders, twisting within the small of her back. Seranai watches as Alexander leans towards her. He whispers something in the gypsy's ear, his lips grazing her cheek as he straightens his spine.

"I'll be fine," Seranai hears the Rogue retort.

"Of course you will." A slanted smirk dances across Alexander's lips "I'll wait all the same."

The Rogue shakes her head, her black curls bouncing wildly across her glittering emerald eyes. "My brother will be here any moment. It would be better for both of us if you disappeared by then. Trust me."

"That man—your Cairan king—he made me promise I would accompany you."

"Yes, to the cathedral," the Rogue reminds him, glancing restlessly over her shoulder. "And here we are."

The look in the gypsy's eyes is resolute. Alexander hesitates, staring back at her. His jaw is locked in consideration. "Fine," he relents. He turns to walk away from her, spinning back upon his heels as he closes the space between them.

"Will I see you again?" he asks. His face is split into a ridiculous grin. Gleaming ivory teeth shine out from a dark, sun kissed face.

From her hiding place, Seranai rolls her eyes.

Before Alexander, the Rogue shrugs. Her shoulders are bare above the sheer, low-cut sleeves of her gown. "You know where to find me."

Tramp, Seranai thinks darkly.

Alexander's eyes narrow as he chews his lips, his unshaven cheeks dimpling. He takes a step backward, nearly tripping over a loose stone upon the street. The Rogue holds up her hand in goodbye, her cheeks tinged with red pinpricks of color.

Seranai watches the pirate turn and disappear down a narrow side street. The young woman is alone. Seranai can feel the heat of her annoyance bristling beneath her skin. Feeling unusually bold, she marches out from the shadows of the alleyway.

"You," she hisses, once she is within the Rogue's line of sight.

The Rogue glances towards her in surprise. "Hello."

Her green eyes study the mud caked to Seranai's gown. Seranai glares down at her face, radiant in the light of the setting sun. Her small, pointed nose offsets her narrow lips, giving her an almost feral appearance. The untamed black curls that tickle her face frame her high cheekbones and tapered jaw. The deviant loveliness of the young woman sparks an even deeper dislike in Seranai.

"I'm Emerala." The young woman sticks out her hand for Seranai to shake. "Sorry about earlier today, I always manage to get myself into the worst situations."

Seranai slaps her hand away. Emerala's green eyes widen considerably. She stares down at her palm, still outstretched, and frowns.

"You had no business doing that—cutting down that body in the square," Seranai snaps.

Confusion cloud's Emerala's pointed face. "He was one of our people. A Cairan."

"So what? He probably deserved what he got. You should have left me out of it. You had no right to drag me into your mess like that."

Emerala's green eyes have narrowed into dangerous slits. She retracts her hand. "No harm was done, I'm sure."

"No harm?" Seranai's voice is shrill. She shoves Emerala hard, pressing her palms into her shoulders. There is a stab of triumph in her gut as the young woman stumbles backwards. "*No harm?*" she shouts again, shoving the girl a second time.

Emerala's eyes flash with rage and she slaps Seranai hard across the face. "Here's a suggestion for you," she seethes darkly. "*Don't* touch me again."

Seranai recoils upon the cobblestone, pressing the palm of her hand to her stinging cheek. "You ignorant wench. You have *no idea* what you did to me today."

The door to the cathedral is thrown open. Horrified, Seranai shrinks back into the shadows. There, standing in the open doorway, is Roberts the Valiant. He is staring down at Emerala the Rogue with apprehension etched across his handsome features. The green eyes that peer out from beneath his messy black curls are so stark that Seranai curses herself, wondering how she did not see the resemblance before. She turns and flees around the corner, tears pricking at her eyelids.

Oh no, she thinks. *No.*

Only when she is safely out of sight does she pause, glancing back around the building behind which she hides. Roberts has descended the staircase and taken Emerala into his embrace. Her arms are pinned down by her sides—her fingers folded into fists. Her stupid, pointed face has disappeared within his undershirt.

"You're hurting me." Her voice is muffled against his chest.

"Good." Roberts releases her and glances around at the empty street. "Whom were you talking to just now?"

Emerala looks about as well, her face scrunched up in consternation. "I don't know, a woman. She was just here." She shrugs, looking agitated as she rubs her shoulders.

"Let's get you inside before someone else comes along," Roberts suggests. He takes her shoulders in his hands and steers her roughly up the looming grey steps. The deep red of the late afternoon sun has draped itself across the street. To the east, a faint twinge of violet dusk pulls at the very edges of the sky.

"Am I in trouble?" Emerala asks. Her voice grows muted as she wanders farther away from where Seranai lingers in the alleyway.

Roberts laughs derisively. "You have no idea."

They are disappearing through the open doorway. There is the squeal of old hinges and a heavy slam and they are obscured from sight.

Seranai stands frozen in the darkness. She curses aloud, her skin stinging with heat. She should have guessed it right away. She should have seen the resemblance.

This will not do.

There is no way she can win Roberts the Valiant over now—not with a sister such as that meddling in their affairs. Whatever it was the Cairan king wanted with him, Seranai will never have the chance to know. She will never

manage to squirm her way into a place of comfortable wealth. Not with her—
not with Emerala the Rogue in her way.

Unless...

She thinks of Alexander, and the way his lips had grazed Emerala's cheek
as he said his goodbye. Pirates never stay in port for long. He will be raising
anchor soon, and Emerala will never see him again. Never, unless Seranai has
anything to say about it. The golden-eyed pirate from the blacksmith's shop
called Alexander his captain. He will know what to do.

I'm not afraid to get my hands dirty, he told her. She thought nothing of
it at the time, so eager had she been to get away from him. She glances down
at her own hands, still covered in mud, and nearly laughs aloud at the irony.

A furtive smile creeps across her blood red lips. Perhaps Roberts the
Valiant is not as far out of her reach as she thinks.

CHAPTER 12

General James Byron

THE RECTANGULAR TABLE before which James Byron sits is covered in various colorful dishes of food. He sits tall against the straight back of the chair, resting his elbows upon the narrow armrests. His intertwined fingers are suspended above his lap. His stomach growls and he ignores it. He will eat later—a humble meal, taken alone in his quarters and away from the eyes of the useless courtiers that line the walls.

"Tell me again."

At the far side of the table, Rowland is chewing noisily at a fat leg of ham. The sound is accompanied by the moist smacking of his lips. He gestures at Byron with greasy, ringed fingers.

"Tell you what, your Majesty?" asks Byron dryly, not quite understanding the order. It has been a long time since Rowland last spoke. They have been sitting together in silence for a long time—an unbearable amount of time, it seems—as Rowland consumed his dinner and contemplated the information Byron brought him only several hours previously.

Rowland swallows thickly, setting down the ham. "Tell me again about the gypsy wench who cut down my body."

Byron clears his throat. Rowland is grasping at the long neck of a gilded goblet. Lifting it to his face, he draws a sip of wine. The crimson liquid dribbles out of the corners of his lips. Byron is reminded, somewhat oddly, of the way the Cairan traitor's blood leaked across the floor of the great hall earlier that morning. He squeezes his fingers tight against one another and wills himself to refocus.

"She was aided by a pirate in the escape," he comments quietly. After a brief pause, he adds, "Although we expect she had more Cairans waiting out of sight."

Rowland swallows with a gulp and hems his throat loudly. "Why is that?"

"When Private Provence and I returned to the square we found that the body had been removed." Byron keeps his voice even as he studies Rowland's face. He knows from experience that the great king does not take well to being opposed in any way. At the far side of the room, he can feel the king's waiting courtiers pressing against the wall in an endeavor to avoid what must surely be his rising rage.

Rowland nods, coughing as a bit of meat becomes lodged in his throat. He pounds his fist against his chest, glancing towards Byron through narrow black eyes. "And what is it you call her?" His words are barely intelligible through his mouthful of food. Projectiles of half chewed meat spit out between his teeth and land back upon his plate.

"The Rogue, your Majesty," Byron reminds him.

Rowland sighs. He places down his knife and fork as he leans back upon his looming, gilded chair. Raising one arm above his shoulder, he snaps his fingers. A nervous looking courtier rushes forward to offer him a clean handkerchief. He takes it, wiping his greasy fingers before dabbing at his lips. He has not managed to wipe away the wine that stains the corners of his mouth. Byron averts his gaze.

"The Rogue," Rowland repeats, his nose wrinkling as though he has tasted something sour. He clicks his tongue against the roof of his mouth and glances upwards towards the vaulted heavens painted upon the ceiling overhead. "Funny things, those gypsy titles, don't you think, James? I never understood it."

The evenness of his tone is alarming. Byron had expected him to be enraged by the Rogue's disappearing act earlier that afternoon—he had expected him to yell, to shout, to storm about the room making unrealistic demands. This quiet reserve the portly king is exhibiting—this contemplative silence that emanates from his end of the table as he scours the smiling faces of the painted cherubs overhead—is more disconcerting than a voluble show of rage.

At least, then, Byron has something tangible to which he can respond. At least, then, he is given an order and sent away. His shift should have been over hours ago. His skin itches beneath the pressing collar of his golden uniform and he fights to keep his gaze blank.

"Neither have I, my liege," he remarks.

Rowland smacks his lips together audibly, his black eyes narrowing as he studies Byron across the lengthy table. "Tell me, James, what actions have you taken?"

Byron leans forward upon his chair, grateful to have received a question to which he can provide a productive response. "We have issued a warrant for her arrest. All of my men have been given her description. It should not be long before we have her in custody."

Rowland nods, appearing suddenly distracted. He picks idly at a bunch of grapes on a golden plate before him. "It will not be enough," he mutters.

Byron leans forward, tilting his ear towards a bowl of hasty pudding. "Your Majesty?"

"The death of one Cairan wench will not be enough to stop this madness," Rowland affirms, popping a grape into his mouth. He bites down hard, the juice escaping from between his teeth and splattering upon the tablecloth. "These gypsies are about as useful to my kingdom as untrained pups."

"It will send a message."

"It will not be enough," shouts Rowland, slamming his fist upon the table. Byron falls silent. "They will continue to defy my orders."

"Yes, your Majesty."

Rowland exhales deeply, his nostrils expanding as he pops another grape between his teeth. "What do you do when you simply cannot train a pup; when it is incapable of following commands and wreaks havoc upon your household fineries?"

Byron can sense where this is leading. "What do you do?"

"You slaughter the beast," Rowland shouts again, louder this time. He slams his fist down upon the overcrowded table with such force that a few plates slide off of the edge and shatter loudly upon the floor. Two courtiers rush forward hastily. They stoop down to clean up the mess.

Rowland croaks loudly. His greatly decorated shoulders heave up and down. For a brief instant, Byron wonders if the king is choking on a grape.

He stares, not knowing what to do. It takes him several moments to realize that the portly king is laughing. Rowland's black eyes pop open. His gaze fixes upon the two men that crouch upon the floor, still attempting to clean the plates. A thin frown spreads across his face.

"What are you doing?"

The courtiers drop the contents in their hands, plunging immediately into humble bows.

"If it pleases his Majesty, we are simply trying to tidy the mess," one of the courtiers mutters.

Rowland leans forward in order to peer down at the floor. The folds of his great stomach crease over the edge of the table.

"Who made this mess?" he demands. No one says a word. He glares around angrily, his cheeks reddening with heat. "No one dares come forth with a confession?"

Silence, again. Byron remains planted stiffly upon his chair. He watches the scene before him with practiced detachment. The courtiers stand frozen against the wall, pained expressions stamped upon their fearful features. Rowland rises awkwardly from his chair. He points one plump finger towards the door.

"Out," he bellows. His face is now a deep shade of violet. "All of you. Get out of my sight. I will not tolerate dishonesty in these walls!"

The courtiers make sudden haste. They bow only slightly before absconding from the great dining hall. They remind Byron of a school of golden fish banding together and turning in unison as they desperately try to out swim a larger predator.

Is my king a predator, then? Or are these men merely spineless guppies?

He knows what his father would say; drawing in his net filled with flopping, silvery prey. He tries not to think about it. Rowland is lowering himself back into his chair. The red drains slowly from his face.

"I apologize for the appalling interruption, James," Rowland grumbles. He sighs, taking another sip of his wine as he rubs at his temple with his free hand. "I have, working within my walls, a horde of incompetent and ungrateful servants."

"Indeed."

"It goes to show you—a man is nothing who cannot command respect. What am I if I cannot control my people? And, like it or not, the Cairans are *my* people. They are under *my* control." He pauses, wetting his lower lip as a laugh ekes out from between his teeth.

"They are my people," he continues, "But they do not respect me. They do not follow my orders. Do you know, James, that they once declared themselves to have a king of their own?"

"I did, your Majesty." Byron shifts his weight upon the chair and studies the dying glow of twilight that spills through the vaulted windows upon the wall. The dust motes that dance within the sleepy red beams remind him of simmering embers upon a hearth.

Rowland goes on as though he has not heard him. "Well, they did. Centuries ago, there was a Cairan queen on the throne. Saynti, they called her. Great After, it gives me the chills just to say her name aloud. The king that married her, he—well, he was under witchcraft of some sort, no doubt. There were old magics in the world back then. Dark magics. He could not have known what it was he was doing."

Byron knows the story well. Only there is no witchcraft in the tale that he was told as a boy. The Cairan queen bore the Wolham king several sons—viable heirs. But the king was slain by Lord Stoward, the first king of Rowland's line. The usurper, he was called, although that name has since been banished from within the palace walls. Lord Stoward took the throne and began his own line of kings—began a lineage that led to King Rowland. The Wolham family was slain. All of them were killed but for a young daughter, who was said to have been carried away by a servant just before the siege of the palace.

It is a well-known story, but it is old—nothing more than a myth. No record exists, in written history or otherwise, of a Wolham daughter's birth. The Cairans and their precious royal bloodline are obsolete, and so is the bloodline of any past kings.

"There is a mock king, even today," Rowland says, startling Byron out of his reverie. The king taps his fingers in agitation against the table, clicking the gold of his rings audibly against the hard surface. Byron is surprised by his claim. He wonders where Rowland received his information. For all of his time spent patrolling the streets, he has never heard such a rumor—not even a whisper of one.

Even so, it would do him no good to oppose his liege. He holds his tongue and waits for the man to continue speaking.

"There is," Rowland says, waggling his finger at the doubt in Byron's eyes. "I can sense him. He is the puppeteer—the orchestrator of this civil disobedience among my people. Even now, he is laughing at me in the dark. I will not have it. The Chancians need to see that I am respected by all. I will have no opposition. I cannot."

Byron chews the inside of his lip as he studies the wild, black eyes of the Chancian king. "What would you have me do, your Majesty?"

"Find the Rogue," Rowland orders. "Bring her to me. She will pay for her actions with her blood."

Byron rises from his chair, scraping the spindled legs audibly against the polished marble floor. "And this Cairan king? What of him?"

A sneer dances in the corner of Rowland's lips. "The girl did not act alone. She will lead me to him."

It is dark when Byron finally arrives at his quarters. He shuts the door firmly behind him—listens for the brassy click of the latch in the strike plate. He stands in silence and stares into the swimming darkness until spots of color begin to blink in front of his eyes. Dragging his boots across the creaking floor, he wanders to the window at the far side of the room.

An obscure fragment of silver radiance pours in through the opening. It illuminates the uneven floor in a warped rectangle of cerulean light. Through the darkness outside of his window he can just make out the white, frothing waves as they crash onto the beach. He smiles, remembering the trouble he went through to obtain an apartment with a view of the ocean.

The wind has picked up outside. It carries with it the pungent fragrance of the shoreline. He inhales deeply, letting the salty sea air fill his lungs. Shutting his eyes, he feels a wave of nostalgia rush over him. He recalls, not without melancholy, countless mornings spent running down the shore after his father. In his memories, he is shouting eagerly to the assiduous old man, his arms waving in earnest as he pleads with his father to wait for him—to take him fishing.

His father was a skilled fisherman—one of the best in Chancey. An honest and hardworking sailor, he always left for work well before sunrise, when the colorless sand was still packed down by the draining tide and the leaden clouds hung low over the murky horizon. Byron loved going along with him in those days, back before his mother died—back before Frederick Stoward, Rowland's eldest son and Byron's closest childhood friend, had talked him into joining the Golden Guard.

His chest feels heavy as he recalls the serene simplicity of his youth. Back then all that mattered to him was the sea. It was all he had been raised to understand. He opens his eyes. The distant rumble of the waves quiet his soul. He watches as the light from the moon dances upon the endless hoary crests of the sea.

Jarring sounds of laughter and merrymaking drift up to the balcony where he stands. He sighs, allowing the indistinct clatter of the inn below to drag him back to the present. That was one of the unfortunate downsides of purchasing an apartment by the sea. He keeps his quarters on the very outskirts of Chancey, wedged in with the riffraff and the commoners. For him, however, the incessant sound of drunkards and harlots is a small price to pay in order to be able to see the ocean night after night.

He turns away from the window and heads towards his cot. Untying his golden cloak, he tosses it carelessly onto the beaten rosewood armchair that perches in one corner of his quarters. He scarcely remembers unbuttoning his shirt and removing his trousers, so enveloped is he in memories. He crawls into bed, pulling the covers over his aching head. The fabric only manages to slightly muffle the cacophony of shouts that echo from below. He takes a deep breath—shuts his eyes.

He thinks of the Rogue, and how her gaze had shone with defiance as she glared back at him across the square. Rowland said he could not understand their culture—could not fathom why they subscribed titles to their people. Byron thinks of the meaning of the word *rogue*, and he understands.

Is she a criminal, Rogue? Is she a traitor? The man she cut down was one of her people. Her blood. Byron tries to remember how he felt when he received the news of his father's death. The notice reached him in the barracks weeks after the old man had passed. *His heart failed him*, they said. *He died alone.* By then it had been over a year since they had spoken.

That's betrayal, he reasons.

Byron thinks, for a moment, that the Rogue is a better man than he.

It is an odd thought. He shakes it away.

There is a rap at the door. He stiffens, wondering who could possibly be calling at such a late hour. He rolls out of bed, his bones aching. It only takes him a moment to cross to the door. Already, the late night visitor has knocked again. He pulls it open and peers out into the dimly lit hallway.

It is his landlord. The man's sallow complexion is eerie in the candlelight. He smiles blandly.

"General Byron." His words are stilted. He bends his head in respectful acknowledgement. "A woman came for you tonight. She informed me that this was to be delivered directly to you."

He brandishes a wrinkled letter from his coat pocket. Byron takes the parchment in silence. With another nod, the emaciated man is off. His tailcoat flaps preposterously behind him as he marches down the carpeted vestibule.

Byron does not remain at the door to watch the man go. This time, when he hears the soft click of the latch, he makes sure to deadbolt the door. A strange feeling of trepidation has blossomed within him. He heads to his desk, feeling the crinkled paper between his fingers. Taking a seat, he lights the oil lamp that sits on his desk. He unfolds the note.

How careless, he thinks.

The woman, and he has a sneaking suspicion he knows exactly who it is, did not even bother to seal the letter. Anyone could have read it.

His eyes scan the delicate cursive writing. His breath catches in his throat.

The Changing Tide

Her name is Emerala the Rogue.
She is hiding out at the cathedral.

-Seranai

Byron tosses the paper aside, remaining motionless in his chair as he stares at the empty desk before him. He thinks of Seranai, and the way she had fled from the square earlier that afternoon. He wonders what it is she hopes to gain through this letter? His favor? His affection? He wishes she would let him go. It was a long time ago, and he had never loved her.

They met upon the beach, but that had not been the first time Byron saw her. Far from it, in fact. She constantly seemed to be present in his memories—always in the background, but always there nonetheless. He wonders, now, after so much time has passed, if perhaps she knew that he would be at the beach the day they met. Perhaps she had followed him there, understanding that he would be the most vulnerable then—the day he received the news of his estranged father's death.

Seranai was always manipulative, even then.

Byron was not a general in those days, but his superiors told him he showed a lot of potential for someone so young. He was in the king's favor, as the closest friend of Rowland's prized heir and eldest son. The officers above him promised him he was going places—that he had a solid future in the palace if he kept working as hard as he did. He never would have let himself disobey protocol so carelessly had he been general. If anyone had suspected his relationship with Seranai, he would have been severely punished.

Byron laughs at the memory of their goodbyes. He had been happy to quit himself of her, so turbulent had their short-lived romance been. These days, he is far more careful with whom he associates. Seranai is as good as dead to him now, and he wishes she would realize that.

Across the city, Byron can hear the bells strike the midnight hour. He rises from his chair as though he has been branded. His eyes scan the letter once more, reading and rereading the name that is written there.

Emerala the Rogue.

So the Rogue has claimed sanctuary at the cathedral. Rowland will not be pleased. It is the one place he does not have jurisdiction. The cathedral rests upon holy ground, and the sacred Great One of the Westerlies binds even his Majesty.

Byron grimaces, crumpling the letter and tossing it upon the ground. He will not think about it tonight. The hour is late, and he is tired. For now, he will sleep, and when he wakes he will decide what he is to do.

He climbs back into bed and shuts his eyes. This time, he is asleep before his head hits the pillow.

CHAPTER 13

Nerani the Elegant

THE LIGHT FROM the rising sun breaks in refracted rays over the clustered buildings that line the street. The swollen bottoms of the clouds are tinted like watercolors, dying the ephemeral strips of coiling white with hazy shades of pink and orange.

Below, in the crisp charcoal shade cast by the remnants of night, walks Nerani the Elegant. Her traveling cloak is clutched tightly about her shoulders. She steps lightly as she hurries along the cobblestone street. The bottom of her whispering lace petticoat disturbs the fallen petals that have blown into the road. They swirl up restlessly about her pale, pearl gown before settling down in her wake.

She glances around cautiously as she walks, aware that at any moment someone may step out from the shaded alleyways and catch sight of her. It is early still, and no one is out and about in the streets. She revels in the solitude of the dawn, glad that she is able to head undetected towards the cathedral.

Glancing upward, she draws to a sudden stop. The wind that has been shoving at her slender figure keeps forward with a vengeance. It bites into her neck and lifts up her cloak and gown. She is momentarily cocooned in the heavy layers of fabric.

A short way away, towering above the crooked buildings, stands the cathedral. Primordial and resplendent among the lesser edifices that surround it, it beckons softly with the deep resonating of bells. She swallows as she lingers in the street. To her, it no longer looks like an architectural wonder at the heart of Chancey. Instead, it is a prison.

Emerala must already be going mad.

Roberts came by the quarters that morning to inform Nerani that it was her duty to make sure her cousin did not leave the safety of the cathedral that day. When she asked what he would be doing in the meantime he did not reply.

It's important, Nerani, Roberts repeated, his face lined with exhaustion. *She cannot step off of the property.*

I know that. I'll watch her.

Nerani feels inexplicably anxious. There is nothing to tie her to Emerala as she stands there in the street. She took special care today—she looks every bit like an unassuming Chancian woman—and yet she cannot help but feel exposed beneath the expanding reach of sunlight. She stares at the exquisite detail of the stained glass windows on the cathedral and tries in vain to quell her nerves.

It is a beautiful prison, if anything.

A dog barks in the distance. The sound sets her heart pumping. She is suddenly and dreadfully aware of the presence of someone else in the lonely grey street. It is the quiet whisper of boots against stone that gives the new-comer away. She wrenches her gaze from the cathedral, tilting her head only slightly in the direction from whence the sound has come.

There is a flash of gold, all too familiar, and she feels her heart seize up in fright within her chest. No longer pretending to be still oblivious to the figure in the street, she turns on her heel to face him. Her pearl gown fans out from her waist as she lifts her chin in a display of quiet defiance.

Standing just a few feet away from her is none other than General Byron. The gold insignia of his uniform gleams beneath the radiance of the rising sun. His handsome face is expressionless as he studies her through aloof brown eyes.

Nerani exhales. Her unsteady breath is loud in the silence. Stale and grey, it hangs visibly between them as she waits for him to speak. The corner of the guardian's lip twitches upward into an unfamiliar smile.

"I have to ask myself," he begins. He takes a step towards her, his boots disturbing the fallen petals around his feet. "What could a lovely woman like yourself be doing in the streets all alone at such an early hour?"

Nerani feels the heat of revulsion curling up her spine at the sound of his voice. It tears at her eyes and burns her throat. She does not respond to his address, but rather, remains with her feet firmly planted upon the ground as she glares back at him through steel blue eyes. She does not know what would have led him to seek her out in the street. She has done nothing wrong.

"No response?" General Byron's brows climb higher upon his forehead. He closes the gap between them, extending his hand. "You're right, I've forgotten my manners. I'm James Byron, General of His Majesty's Golden Guard."

Nerani feels the revulsion ebbing away within her as stark confusion takes its place. Certainly he does not recognize her as a Cairan. She has broken none of the decrees. Still, she cannot understand what would lead an officer of the Golden Guard to treat her with such civility. Her hand trembling, she places her slender fingers within his grasp. She watches, her heart pounding within her chest, as he leans down and grazes his lips against her knuckles. His dark gaze remains locked upon her face as he does so.

"D-delighted," Nerani stammers, throwing out the phrase she often overhears Chancian women chirping at the young men who stop to greet them on the street. General Bryon straightens and drops her hand with a light smile.

"Am I not to receive a name in exchange for giving you my own? It's polite, you know."

Nerani forces a timid smile back at him. "I'm afraid not." A frantic lie is formulating in her mind. "My father has instructed me to keep to myself and not converse with strangers."

"Your father?"

"Yes." Confidence is knitting her bones back together. She straightens her posture, attempting to look like a young lady of considerable wealth. "My father is one of the merchants that sailed to your island with the spring tides."

General Byron cocks an eyebrow in interest. "Curious," he muses.

Nerani frowns. "How so?"

The general proffers a light shrug, his golden cloak dancing upon the tugging wind. "You don't often encounter the fine daughters of the foreign merchants wandering about the city without an escort of some sort accompanying them."

"Of course. I left without permission," Nerani says quickly, realizing that he is correct. "The accommodations of our inn are rather poor compared to what I am used to." She wrinkles her nose in mock distaste as she speaks.

"Ah." General Byron studies her through narrowed eyes. His teeth graze his lower lip as a charming smile cuts across his face. "Well, then you must permit me to accompany you on your walk."

"There's no need," Nerani disagrees, biting back a scowl. "I'm headed to visit your cathedral, just there. I wanted to see how the morning light looked when it fell through the stained glass, and you are holding me up."

Nerani does not know when she got so adept at lying. Her whole life she floundered and giggled and eventually confessed the truth. It is Emerala who is able to bluff and manipulate her way through any situation.

General Byron is watching her through unreadable eyes. The smile lingers above the square line of his jaw as he chews lightly upon the inside of his lip. "I'm afraid I'm going to have to insist."

He moves to stand at her side, holding out his arm for her to take. Nerani tries to appear calm as she frantically wonders what to do. If she allows him to lead her to the church, surely Emerala will see them approaching. She knows that her impetuous cousin will not be able to resist racing down to the foyer of the great cathedral to stick her nose into trouble. She will be all too curious, and her presence will condemn Nerani before the Guardian.

He will know that she is not really the daughter of a merchant.

He will arrest her and throw her into prison for falsifying her identity.

She could be hanged for her crime.

Nerani's fingers do not cease to tremble even as she slips them lightly into the crook of his elbow. If General Byron notices her hand quivering upon his arm, he does not acknowledge it. Instead, he smiles graciously down at her as he begins to lead her down the cobblestone street.

The morning has dawned in full about them. Sunlight falls in shaft of radiance between the clustered buildings A few sleepy occupants have stumbled out of their homes to begin their morning routines. Nerani does not notice them—she does not hear them—she is only conscious of the stalwart guardian that walks at her side. Glancing out of the corner of her eye, she studies his face. He is staring forward into the street, a cryptic smile twitching in one corner of his lips.

She wonders if she should dismiss him in pretentious irritation. She quickly thinks better of it, realizing that even a wealthy merchant's daughter would have understanding enough to know the type of power held by the general of King Rowland's Golden Guard. She is walking with a man who commands the utmost from everyone, regardless of class. He will expect nothing less from her as they say their goodbyes upon the looming grey steps of the cathedral.

"Have you graced the island of Chancey with your presence before?" General Byron's question startles Nerani out of her panic-stricken thoughts.

"No," Nerani says, and then realizes that her answer sounded far too blunt. Tugging at her petticoat with her free hand, she adds, "I have not yet had the good fortune to travel with my father."

General Byron nods, biting the inside of his lip. He tilts his chin upward, glancing towards the rising sun. The golden light spills into his dark brown eyes and he pulls them nearly closed, causing shallow grooves to splinter out across his face. The effect manages to only heighten his charm, and Nerani finds her stomach plummeting in an unfamiliar drop in spite of her clutching terror.

Keeping one eye squeezed shut against the sun, General Byron returns his gaze to her face. "I imagine it must have been quite the experience to be stuck onboard the ship for so long."

"It was rather cramped," Nerani agrees, pulling her gaze away from the smile in his eyes. The sky overhead is crisp and clear. Her breathing is beginning to normalize as they walk.

"I don't believe I caught where you sailed here from."

The question is asked innocently enough, but Nerani feels her insides clench in fright all the same. Her thoughts pitch about wildly in her brain as she searches for a believable reply.

"Rosanda," she stutters. Her blue eyes remain trained upon the hem of her gown. *Don't be silly. Raise your chin, you are a lady*, she admonishes herself silently. A wry voice deep within her adds, *or at least pretending to be one.*

"Rosanda?" General Byron repeats, the first hint of suspicion tingeing the edge of his words. They are at the first step of the cathedral. Nerani is certain she can feel Emerala's eyes boring into her from somewhere above—or does she imagine that? Her skin itches. She fights the urge to fidget.

"Yes, Rosanda." Nerani forces her gaze to meet the general's. Her breath catches in her throat as she realizes how close he is. His eyes flicker back and forth across her face in uncertainty.

"There are no merchants here from Rosanda this season," he says confidently.

"Of course there are." Nerani tries to laugh and fails. His proximity is unnerving. "My father sailed in just yesterday. Perhaps it is not yet documented."

The guardians are very precise about the documentation of all foreign ships that sail into port. Still, pirates manage to slip in their midst every year. Why could a merchant ship not have gone unnoticed?

"Impossible."

"Why?"

"No new ships docked in port yesterday, documented or otherwise."

Nerani swallows. General Byron's arm drops. Her fingers fall back against her heavy gown.

"Who are you, really?"

"I told you." Nerani's voice grows strangled in her throat. Perhaps she has not become a skilled liar after all.

"You didn't. You gave me no name," General Byron reminds her.

Panic claws at Nerani's heart. She stands immobilized before him and wonders what her next move should be. She can turn and run up the steps. Once she is within the walls of the church, she will be safe. It will not matter whether or not he discovers her to be a Cairan.

He is staring at her with such intent, waiting quietly for her to provide him with some sort of response. She clears her throat, her mouth falling open. No answer rises to her lips. Fear bubbling in her chest, she turns to run. She does not make it up the first step before she feels her hand catch in his.

"Wait." There is no trace of menace in his voice, and yet Nerani feels herself tremble all the same. He draws her back slowly, forcing her to turn and face him. Her pearl gown trails down the steps like water. "Why are you running?"

"I—" Whatever Nerani had been getting ready to say dies upon her tongue. The door to the cathedral is wrenched open with an ugly squeal of the rusting hinges.

"Get your hands off of her," spits an all too familiar voice. Nerani flinches, heat rising into her cheeks. She does not need to turn her head to imagine the picture that General Byron now sees before him—Emerala the Rogue, her green eyes as dark and as wild as her unruly black mane, her lips peeled back in a feral sneer.

"Rogue," General Byron says, startled.

"Unhand her." Emerala's voice is low and dangerous. Nerani glances upwards at the general and finds him staring back down at her. Slow realization steals across his face.

"So you *are* a Cairan," he mutters, as if confirming a previously held suspicion. His grip upon her hand slackens. His fingers brush against hers as he withdraws his grasp.

"Yes," Nerani admits. She takes a shaky step backwards.

"You can't harm her," snaps Emerala. "Not once she's within the cathedral—not once she claims holy sanctuary."

Silence hangs between Nerani and General Byron as she lingers upon the steps before him. His searching gaze has not left her face.

"Claim holy sanctuary," Emerala's voice hisses down at her.

"Sanctuary," Nerani echoes. Her voice cracks.

General Byron clears his throat, blinking as though he has been startled out of a trance. "No harm will come to her." His eyes have fallen back into unfathomable darkness. His jaw is locked. His stature is stalwart and cold. "She's done nothing wrong."

"Of course she hasn't," Emerala retorts. Nerani turns and flees up the stairs. Her heart pounds in her ears as she slows to a stop by Emerala's side. General Byron is still watching them closely, his golden clad silhouette out of place upon the cool, grey steps.

"Emerala the Rogue," he says. He gathers his hands together in the small of his back. His shoulders are erect. Nerani feels something freeze within her. *He knows her name.* "You are the reason I came here this morning. I received a tip regarding your whereabouts last night. It came from one of your own people, actually." He pauses, smiling, and adds, "I suppose there is little honor among outlaws and criminals."

Emerala's lips curl into a sneer. "Do you have a point?"

"As a matter of fact, I do."

"Then make it."

Nerani cringes at the defiance that punctuates her cousin's words. She wishes Emerala would be more respectful. She is already in enough trouble as it is.

"His Majesty has placed a warrant out for your arrest. You are a wanted woman, Emerala the Rogue. The cathedral may keep you safe for now, but watch your step. If so much as one toe touches ground that is within King Rowland's province, you'll be mine."

Emerala offers him a small curtsy. "I look forward to the day, General," she says with a smirk. She grabs hold of Nerani's sleeve and tugs. "Let's go."

Quietly, and without another look at the general, Nerani allows Emerala to lead her away. She jumps as the great doors to the cathedral fall closed at her back. A cloud of dust is kicked up around her feet. She perches numbly in the foyer, shuffling her feet upon the cold marble floors. A vast multitude of candles are lit. She stares at the dancing flames as they flutter like a silent symphony, and thinks that the very room seems alive. The walls dance between shadow and light.

"Why were you talking to that pig?"

Emerala is suddenly in her face, her angry glare consuming her field of vision. Her curls are outlined in warm orange light.

"I couldn't help it, could I?" Nerani asks, feeling unnaturally defensive. "How am I supposed to simply dismiss an officer of the Golden Guard?

"I did."

Nerani scowls. "Yes, and you have a warrant out for your arrest." She scoffs in disbelief. "A warrant! Roberts is going to be furious."

"He already knows," Emerala says, dismissing her cousin's concern with a shrug. She studies Nerani with conviction. Nerani places a shaking hand upon her cheek. Her skin is burning.

Placing a hand upon her hip Emerala asks, "What is wrong with you? You're the color of a tomato."

"I am not."

"You are."

Nerani hesitates before admitting, "He was kind to me."

Emerala's eyes widen into perfect circles. "Don't be mad, Nerani. He didn't know who you were. He would never have given you a second glance had he known you were nothing more than gypsy scum."

"Don't say that," Nerani snaps, feeling irritation with her cousin taking the place of her nerves.

"It's true, that's what he sees us as. Scum. Filth. He wasn't kind to you, he was kind to the woman he thought you were."

Nerani sighs. Her hand drops down to her side. "I know that. It's only that I wasn't in any danger until you showed up, that's all." She did not come here to pick a fight with Emerala. She came here to keep her cousin company. The last thing she needs is for things to be tense between them. She is certain Emerala is already going mad with boredom. The echoing cathedral is lonely and dark and Emerala never did well indoors.

Already, Emerala has lost interest in the conversation. She wanders away, her eyes taking in her surroundings with subdued interest. Her fingers run lazily along the stone garments of a stern looking statue—a saint, maybe, or perhaps a god. Nerani never cared much for religion. All those that claimed to be godly have always scorned her, or meant her harm.

She stares after Emerala. "Where are you going?"

"To the bell tower," Emerala calls over her shoulder. "The archdeacon has promised to let me help him ring the bells at noon if I stop harassing the nuns."

Nerani rolls her eyes. The last bit of trepidation falling away from her, she allows herself to follow her cousin farther into the shaded depths of the cathedral.

CHAPTER 14

Emerala the Rogue

IT HAS NOT even been a full day, and already Emerala is bored out of her mind. It seems the most exciting thing to happen to her is destined to be her brief interaction with General Byron earlier that morning.

She slumps down further in her pew. Her backside is aching. How long has she been sitting here in the dusty shadows? She stares directly in front of her, watching the tinted sunlight fall down in fragments through the stained glass window overhead. It is pretty enough, she supposes, but artwork has never captivated her interest. It is manmade. Stagnant. She much prefers the sea—its surface always glittering in the light, always changing its shape.

Nerani wanted to spend all morning looking at stained glass—all morning wandering from one dusty corner of the cathedral to the other, *oohing* and *ahhing* and commenting on the details. It was laughable, really. The hand painted images depicted holy saints and famous legends of the god of the Westerlies— all things that Emerala is certain her cousin knows nothing about.

She sulks, running her fingers through the snarl of curls atop her head. Her stomach growls hungrily. Rob said that he would be back with food, but he never said when. She is getting impatient.

"There you are!"

Nerani's voice is cringe inducing in the silence that has settled upon Emerala's ears. It has been nearly an hour since the Elders made their last prayerful round, the smoking ball of incense swinging consistently back and forth. Emerala glances over her shoulder to see Nerani with her hands upon her hips. Her chest heaves a sigh of relief beneath her low-cut pearl bodice. Her blue eyes are wide with worry. Emerala knows that Nerani has been dreaming up the most plausible story to tell Rob when he returned and demanded to know how she managed to lose Emerala once again.

I can't get very far, Rob, Emerala thinks bitterly. *You finally have me in a cage.*

"I've been looking for you everywhere!"

"Have you?" Emerala sits up straighter in the pew. "What a coincidence. I've been avoiding you everywhere."

Nerani scowls down at her. "I'm not the one stuck in here, Emerala. I can come and go as I please if you don't want me around."

"You can do no such thing. I know Rob made you promise to stay and keep an eye on me while he's gone."

"He did," Nerani admits. "Anyway, he's back now. He's been looking for you as well."

Emerala jumps up from the seat, ignoring her aching backside. "Where is he?"

They find Rob waiting in one of the prayer rooms. The palms of his hands are upturned within his lap. His eyes are closed. He looks tired, as though he has not slept. Emerala thinks as she enters that the prayer room looks more like a cell than anything, with the wrought iron bars and the windowless walls. She supposes it is suiting. After all, the cathedral has become her holding cell in a matter of hours. She frowns at the thought, glaring down at her toes.

"Roberts." Nerani is shaking his arm lightly. He startles. His eyelids flutter open. "I found her."

His green eyes drift to Emerala's face, his brows lowering in consternation. "Where have you been?"

"What do you mean, where have I been?" Emerala asks icily. "I've been here—wasting away to dust."

Rob purses his lips and says nothing, clearly deciding not to pursue an argument. Emerala feels relief rush through her. She is tired of arguing—it seems to be all they do lately. It was certainly all they did the previous night, as he berated her for having climbed the post in the square.

It was none of your concern, Emerala, he shouted. His voice echoed against the barren stone walls. The eyes of the saints followed them as they paced among the low-burning candles. *Cutting him down didn't bring him back to life!*

No, she retorted angrily, *but it was the right thing to do. You would have done the same, Rob, don't try to deny it.*

She blinks, remembering. She tries to decide if it was worth it. She exhales deeply, her lungs deflating. The air tastes stale upon her tongue. Already, she is beginning to forget what her motivation had been. What has she accomplished? Nothing. But she will never admit that. Not out loud, anyway.

"Roberts the Valiant?"

An unfamiliar man has appeared in the prayer room with them. *Unnerving,* Emerala thinks, scowling darkly at the stranger. She had not seen or heard him enter. He is tall—uncommonly so—and the buttons of his tight red doublet look as though they are about to pop off.

Rob runs a palm down the length of his tired face. "Hello, again."

"Your audience is requested," grumbles the stranger.

Emerala feels thoroughly confused. She stares back and forth between the man and her brother. Is this the secret he has been keeping from her? It is part of it, anyway—it must be. She is certain that she and Rob know all of the same people, and this man is not one of them. She fidgets; growing excited, and tries to remain still. Next to her, Nerani appears just as lost as she. She chews absently at a hangnail upon her pinky, her blue gaze studying the stranger with unabashed curiosity.

Before them, Rob has risen from his seat. He shoots a sideways glance at his sister and his cousin.

"I have some business to take care of. You two stay here."

"But you've only just returned," Nerani protests.

"And you promised us food," Emerala reminds him, wondering if anyone else can hear her stomach growling.

Rob is about to open his mouth and offer a rebuttal when the stranger speaks. "Your sister's presence is requested as well."

"Really?" Emerala asks at the same time as Rob. Their gazes meet and he scowls. She resists the sudden, childlike urge to stick out her tongue.

"What about me?" Nerani inquires. Her blue eyes are wide with apprehension. Emerala knows she is dreading being left to her own devices amid the formidable stone cathedral. It is getting dark outside. The light is fading from the stained glass windows. In the darkness, the innards of the church are transformed. The shadows take on different shapes—darker shapes. She would not like to be left alone, either, and she is much braver than Nerani.

Before them, the stranger eyes Nerani impassively. "Are you the cousin?"

"I am."

"I suppose an exception can be made," the stranger assents, staring into the shadowed space above Nerani's head. "Follow me, all of you."

Emerala and Nerani exchange silent glances as they fall into step behind the strange man and Rob. They are led through an unassuming doorway that sits concealed beyond a vast marble pillar. From there, they descend a dimly lit and creaking staircase. The air is cold against the skin of Emerala's exposed arms. She shivers, crossing her arms tightly across her chest.

It is not long before they reach the bottom step. They pass through a narrow archway, entering an empty room with a low, exposed-beam ceiling. Emerala glances around the expanse, feeling confusion broiling within her.

In the heavy shadows before them, stands a regal looking figure. He approaches the group with a wide smile upon his narrow face. His black hair is pulled away from his neck in a leather tie, accentuating the razor sharp line of his cheekbones and the sculptured bridge of his nose. One gold earring dangles from his earlobe.

"Welcome, all of you." He takes Emerala's hand in his—gives it a vigorous shake. His skin is warm against hers. "Welcome to the catacombs."

"*You're* the Cairan king?" Emerala asks. She recalls the disembodied voice that instructed her and Captain Mathew the morning she cut down Harrane's body from the post. He had identified himself as the king of the Cairans. Emerala denied it at first; she had never truly believed that the Cairans had a king. It was the stuff of legend; the type of games children played in the streets. King of the Cairans—with sticks for swords and slingshots for pistols.

"He is." Rob's tone is a silent warning for Emerala to be respectful. She does not acknowledge it. She wishes the man before her would let go of her hand.

"I am Nobody on the streets," the man explains. "But my mother named me Topan."

"Yes, well—hello." Emerala attempts to discreetly dislodge her palm from his grasp.

"It's wonderful to meet you in person at last, Emerala the Rogue. I must say, I was impressed with your bravery in the square."

A wry chuckle escapes from Rob's lips. "Don't encourage her."

Topan's deep blue gaze roves to where Nerani stands, out of place and silent in the shadows. "And who is this?"

Emerala seizes the opportunity to place Topan's firm grip into Nerani's hands. Shaking out her fingers, she says, "This is my cousin, Nerani the Elegant."

"Ah." Topan beams. He leans down to brush his lips against the back of her hand. Her violet eyes remain transfixed upon her face. "Roberts told me all about you. You're even lovelier than he said."

Nerani gives a small smile, her cheeks flushing with pink. "I know I wasn't summoned here along with my cousins," she says, ever polite. Emerala fights the urge to roll her eyes. "I hope I'm not intruding."

"Not at all. You're always welcome here." Topan gives her a small wink before turning his attention to Rob. "The other day you told me that you wanted to speak with Mame Noveli."

"I did," Rob assents quietly. "I do."

"Come this way, she's right in the next room." Topan turns his back to them, heading off through a narrow doorway at the far side of the room. Emerala starts to follow in his wake, but is dragged backwards by a firm grasp upon her shoulder. Rob's fingers dig into her skin like claws.

"*Be polite*," he snarls in her ear.

"I'm always polite."

His next word slips out in a warning hiss. "Emerala—"

"I know, I know—I'll be the picture of perfection, Rob."

Her brother releases her, heading past her without another word and disappearing through the shadowed door. Emerala shoots a sidelong glance at Nerani, a smirk curling at the corners of her lips.

"What?" Nerani demands.

Emerala shrugs. "Topan thinks you're lovely."

Nerani exhales sharply, her gaze darkening. "Stop that," she snaps, and frowns. Pink heat rushes back into her cheeks and she ducks through the doorway without another word in Emerala's direction. Emerala follows her cousin, glancing over her shoulder. The towering man in the red doublet is gone.

Strange—she had not heard him go.

The room that Emerala enters is several times smaller than the last. Rob stands hunched beneath the cracked trowel ceiling, his curls brushing the cool stone above his head. Around his feet, several plump and vibrant pillows have been strewn about the floor. Incense rises from hand painted glass jars in colorful, reeking curls of smoke.

At the head of the room, a tiny old woman crouches upon a hand woven wicker chair. Emerala recognizes her immediately, although time has not been kind to the petite Mame. She has become a crippled old woman, bowed and bent nearly in half by time. Her long white hair cascades down her shoulders and pools upon the floor at her tiny feet. Her hands—like eagle-talons—grip at the armrests as though she is fighting to keep her hollowed bones from floating away. Her wide blue eyes watch the group without blinking as they move further into the expanse.

"Sit," Topan urges them. "She won't speak until you've made yourselves comfortable."

They obey, taking seats upon the pillows. Emerala wonders what it is they are doing here, so far beneath the earth. She frowns, hoping that Mame Noveli will at least have a story to entertain her. It has been ages, it seems, since she heard a yarn from the elderly woman. Emerala was no more than a child, then, and still the storyteller had been old. Emerala reflects upon this, and realizes that she thought the old woman to be dead.

"I'm not dead," a voice croaks from the direction of the chair. Emerala looks up, surprised. *Did she read my thoughts?*

The woman is glaring at Nerani, who has recoiled from the scathing accusation on the old woman's tongue. Her wide eyes are apologetic—her cheeks are red as tomatoes. Emerala notices with mild amusement that Topan has taken care to sit directly next to her cousin. At the front of the room, Mame Noveli glares down at Nerani through glittering eyes. "You're looking at me like you're surprised to see me alive, girl."

"I—" Nerani stammers uselessly for a moment, searching for the right words of apology. Mame Noveli has already turned her attention elsewhere. Her bright eyes rove the room, studying each occupant in turn.

"Why are you here?" Her voice crinkles out of her like paper.

It is Rob who speaks. "I was instructed to seek you out." He is quiet—respectful—as he watches the Mame with reverence in his emerald gaze. Emerala's eyes dart in his direction.

When was he instructed to do so? And by whom? She frowns at him, hoping he can feel her eyes like daggers in his skin. *More secrets.*

"By whom?" Mame Noveli whispers, mirroring Emerala's thoughts.

"Mame Galyria."

"That mad old hen?" Mame Noveli croaks out a laugh. The sound quickly becomes a wheezing cough. "She can't tell you the future, so she pawns you off on me with some absurd dogma about looking into the past, tell me I'm wrong."

Rob clears his throat, looking decidedly uncomfortable. "That's, uh, just what she said."

The old woman squawks in delight. Her talons tighten upon the armrests. Her knuckles whiten. "I knew it."

"I went to see her regarding the burning at Toyler's. I wanted answers."

Mame Noveli leans forward in the chair, allowing her white hair to spill over her shoulders and tickle the floor at her feet. "And? Did she give you any?"

"Well—no," Rob admits.

"Mame," Topan says, glancing at Rob out of the corner of his eye. Emerala does not miss the twinkle of implication in his gaze. "If you're impartial, I have a story I'd like to hear. I think Rob might like to hear it as well."

Mame Noveli's blue gaze fixates upon Topan. Her smile wavers slightly. "Do you, now?" Her wrinkled nose scrunches drastically, twisting the features upon her face. "Well, I'm tired."

"It's just one story, Mame," Topan insists. "One story, and then we will leave you in peace."

Mame Noveli considers this, her nose still crumpled in thought. "Fine," she grumbles at last. "Out with it, boy—what do you want to hear?"

"Can you tell us about the Forbidden City?"

Topan's question catches Emerala's attention. She shoots him a sideways glance, feeling puzzled. Emerala has heard of the Forbidden City once before, back in the days of her childhood. Her uncle had regaled them with the dark story over dinner. She remembers the night clearly—remembers the way his eyes had glowed wild in the light from the fireplace—remembers the shivers that dripped down her spine.

Gerwinge, you're frightening the poor dears, her aunt had scolded at last. Emerala had not been frightened—she'd been mesmerized. But the story was fiction, nothing more. It had been dreamt up ages ago and passed down through the generations. There is no Forbidden City—there was never a Forbidden City. It is a legend, told purely for entertainment and nothing more. She wonders why Topan has requested such a fantastic story of the old woman. It seems ridiculous to her—odd, even, in light of the events that have taken place over the course of the last few days

At the front of the room, Mame Noveli tugs at her hair with her knobby talons. "I do like that old tale. I haven't told it in ages."

"We'd like to hear it now," Topan urges. Mame Noveli's left eye flutters shut and she peers at him from her right. The tiny, pink tip of her tongue darts out from between her lips. She surveys him in silence for a long moment before turning her attention back to Rob.

"You're half-blood, boy, aren't you?"

Rob appears startled by the question. "Y-yes." His voice cracks and he clears his throat. "Yes, I am."

"And your sister? You share a father?"

"We—"

"She's half-blood, as well?"

"Yes, she is."

"The eyes," Mame Noveli barks, jabbing one, knotted finger at Emerala's face. "Green as the storming sea. That's uncommon in these parts. Singular. Who are they from? Your mother? Your father?"

The question sends a jolt of adrenaline through Emerala and she sits up straighter. The pirate in the square—the one with the golden eyes and the wicked grin—had asked her the same exact thing.

Next to her, Rob's expression has darkened considerably. He does not like to speak of their father—hates to even be reminded of the man. He chews his lip for a minute before responding, his words frosted with ice.

"Our father had green eyes."

Mame Noveli nods enthusiastically, sending tendrils of white hair flying off in all directions. The conviction in her bright eyes suggests she already knew the answer to her own question. A gummy smile appears on the lower half of her face. Her skin crinkles, folding like raw dough over the pale blue of her eyes.

"Quite right, my boy, quite right." She licks her lips, and sighs. "The Forbidden City, eh? A fitting tale for a fitting audience, I should think."

Emerala glances sideways at Topan. His hands are folded in front of his lips. His face is still and unreadable, like the flat surface of the sea before a stone is cast into its depths. She dislikes the quiet reserve of the Cairan king—dislikes the way the Mame is studying her, as though she and her brother are some sort of magnificent specimens.

"GIRL," Mame Noveli barks, startling her. Next to Emerala, Nerani jumps. A gnarled finger is prodding pointedly in her cousin's direction. "Fetch me the vial of amber incense. You'll find it on the corner of the table behind you."

Nerani obliges dutifully, clambering to her feet and snatching at a crystal-line vial filled with lightly smoking sticks of gold. The pale smoke that rises from the ampoule has a deeply honeyed scent, and it tickles the inside of Emerala's nose as Nerani carries it gingerly towards the Mame.

"Set it here," Mame Noveli commands. "No—not there, by my feet, girl."

Nerani obeys, setting the glass down with a quiet clink and rushing back to the relative safety of her pillow. At the front of the room, the old woman clears her throat. Her heavy eyelids drift slowly closed, her fingers relaxing upon the armrests of her chair. When she speaks, her voice is no longer crinkled with age, but strong and honeyed. The sound of her words lull Emerala into a deep sense of calm. Upon the floor, the pale smoke thickens, blanketing the room in a smoldering aura of gold.

"To tell the story of the Forbidden City, I must tell it all," Mame Noveli says. "I'll begin at the beginning, as stories go."

She launches into a yarn, then, but her words, to Emerala, sound like a foreign language. The whispered tongue curls around Emerala's thoughts, lulling her downward into darkness. The thick, cloying smoke fills her eyes, and with a swooping motion she finds herself plummeting downward through the dark.

"Watch, child of Roberts," instructs a deep and terrible voice. "Do not look away."

Emerala is suddenly standing upon the deck of a ship. Overhead, the sky is painted gold. Streaks of sunlight spill across the sea in shafts of unfiltered brilliance. Before her stands a man, tall and broad shouldered, with stormy green eyes staring out from a pale, pointed face.

"*What do they call you?*" His voice is swallowed by the endless sea.

"*Saynti,*" Emerala hears herself say. There is a tremor in her voice. "*Have you come to kill us?*"

The man before her shakes his head. She notices that he is donned in the fineries of a king. He drops to one knee, his green eyes never leaving her face.

"*I'm here to rescue you and your people, lady Saynti. Your captors have all been slain. You are free to go. Although if you stay, I would take you as my wife. Your people will want for nothing as long as I reign.*"

Emerala is falling again, plunging through water like ice. She claws at her throat—kicks frantically for the surface. Overhead, the sun is a muddled circle of rippling white on the top of the sea. She sinks deeper and deeper still, landing finally in the soft, white cotton of a four-poster bed. Her curls are plastered to her cheeks. Her fingers are knotted in the fabric. A scream erupts from her chest, violent and hoarse. Somewhere nearby, she hears an infant's wail.

The green-eyed man appears besides her, clutching at a tightly swaddled infant, red and howling. A crown rests upon his wild head of curls. His face is filled to the brim with elation.

"*My queen—Saynti—look, it's a boy. You've given us a beautiful boy.*"

Falling again.

This time, she lands upon a throne of solid gold. Overhead, fat cherubs ogle her from the painted heavens. The green-eyed man sits beside her. Two young boys stand at her side. Her knuckles are white against the armrests. Her palms are slick with sweat.

"*What news do you bring from the marketplace?*" she hears herself ask. Her voice is high and clear. Before her stands a nervous looking valet. He glances from the king to her and back again.

"*Your Majesties—it is just as you feared. The riots have begun. We are on the verge of a civil war. The Chancian people have risen against the Cairans.*"

"*I knew it,*" she says, her voice a breathless whisper. "*I knew this would happen. Your people have never accepted a Cairan woman as their queen.*"

The green-eyed king at her side rises from his throne. "*Saynti—*"

"*Don't say a word.*" She cuts him off, mirroring his movements. They are face to face beneath the painted heavens. "*Don't you say a word. You promised me we would be safe under your rule. You are a powerful man, Lionus, but even you cannot change the hearts of men. They are given to hate. They are prejudiced against us.*

"*Have you heard what they are calling me in the streets? Witch. Sorceress. They say I've spelled you into taking me as queen. A hate that burns as deep as theirs does not sputter out, my king. When you die, that will be the end. They will never accept a half-blood king. They will never accept the rule of my sons.*"

Lionus's green eyes flash with anger. "*They are my sons, too.*"

"*And my people? Are the Cairans your people as much as the Chancians?*"

"*You know that they are, Saynti.*"

"*Then protect them. It is too late for us—too late for our boys—but the rest of them—*"

She feels the words choke and die upon her tongue. Lionus's gaze fills with determination.

"I will build them a sanctuary, safe from the eyes of the city. You are right, for all the power that I have invested in me, I cannot change the black hearts of men. Only time can do that."

Emerala nods. *"The Forbidden City,"* she whispers, taking Lionus's hands within her own.

"It will be done at once, my love."

The room changes as the sun outside the window rises and falls and rises again. A flicker of untainted life pulses in Emerala's womb. She presses her hand to her distended stomach, suddenly wrought with such a warring clash of grief and love that she nearly collapses to the floor. Before her stands an elderly Mame, bent at the shoulders and leaning on a cane. When she speaks, it is Mame Noveli's voice, sweet and loud and clear, that reaches Emerala's ears.

"Who are you, the seer asked, that knows his fate is set?

Your day will come. Your line will fall. Your people will abet.

But in the babe, so soft and pure, your bloodline will be spared.

She'll fall to dust and dust she'll be, forgotten by the erred.

And when the years, they roll away knowing what's to come,

Her blood with blood will mingle true—a queen she will become."

The scene changes and Emerala is back in the four-poster bed, biting hard upon her lower lip.

"Don't scream, Your Grace," whispers a frightened voice in her ear. *"They will come for us if they hear you."*

Blood trickles down her chin and she moans.

"My sons," she cries. The pain is blinding, searing at her insides. She feels as if she is being ripped open. *"Where are my sons?"*

A long pause follows her question. Her ragged panting fills the silence, broken only by the murmuring of midwives. Far beyond the stone, she knows the world is burning.

"They are slain, Your Majesty. They were killed besides their father. The people are at the gates."

A disconsolate cry escapes her, ripping free of her chest in a broken sob. It is echoed by the wail of an infant, piercing and shrill.

"*Quiet her at once,*" instructs a midwife. "*Wrap her and take her away.*"

"*My daughter,*" Emerala sobs. "*Let me see my daughter.*"

"*Your Majesty,*" whispers that same voice. "*The girl must go. Arden will take her somewhere safe. Lord Stoward's men have stormed the bailey. You must go out to meet them. Your people need to see that their queen will not cower in the palace while they burn.*"

Beyond the thick stone walls, Emerala can hear the distant sound of hammering boots—the war cry of soldiers dying. Steel rings against steel in a shivering ballad. Across the room, the blue-eyed midwife—a Cairan woman, and loyal still—watches Emerala sadly.

"*She's got green eyes, your Grace,*" the midwife says. "*Like her father.*"

"*Take her away,*" Emerala hears herself order. "*Hide her. I will meet my fate upon the steps with my sons.*"

With a loud grunt, Emerala hits the lumpy pillow of the catacombs. She is seated between Roberts and Nerani, staring up at the sleeping figure of Mame Noveli. Next to her, she can feel Nerani staring pointedly at her, a look of accusation in her eyes. Her stomach churns slightly beneath her corset. Her mouth feels dry.

"What?"

"You cried out aloud," Nerani says reproachfully. "You fell asleep right at the start of her story."

"I—" Emerala starts and stops, unsure of what to say. Confusion broils within her gut. "You didn't see things? In the smoke?"

One shapely eyebrow rises upwards on Nerani's forehead. "Of course not, Emerala. Unlike you, I managed to stay awake."

On Emerala's left, Roberts has gone as pale as a ghost. His lips press together in a thin line as he studies the open palms of his hands upon his lap.

"What about you, Rob?" Emerala asks. He glances up at her as if surprised to see her there. A shallow groove has rooted between his brows, casting his expression into a permanent frown.

"What about me?"

"You know—did you see something in the smoke?"

Rob glances over her head towards Nerani and Topan. "No," he retorts, his answer coming too quickly to be believed. "No, I didn't."

"Wipe your chin, Emerala," Nerani instructs. "You've drooled a bit."

Emerala shoots her cousin a scathing glance, pawing at her face with the back of her hand. At the front of the room, Mame Noveli lets out a loud snort. Her blue eyes pop open one at a time.

"Have you no respect for the elderly?" she snaps. Her lower lip quivers. "Can't you see I'm resting?"

Next to Nerani, Topan rises to his feet, offering her his arm as he does so. "We're terribly sorry, Mame."

"Don't apologize, just get out." She waves her hand in the direction of the door. "Be gone with you all."

They obey immediately. Emerala is all too eager to be free of the dimly lit room. She feels as if she is going to be sick. Already, the images in her mind are fleeting, catching on the corners of her memory and fading away to the place where dreams are stored.

Had she fallen asleep?

She supposes it is entirely possible that she had been dreaming. The sleepy darkness of the catacombs is enough to lull anyone into the depths of sleep, and she has never been good at paying attention during long-winded stories.

Still, the dream had felt so real—the images had been so stark. Deep within her, her aching womb feels raw and empty. She thinks of Queen Saynti, and how the Cairan queen had been stripped of her fineries and burned at the stake before all of Chancey. A visible shudder runs through her.

Next to her, Rob is as silent and as grey as stone. His black hair is wilder than usual—the front sticks up at odd angles as if he has been pulling at the roots.

"Are you alright?" she asks him finally, nudging him with her elbow. He jumps as if he has been branded with a hot poker.

"I'm fine," he snaps, not sounding fine at all.

She scowls up at him, unconvinced. "What did you think of the story?"

"It was a fine story," he mutters darkly. "I've heard it before."

"And do you think it's real?"

He meets her gaze head on at that, his scowl deepening. His green eyes are haunted. "It's a legend, Emerala. The Forbidden City has always been nothing more than a legend."

With that, he turns and walks away, heading off quickly into the shadows alone.

Emerala leans back against a low table and watches him go, wondering about the existence of the Forbidden City. Topan had implied that it was a real place. And if what she saw in the smoke had been more than an idle dream—

If the city is more than some legend buried by the years—if it is a tangible dwelling hidden away from the Chancians, then she would like to go there, she should think. She frowns up at the mildewed stone above her head and feels herself shiver against the unremitting chill. Anywhere would be better than this stifling prison of stone.

CHAPTER 15

Seranai the Fair

SERANAI LETS LOOSE the breath of air that she has been holding. She glances around the darkened street, her grey eyes wide. She is going to have to be more careful.

The man that meandered around the corner mere moments before had nearly stepped directly upon her feet in the dark. She cannot chance being recognized—not here, as close as she is to the brothels and the slums. But this is where the golden-eyed pirate has taken up residence, she is sure of it. She cannot think of a better place to meet.

She pulls her traveling cloak tighter about her body as she walks. Keeping close to the walls, she trails her soft fingers against the abrasive exterior of the crumbling brick. The murky shadows of the alleyway provide a strange sort of solitude.

Overhead, the sky is growing lighter. The grey dawn bleaches the corners of the horizon, fading the black night overhead into varying hues of violet. Seranai knows she only has a few more hours until sunrise. She pauses at the edge of the alleyway and glances down at the attire that bulges out from beneath her cloak. The suit is of a blood red hue—the skirt billows out so far that it trails uncooperatively behind her. The material is finely made—foreign, she should think. Whoever bought it probably paid a pretty penny to have it made. She pets it softly, running her fingers down the whispering taffeta. She wonders how much more regal she would appear if the gown had been tailored specifically for her. She frowns down at her feet. Beneath the gown, the ruffled white petticoat is hers. The hem is muddied and torn in places.

Slowly, she pulls off her fitted red jacket. The ruffled white sleeves are beginning to fray at the ends. She eyes them with disdain as she lets the jacket drop to the ground at her feet. The cold night air tickles the exposed flesh of her shoulders and she shivers. Her crimson corset is tightly laced with gleaming, black stays. It cinches her waist almost to a point. Her bosoms heave over the bone lined edge.

She wants to be away from the brothels long before sunrise. That is when James Byron's shift begins. She does not want to chance running into him again, not after he had treated her so poorly the last time. She knows how she looks today—knows what he will think of her if he sees her exposed and dressed for seduction, lingering beneath the shadows of the brothels. Even in his self-indulgent days as a private he was too good for a whore.

Her grey eyes narrow into slits as she thinks of him. She wonders if he is awake yet, and if he has received her letter. The landlord promised that he would hand deliver it to his quarters. She wonders if James will act upon the information she provided him. She wonders if he will think better of her, now. She has cooperated with the guardians. She has separated herself from that vile Cairan wench.

Emerala the Rogue.

She sneers at the thought of the dreadful young gypsy. It is Emerala who has brought her to this point—it is Emerala who has led her to Mamere Lenora's. It is Emerala—that wicked, rotten girl—who has made things difficult for her.

Seranai needs her gone.

She needs her gone, and there is only one man she can think of who can carry out her wishes.

The vociferous catcalls start as soon as she rounds the corner. Seranai flashes a winning smile at the drunken men that mill about between the brothels. Raising an idle hand, she pushes her white blonde locks over her shoulder.

She finds a familiar looking girl seated upon the front step to Mamere Lenora's. The girl frowns as she studies Seranai's deep, crimson gown. Reaching up with dirty fingers, she fixes the steadily plunging neckline of her own ripped cotton chemise, which she has slipped carelessly over a cream colored petticoat. Her black corset is moth bitten and misshapen. Seranai's dainty nose turns up at the sight of her.

"Good evening, Whinny," she says, and sniffs.

"What do you think you're doing here?" Whinny demands bitterly. Her two, overlarge front teeth protrude from behind parted lips.

Seranai fidgets absently with her petticoat, refusing to meet the harlot's gaze. "I told Mamere I'd be coming by."

Whinny's only response is to spit at her feet. Seranai glowers down at the spot of saliva before her slippers, repulsed.

"I'll just go in, then." She sidesteps Whinny, gathering her gown within her fists and holding it off of the soiled ground underfoot.

You'll find him in the third door on the left. That was what Mamere Lenora had told her, her black eyes glittering hungrily as Seranai dangled one of her mother's old bracelets before her. *Be quick about it, Fair. Can't have you pulling focus from my girls.*

Seranai wanders down the narrow hall, keeping her eyes towards the floor. The cloying smell of lavender and old cologne permeates the musty foyer. She wrinkles her nose, holding her breath. As she walks, she counts the doors. Mamere had promised it would be left unlocked.

The soft glow of a candle shines out of a crack in the doorway. *Door number three.* Seranai draws to a stop, staring at the slanted beam of gold that lies across the fusty carpet. She slips through the opening and pulls the door closed behind her. It latches with a click, shutting her inside the cluttered room.

"Finally," a male voice says.

Seranai plants a smile upon her face, taking several steps further into the room as she catches sight of the pirate by the window. His back is to her and he clutches at a decanter of liquor. The fingers of his free hand trace circles upon the soiled glass panes. She wonders if he is drunk. For her sake, she hopes not.

"I apologize for taking so long."

The Hawk turns around, surprised at the sound of her voice. He surveys her with suspicion, his golden eyes glittering beneath the flickering light. He is handsome, she realizes. The chiseled jawline of his face accentuates the lop-sided grin and deep, shaded dimples that root permanently upon his cheeks. His sharp gaze pierces her pallid skin. She feels a small prickle of pleasure at the sight of his eyes. She remembers them distinctly from the blacksmith's workshop. How could she forget? She has never seen anything quite like it. Her intuition has once again led her to the right place.

"You're not at all who I thought," he grumbles. Shadows pull across his face as he frowns and takes a swig of his drink.

"Mamere didn't tell you I'd be coming?"

"Not expecting you, am I?"

"I suppose not."

There is a prolonged moment of uncomfortable silence as the two strangers survey one another across the room. Seranai wonders what he is thinking. Does he remember her? It was only a few days ago that they encountered one another, and he does not seem like the type to forget a face. She squares her shoulders and steps within the throw of the flickering lanterns that line the wallpapered room. The warmth tickles her exposed flesh. Raising a languid hand, she flicks her wrist so that her white locks drape across her shoulder. She smiles softly—bats her thick, black lashes.

"You're not a prostitute," the Hawk states simply, setting down the decanter of liquor upon the windowsill. Stray locks of his black hair fall out from beneath his tricorn cap and sweep across his brow. Seranai drops her hand to her side, a scowling pulling her lips downward.

"Of course I'm not," she snaps.

The Hawk glances implicatively around the room before turning his gaze back towards Seranai. "Aye, well this is a brothel, love."

"This was the safest place for us to meet."

He scoffs. "Where's Lenora?"

He brushes past Seranai, heading toward the door. Steadily—her heart pounding against her ribcage—Seranai places one cool hand upon his chest.

"Wait," she commands. She fights to keep her voice even. She cannot afford to lose his attention—not now. Not when she finally has a plan to pull herself out of a lifetime of undeserved poverty.

The pirate glares down at her hand, held fast against the moth bitten black fabric of his jacket. His lips curl into a sneer and he peers closely at her face.

"I know you," he says at last. At this proximity she can smell the ale upon his breath. It tastes rancid upon her tongue. She tries not to wrinkle her nose in distaste. She allows a small laugh to fall forth from her lips. The sound is light—alluring.

"I believe you do. We've met before." She is gaining control of the situation—can feel him relaxing beneath the palm of her hand. The pirate grabs one delicate wrist in his dirtied fist. He backs her hard against the door, his face drawing nearer to hers.

"If I remember correctly, you said you don't consort with pirates then, love."

"I do when it's a matter of convenience."

"Aye?" She watches as a lewd smile stretches across his face. She can see his gold-capped tooth catch in the light. "And just how am I convenient for you?"

Seranai allows herself a genuine smile, pleased that the pirate is choosing to play along. "You mentioned the other day that you were the kind of man willing to get your hands dirty."

"Aye, I suppose I did."

"It just so happens that I have dirty work that needs doing."

The Hawk tightens his grip upon her wrist, drawing her close to his chest. She can feel the warmth of him through his clothes. "It doesn't come free, you know."

She pries herself out of his grasp, putting space between them. Meeting his gaze, she smiles. "You will be compensated for your efforts, believe me."

The tip of his pink tongue darts out between his lips. He reminds Seranai of a coiled snake lying in wait for its prey. His golden eyes flicker back and forth across her face.

"You have my attention."

"Have you ever heard of the Cairan fortune? Queen Saynti's buried treasure?"

He grimaces, studying her in unreadable silence for a long time. After a moment, he shakes his head. "No."

"No?" Seranai echoes, smiling wider. "If you do this job for me, you'll be helping me access it."

The Hawk mirrors her smile, taking a slow step in her direction across the fetid carpeting underfoot. "And what kind of fortune are we talking about?"

"Gold," Seranai says without missing a beat. "Lots of it."

She watches as the pirate considers this for a moment, his tongue pressed in the corner of his lips. His unblinking golden eyes linger upon her pale, grey gaze. He presses the unbuttoned cuffs of his sleeves up around his elbows, and she sees the black silhouette of a soaring bird inked across his forearm.

"What would you have me do?"

Seranai exhales sharply, smothering her relief. "There is a woman—Cairan born. I want her gone."

"You'd have me kill her?" The eager way in which he asks the question sends a shiver down Seranai's spine. She blinks rapidly, trying to wipe away the bloody image of the butcher's tools that has suddenly imprinted itself upon the insides of her eyelids. She can see her father's grave—freshly dug—can feel her trembling fingers at her sides.

Murderer, she hears her mother whisper.

"Murder isn't a game, pirate," she says before she can help herself.

He laughs at that, his eyes crinkling at the corners. "It is if you know the rules."

"And you do?"

"Aye, love, I wrote the rules."

Something in his voice unsettles her deeply. She clears her throat, flicking a stray lock of hair out of her eyes. "I don't want her killed. I just need her to disappear.

His eyes narrow into slits. "Disappearance isn't as easy as death. It'll cost you more."

The smile flickers momentarily from Seranai's lips. She pretends to consider this—turning her back upon the pirate. As she walks, she traces one lazy finger along the peeling molding that stretches along the length of the wall. She can feel those golden eyes glued to her as she goes.

"Fine," she relents at last, glancing over her shoulder at him. Her pale hair trickles down into the small of her back. "However much you want, you'll have it."

"And not later," the Hawk adds, cutting her short before she can continue speaking. "Now. You'll pay me upfront for disappearance."

Seranai pauses, scowling. "I don't have access to the Cairan Fortune yet."

He shrugs, and a bawdy grin splits his face in half. "I accept all manners of payment, love."

Seranai sniffs, feeling her skin prickle with impatience. "As long as you do it right, you can name your price."

The Hawk lets out a long, low laugh. "This Cairan really did you wrong, did she, love?" He winks at her, his glimmering, golden eye disappearing and reappearing upon his face.

Seranai ignores him. "It cannot be traced back to me, that is the most important."

"Of course not," the Hawk agrees, grinning lecherously. In spite of his agreeability, she cannot help but feel as though she is being mocked. She swallows. Continues.

"In any case, I believe I can help you with the disappearance. It shouldn't be too difficult—your captain has taken a liking to this Cairan woman. I'm sure he would be all too eager to take her with him when you lift anchor in a few weeks."

One dark eyebrow rises upon his forehead—disappears beneath the ends of his tousled, black hair. His face becomes serious for the first time since she entered the room. "Aye, is that so? Tell me, who is this Cairan girl?"

"Emerala the Rogue."

Those golden eyes widen into circles like coins. A laugh like a crow escapes from between his lips. Seranai bristles, turning to face him.

"Emerala the Rogue?" he repeats.

"Yes."

The laughter grows louder. Seranai resists the sudden urge to slap him.

"What's funny about that?"

The pirate shakes his head as his laugh dies upon the air. "Nothing at all, love," he says, fighting to catch his breath. "Nothing at all. It's Emerala the Rogue's disappearance you desire?"

"It is."

The Hawk bows low, sweeping his hat from his head. Tangled black hair falls down into glittering yellow eyes. "Your wish is my command."

CHAPTER 16

General James Byron

THE KING IS going to the cathedral to pray.

Byron watches the flurry of activity from his post at the grand golden door and tries to shake away the grey remnants of sleep. He was summoned from his quarters well before it was time for him to report for his morning shift. The private that retrieved him was apologetic as he reported the reason behind his visit.

He wants what? Byron asked, not comprehending. There was no trace of the sun upon the eastern horizon. The birds were silent—sleeping beneath their wings.

He wants to observe mass at the cathedral this morning.

I heard you, but why?

He hardly needed to ask. He knows exactly why. The night before, he himself had bowed low before the throne and reported that Emerala the Rogue had claimed sanctuary within the walls of the cathedral. He saw it himself, he said. Rowland laughed at that. He laughed and laughed until his face turned violet and he could no longer catch his breath.

Well, he said at last. *At least now we know where she is.*

Byron thought for sure that the king would have been enraged. He thought he would demand that the Golden Guard take immediate action.

Instead, Rowland merely dismissed him.

Go home, James. Get some sleep. You look tired.

Rowland has never visited the cathedral in the square for any reason. Not even in the days of his youth, when his father, the former king, passed in his sleep. That day, the men and woman of Chancey spilled out of the cathedral like ink. They lingered upon the great grey steps in the pouring rain in order to mourn his death. Byron remembers it clearly. His father had dragged him there by the wrists as he dug his heels in the dirt. He had not wanted to go, but it was their duty, his father swore. It was respectful. It was right.

Young Rowland remained holed within the court that day, demanding his immediate coronation.

Neither did Rowland Stoward visit the cathedral following the death of his wife. The bells tolled day and night after her passing, so beloved had she been by her people. Instead, the great king drank himself into oblivion— alone. He spent the day squatting in her garden, pulling up her prized flowers by the roots.

He is afraid, Byron muses, of the people beyond the palace walls—what they might think of him. What diseases they might carry. *Who knows of what,* he thinks, *but he is afraid.*

Byron wonders if bells will toll when Rowland Stoward dies. He wonders if the cathedral will be full. Or, if perhaps, the only men that will attend the memorial are his guardians—a fleet of gold surrounding his tomb. It is cold. It is fitting. He frowns.

"Is the carriage ready?" Byron asks Private Provence. The young guardian has materialized at his side. Swollen circles underline his eyes. The private has a new wife, he remembers. Married as the flowers unfolded upon the trees—a spring wedding.

He must not get a lot of rest.

"It is, sir. Several guardians flank it on either side. His Majesty will be safe."

"I know." Byron takes a cautious step deeper into the foyer. The king— his brave liege—is lurking in the shadows, well out of the way of the bustling activity. His dark eyes are watching the morning sun spill through a quatrefoil upon the wall. Speckles of dust swirl upon the air, dancing between the light and the dark. "Your Majesty?"

"Hmm. Yes?" Rowland appears as though he has been startled out of a dream. He seems unhappy. Worried. The splintering lines upon his forehead have doubled.

He can hold Mass here, Byron reasons. He has a chapel of his own—and an accomplished Elder. Mass is held whenever he deems it necessary.

"Your carriage is ready." Byron bows respectfully, gesturing towards the door.

Rowland Stoward is not going to the cathedral to pray. It is a guise, and a poorly disguised one at that. He wishes to catch a glimpse of Emerala the Rogue.

What will you do, my king, when you find her? His royal hands are tied beneath the watchful eyes of the ageless saints. It is tempting fate, Byron thinks, to get so close to her.

The ride to the cathedral is uneventful. Quiet. Rowland insists that Byron ride with him. *He is frightened,* he thinks. Outside, the citizens of Chancey have gathered in the streets. Everyone desires to catch a glimpse of the elusive king outside of his impenetrable fortress. Byron keeps the violet curtains drawn. The heavy fabric mutes the sunlight. The air inside the carriage is thick and stuffy. He can hear the rhythmic sound of boots upon the cobblestone—the familiar cadence of a handful of men marching in time.

"Keep back," a voice calls. He cannot tell from what side of the carriage the voice emanated. Rowland shuffles his weight upon the cushioned bench where he sits. It is strange, Byron realizes, to be so close to the king. He has known the man all his life, and still he has never been as near to him as he is now. From this proximity Byron can make out the sheen of sweat upon Rowland's brow. His pores are pinpricks of black upon his pale flesh. He is less of a presence without the ornate backing of his gilded throne encapsulating his figure—without the choir of painted cherubs genuflecting at him from the heavens.

This is not a god who sits before him—it is a man. Byron forgets that sometimes, he thinks.

The carriage draws to a stop.

"W-what?" Rowland's fingers curl into fists. His black eyes dart around the musty interior of the carriage. "What's happened, James?"

There is silence beyond the violet curtains. The rhythmic beating of boots against pavement has ceased.

"We have arrived, your Majesty."

A trumpet sounds, expunging three energetic blasts. Byron tries to picture Emerala the Rogue waiting in the shadows, watchful and alert. The face that swarms into focus in his mind is not hers. Instead, it is the blue-eyed Cairan he met on the street. His stomach does an unfamiliar flip at the thought of her with her hand in his—her steely gaze riddled with disdain. He shakes his head. The image of her blurs against his eyelids—blocks of color drifting apart, fading back into black.

The door to the carriage is pulled open. A guardian bows low, gesturing for Rowland to exit into the street.

"Is it safe?" Rowland's eyes rove from the guardian to Byron. He has never seemed more like a child. Byron tries to picture him as a young king, demanding his coronation even as his father was lowered into the earth.

It is easy, he thinks, *to be brave behind stone walls.*

"It is perfectly safe, your Grace. The Archdeacon has ordered the church be emptied of everyone but its humble, holy residents."

He follows Rowland out onto the great, grey steps of the cathedral. His men have done a good job of clearing the streets of stragglers. It is silent. Empty. Even the sun has drawn back behind the thin wall of white clouds that coat the sky. He glances up at the hazy circle of yellow, blinking his eyes in the glare. *It is going to rain soon*, he surmises.

Rowland nearly jumps out of his skin as the heavy double doors of the cathedral fall closed at his back. Only a handful of guardians have entered the cathedral with them. The rest have placed themselves at each entryway. They have been ordered not to let anyone enter, but each of them knows their true instructions.

If she tries to leave, arrest her.

Byron does not think the Rogue would be so foolish. He follows Rowland as he ambles cautiously across the floor. Even the Archdeacon and the Elders have absconded into the shadows. He watches as the king scrutinizes the dark corners of the main room. What does he expect to see? All of Chancey knew about his visit to the cathedral. Byron is certain Emerala the Rogue has made sure that she is well concealed.

"I want to pray."

Rowland's voice is loud in the silence. A cluster of tall candles dance before the breath upon his lips. He has drawn to a standstill before a looming grey statue. Saint Alistair—the patron saint of good fortune. His stone face smiles blindly upon floor.

It takes two guardians to help lower the king to his knees. It is a strange sight—the crown king of Chancey kneeling upon the floor. His heavy fur cloak—bear, Byron thinks—trails behind him. He looks more animal than man in the gloom. The flame from the candles catches in the corners of his golden crown. His eyes drift close. His lips are moving, but no words reach Byron's ears.

Byron is distracted, then, by a sudden movement to his right. He does not glance over his shoulder. Instead, he takes a few idle steps backward. His boots squeak against the polished floor. The golden candlelight seeps from his cloak as darkness pulls at his uniform. He sees another movement—farther in the shadows this time. From the corner of his eye he can make out the hem of a gown sweeping against the floor as its wearer—decidedly feminine—disappears through a narrow doorway.

He follows. Rowland will persist at his prayer for a while. Byron's absence will hardly be noted.

The doorway leads to a narrow spiral stairwell, dimly lit. He frowns up into the gloom. He can just make out light footfalls upon the steps. The sound is coming from a short way ahead. Byron starts up the steps, careful to keep his boots from making too much noise. The air is thick with dust. The shadows play tricks upon his eyes.

He catches up to his mark at the second landing. She is waiting for him, her familiar blue eyes furious in the shade as she glares down at him across the bridge of her narrow nose. Her dark brown hair is drawn back from her face in a pastel ribbon. Stray ringlets curl down around her cheeks, framing her face. Pale white light falls into the stairwell from a narrow slit in the stone high above their heads. It drapes across the grey steps, trickling down like water.

"Why are you following me?" The young Cairan woman is donned in the same gown she was wearing when he apprehended her upon the street the previous day and he finds himself wondering whether or not she has left the cathedral. It is not she who has a price upon her head, after all.

She does not wait for him to provide an answer. "If you think by following me I am going to lead you to my cousin, then you're mistaken."

Byron swallows. *Cousin?* His hand grips the splintering railing as he stares up at her from his lower position upon the curving steps. "Emerala the Rogue is your cousin?"

"She is."

"Is that why you lied to me the other day? To protect her?"

The woman hesitates. He can see the wheels in her head turning—can visualize the words upon her lips as she grapples with whether or not to respond to his question.

"No." Her voice is curt. "I had no idea she would be there when we arrived."

"Then why did you try to mislead me?"

"To protect myself." She states the answer as though it should have been obvious to him. One slender eyebrow arches upward upon her forehead. Outside, the sun is inching across the sky. The pale pitch of light has draped across her face in the gloom.

"You were never in any danger," he assures her. "You had done nothing wrong."

"These days it is a crime to be a Cairan."

"You were afraid of me." It is not a question. She glares back at him. The sunlight catches in her eyes. Her pupils constrict—light dances in the silver slivers that splinter through her dark blue irises. She does not respond. She does not need to. It is written all over her face.

"I am a man of the law, but there is nothing evil about me." Byron does not know where the urge to defend himself has come from. It builds up in his chest—pushes against the wall of his heart. He thinks of his father, how he had turned away his gaze when Byron told him that he was leaving him to pursue the life of a soldier. He thought the old man would be proud.

It's not evil, father. It's not something to be feared. I will be working for the greater good.

146

His words, then, had fallen on deaf ears. Before him, those blue eyes are still studying him, waiting for him to continue. Does she hear him now? A wrinkle has creased the top of her nose. He wishes she would speak.

"It is my job to maintain the peace," he says.

This spurs her to respond, eyes narrowing. "Was it an act of peace, then, what was done to that Cairan man in the square?"

He bristles at the question, recalling the way the man's body had slumped upon the polished palace floors—remembers the pungent scent of gunpowder singing his nose.

"That was different. He attacked my men. The law of the Great One states that violence may be answered with violence."

A smile curls in one corner of her lip. "I don't believe in your god."

A funny thing to say, he thinks, *hidden in His house.*

"What *do* you believe in?"

She scowls, turning away from him without responding. Annoyance splays through him at the sight of her insubordination. He is not accustomed to being ignored. He charges up the steps two at a time, grabbing her arm between his grasp and wrenching her about to face him. They are nose to nose upon the spiraling, narrow stairs—the sound of their breathing whispering back at them in ghostly echoes. He glares down into her face and finds her staring back up at him with contempt.

"I asked you a question," he snaps.

"I heard you."

"I expect it to be answered."

She is silent before him, her chest rising and falling beneath her bodice. Her cheeks are aflame and he wonders if her skin would burn his palm were he to take her face within his hands. His breathing catches in his throat.

"What do you believe in?" he repeats.

"Justice."

This time, her answer comes immediately, like the snap of a whip. It catches him off-guard. His breathing catches in his throat. There is no time to think of a response. He can hear footfalls upon the stairs at his back. Someone is ascending rapidly.

"General Byron!" The voice is familiar—another guardian. The gypsy before him scowls up at him, the high color leeching out of her cheeks. She wrenches her arm from his grasp, turning upon her heel and disappearing around the corner. He watches her go, feeling his temper beginning to abate.

"Sir!" It is Provence. The young private draws to a stop a few steps below.

"What do you want?"

Provence's gaze flickers around the narrow, grey expanse. "To whom were you speaking just now?"

"What?"

"I heard a voice."

"I wasn't speaking to anyone, private."

"But—"

He cuts the private off before he can finish his thought. "I was looking for Emerala the Rogue, as you're supposed to be doing."

"Oh." The private's brow is wrinkled in consternation. He stares uselessly at the slant of white light that has fallen back against the steps.

"Has his Majesty finished his prayer?" Byron asks.

"He has. He is ready to go. He, uh—he says he's grown weary of staring at shadows."

As have I, Byron thinks wryly. He follows the private back down the steps, listening to the sound of his footfalls upon the stone. Corporal Anderson is waiting for them at the bottom. He stands amid a cluster of dripping wax candles. The light pulls across his face, causing pools of darkness to contort his features. He is eerie in the gloom—demonic, even. He studies Byron as he approaches, a furtive smile creeping across the lower half of his face.

"Where did you disappear off to, sir?"

"Nowhere."

"Indeed?" Anderson's smile widens. He remains planted to the floor, his golden cloak pooling upon the colorless stone underfoot. Byron pauses in front of him, holding his inferior officer within his unreadable gaze.

"Is there a problem, corporal?"

"Not at all, sir," Anderson insists, still smiling. "It's only that I saw you following a figure out of the room."

Why did you ask, Byron wonders, *if you already knew the answer?*

"I wanted to make sure there were no stragglers attempting to get near to His Grace," Byron explains

"And were there?"

Byron allows himself to smile back at the corporal, his lips twisting into a practiced grin. "No. It was only one of the Elders, trying to stay out of sight as he made his way to his personal quarters."

Anderson tilts his chin upwards, surveying Byron over the bridge of his nose. He says nothing. *As he should,* Byron muses. *I am his superior. It is not his place to question me.*

"Where is Rowland?" Byron turns his attention away from Anderson's watchful stare.

"He's already been escorted to his carriage. He's asking for you."

"Then let's not keep him waiting." Byron heads out of the cathedral, gesturing for the two guardians to follow suit. As he walks, he replays the odd conversation with the gypsy again in his mind.

What is justice? He frowns down at his boots. It is fair. It is impartial. It is the assignment of merited punishments in response to negative action. She does not understand justice. She cannot.

He is a man of the law, and justice is his duty. He thinks of the body that hung limp in the square. He thinks of his father wringing his cap in his hands, turning away. He thinks of the bear king—of the man-who-would-be-god—kneeling on the floor and praying for luck. Pulling up his dead wife's flowers by the roots.

What is justice?

CHAPTER 17

Evander the Hawk

IF A VIOLENT storm blossomed from the depths of the sea and drowned the godforsaken island of Chancey, Evander the Hawk could not say that he would be sad.

He had spent so much of his youth hating the island and all it was worth. He hated his mother for always smothering him—for keeping him from experiencing any remote bit of fun. He hated his people for being so different, so unwanted. More than anything, he hated the Chancians for casting them out—for making his mother lead a life of fear.

He hated jumping at shadows, hated living off of breadcrumbs, hated sleeping on the floor with the rats. Hate. Hate. Hate.

There was an entire world out there—out on the endless, glassy sea—and there was no need to sit around and live with such hate; to tolerate so much abuse.

And that was all it ever was, abuse.

He leans back against the brick building before which he stands and expels stinging smoke through his nostrils. His golden eyes follow the grey tendrils as they rise upon the afternoon and dissipate in the air. Across the way, a cluster of Cairans plays their instruments. An older man—plump, his nose too big for his face—is plucking at the strings of his guitar. Next to him perches a slender young woman. A tambourine is grasped within her bony fingers. She moves it fluidly, her gown pulling against the cobblestones underfoot. At her feet sits a boy and his drum. His bright blue eyes are wild as he palms the pulsating skin of the instrument. His fingers move quickly and fluidly. They appear translucent, lingering above the skin of the drum. It is well done, the performance. A small crowd of Chancians has gathered to listen.

Evander the Hawk lingers on the outskirts, invisible. He peers up at the sky. The day is overcast—the sun has been suffocated behind a screen of clouds for hours.

It is going to rain soon.

Maybe it will be enough to flood the island of Chancey—to wash everyone into the sea.

He scoffs, lifting his pipe to his chapped lips. One can only hope.

He squints at the clouds and thinks of the word suffocate.

Choke, he thinks.

Throttle.

He spent his youth upon Chancey being slowly strangled to death—like a criminal slipping against his noose, clawing at flesh. His only solace was the sea. He remembers the countless days spent with his toes immersed in the sticking mud beneath the waves— remembers holding his face beneath the surface and counting his heartbeats until he was forced to come up for air.

One, two, three…

Even now, he recalls the sound of his heart beating in time with the buffeting of the white-capped waves against his bare torso.

What had he been trying to do?

Grow gills and swim away? Drown?

Looking back, he thinks he would have accepted either fate.

It is no surprise that he had jumped at the chance to join Samuel Mathew's crew of pirates the day the Rebellion first dropped anchor offshore. The captain's scullery boy had died at sea, and the crew needed a new lackey to do their dirty work. Evander had agreed in a heartbeat. Anything would be better than wasting away on the island of Chancey.

He did not even bid his mother farewell.

He sighs. Smoke tickles at the back of his throat. He thinks of Seranai the Fair and of her request: make Emerala the Rogue disappear.

Strange, when he had come on to Seranai the day before in the blacksmith's shop he had not anticipated that she would seek him out again. If she did, he assumed it would most certainly not be regarding Emerala the

Rogue. He frowns down at his fingertips. It is not often that he finds himself so caught off-guard.

Of course, things could not have worked out better for him thus far. There is no way that Seranai the Fair could possibly know his ties to the island of Chancey. She cannot know that the very reason he came back to this forsaken island—the only reason he allowed himself to set foot on its wretched soil again—was for the same green-eyed Cairan Seranai wishes to disappear.

Evander needs Emerala the Rogue, and he needs her even more than Seranai wants her gone. Only now, he is going to be paid handsomely to carry out what has been his plan all along.

It will be easy to convince Emerala the Rogue to disappear. He recognizes the longing in her eyes—she hungers for adventure the same way he did all those years ago. It does not take a fool to see that she is starved for freedom. She is a captive to Chancey, and she resents it. She is not that different from him, it would seem.

He smiles into the street before him. Smoke seeps out between the gaps in his teeth. He has been dealt a wonderful hand and it is important that he does not give the game away.

Down the road a ways, he can hear the heavy clattering of turning wheels upon the uneven street—boots pounding in time against stone. A horse whinnies. Instinctively, Evander drops back into the shadows. He sees a gilded carriage turning the corner. The lively music from the Cairans sounds discordant paired with the numerous, steady footfalls of the guardians that surround the royal coach.

"Halt!"

The boots shuffle into immediate silence. The horses draw to a stop. Evander watches from the shadows. Even their reins are painted gold. Ridiculous gilded plumes rise from their halters. They paw restlessly at the earth, chewing at their bits.

The door to the carriage flies open. Two men clad in gold cloaks exit. Guardians of a higher rank, no doubt. The Chancians are backing away, returning to their shops. They do not look at the golden carriage in the street.

The music settles into silence. The plump Cairan places a hand over the strings of his guitar.

"What are you doing?" The question comes from a guardian with slick, silver hair. He is smirking at the Cairans before him. Even from where he stands, Evander recognizes the intense disdain in his eyes.

"Performing," the slender woman says. Her thick brows are lowered over her fearful blue eyes.

"There's no law against it," says the man. He offers the guardians a polite smile. The boy sits silenty at his drum.

"You're quite right," comes a voice from within the carriage. Evander cranes his neck to see into the dusky interior of the coach. A shadow is moving within. It does not come into view. It is the king, perhaps, or maybe one of his lords. Evander feels himself coiling like a spring.

Inside the carriage, the voice is speaking again. "There is no law against music." The words slip into the air like smoke.

"General Byron," the voice barks. The second guardian wrenches his eyes away from the Cairans before him.

"Yes, your Majesty?"

So it is the king. Evander relaxes slightly, but only just.

"Arrest them."

Words of protest arise from the group of Cairans. They do not move from where they stand. There are too many guardians about them—they will not make it far if they run. The general is frozen upon the stone. His dark eyes are cold. His muscles are still. He stares into the darkness of the carriage.

"Your Grace?" he asks, as though he has not heard.

"Arrest them, James. If Emerala the Rogue will not hand herself over willingly, so be it. There are other ways to draw a rat out of its hiding place."

Evander feels himself start at the mention of Emerala's name. He frowns. Strange, that the king wants her as well. It is a small world—he has always known that. But this small? It seems like too large of a coincidence.

He wonders what Rowland Stoward knows—how much of the truth he has managed to uncover.

He must fear the prophecy, Evander muses, studying the scene before him. *Only a fool would question the fates.*

General Byron is silent before the shadow of his king.

The voice that leaks from within the carriage is fueled by anger. "I will execute every single Cairan in Chancey if I must. Is she so important of a woman that her mock king will allow his people to die in her place?"

Again, no one speaks.

"No one is that important! ARREST THEM!"

"Right away, your Grace." General Byron snaps his fingers. Several guardians march forward as the carriage door is slammed shut. A whip snaps. The horses whinny. With a squeal and the clatter of hooves against stone, the carriage takes off down the street.

"Run, Benten," the Cairan woman orders. The boy drops the cylinder instrument to the ground. It hits the stones with a resounding crash as he takes off down the street. His bare feet kick up the fallen petals of spring blossoms as he runs. The sound of the drum reverberates through the street—bounces between the walls of the surrounding buildings. One of the guardians moves to chase after the boy. General Byron holds him back.

"Let the boy go."

"Yes, sir." The guardian falls back. Trained to obedience, Evander notes.

"Bind them. Take them to the palace." General Byron's voice is devoid of emotion. His commands are immediately followed. It takes only a handful of guardians to shackle the remaining two Cairans.

"This isn't right," the man calls out to the officers. "You know this isn't right!" He fights uselessly against his restraint. The woman is sobbing openly; a shrill shudder wracks her tiny frame. Tears trace lines through her makeup and pool beneath her chin. Evander watches, invisible, as they are led away behind the clattering carriage.

The sound of the carriage settles into silence upon the crisp, spring air. Only General Byron and the silver-haired guardian are left. They stand in the street, staring one another down. Even from where he stands, Evander can taste the tension in the air.

"Word will have to be delivered to the cathedral." General Byron's voice is impassive. "We can't rely upon the boy to get the message to Emerala the Rogue. He may not even know who she is."

"And you want me to go?" The challenge in the silver-haired guardian's voice is succinct. His dark eyes are narrowed. General Byron frowns at him.

"Will that be a problem?"

The guardian flashes his superior officer a barely suppressed smirk. "Without overstepping my bounds, sir, I think it should be you."

"Do you?"

"I do."

"And why is that, corporal?"

"Because you lied to me, sir. You spoke with one of the Rogue's people in the cathedral—a Cairan woman. I saw her leaving the foyer. I saw you follow her up the stairs."

General Byron's eyes narrow dangerously "That doesn't mean I spoke with her."

"I'm sure his Majesty will think that you did, should I bring this information to him. He went into the cathedral looking for Cairans and came up empty. How would he feel if his most beloved soldier came across one on his own and kept it to himself?"

General Byron's dark eyes are like stone. Evander notes how he clasps his hands behind his back. His knuckles constrict—stretch his flesh to white. The corporal is cold—calculating. He knows that he has the upper hand.

General Byron says nothing. Instead, he walks away, turning his back to the guardian in the street.

"Where are you going?"

General Byron hesitates mid-step. He glances over his shoulder and smiles cordially. "Home. I believe my shift is over."

"And the king's message?"

"I'll take care of it."

Without another word, General Byron heads down the street and out of sight. The corporal watches the space where he disappeared, fuming into the empty expanse. After a moment, he, too, turns and walks off.

Evander the Hawk is alone in the street. He emerges from the shadows, beaming ear to ear. Cool slivers of water prick his flesh and roll off of his skin.

It has begun to rain.

So Rowland Stoward wants Emerala the Rogue. Evander does not know what for—not yet, not really—but it is clear that the Chancian king wants her terribly. Executing innocents? She must have done something quite naughty.

He nearly laughs aloud. He hates Chancey, yes, but thus far the island has been doing a wonderful job of playing along in his game.

Another good hand, he thinks. *Just a few more, and I take home all the winnings.*

A plan is formulating in his mind. The wheels in his head are turning.

Emerala the Rogue is a wanted woman. A life as a pirate has taught him what that is like. It has also taught him the best remedy for a price upon your head.

Disappearance.

CHAPTER 18

Nerani the Elegant

NERANI HOLDS HER breath and studies the stained glass window over her head. It is dark, drained of its color. The sun ceased to shine earlier that afternoon as the weather gave way to rain. The thick black lines that separate each individual shard of colored glass dance before her vision, so long has she been staring without blinking. Her eyes are watering. Her head aches. She cannot remember the last time she slept peacefully through the night.

The dim cathedral about her is brimming with silence. She sits back against the polished wood railing against which she has taken her seat and allows her eyes to drift closed. She is grateful for some time alone. Roberts and Emerala spent the entire morning bickering. All they do lately is fight. She is sick of it—is sick of listening to the yelling, sick of trying to mediate between the two. She loves both of them dearly. They are all that she has. She wishes, more than anything, that they would stop tearing one another down.

What will it help? Fighting will not make Rowland Stoward change his mind. It will not render Emerala safe in Chancey, if there is such a thing as safety for a Cairan in these treacherous times.

She thinks of the previous summer—thinks of following an exuberant Emerala down to the beachfront. Her cousin had been determined to visit the pirate ships anchored just offshore—had sworn to Nerani that she would get on a ship and never look back.

Nerani remembers the terrible heat that summer. She recalls the sand beneath her feet, the sun-cooked granules hot between her toes. She had, for a while, feared that Emerala's threats to leave for good were very real. She pursued the wild girl all through Chancey, begging her to see reason.

She thinks of Emerala's persistence that morning. In her mind's eye she can see that coiled black hair bouncing in the sunlight, taking on a life of its own. The pirate ship bobbed upon the ocean. Golden rays of light bathed the glassy surface, radiating off of the murky green water in a dazzling display of blinding light that ebbed and flowed with the waves.

They did not make it out to the ship that day, nor did they speak with a pirate. Emerala had merely stood motionless before the ship, staring at the unfurled sails as they billowed and snapped in the wind.

Later on, Roberts had been furious with them.

What were you thinking? he shouted at them—both of them, as though Nerani had been involved all along.

It was harmless, Rob. We were just having a bit of fun.

Nothing involving pirates is harmless! You could have been taken captive. I've told you not to go that close!

That day, she had wanted nothing more than to curl up into a ball and disappear. Now, she wishes a pirate ship were the worst of their troubles. Pirates are dishonorable, yes, but they are also drunkards and flirts. They have no authority upon the island of Chancey. They cannot hold a candle to the Golden Guard, nor to the tyrant king.

Nerani thinks of the indignant look that had been etched upon Emerala's face that day as she fought tirelessly with her brother. She can still see the stout lower lip, the narrowed green eyes. She wonders if General Byron saw the same stubborn resentment in Emerala's gaze the day she cut down Harrane's body in the square.

It is no wonder they have called for her arrest.

Somewhere in the distance, she hears the sound of a heavy door scraping against the floor. It slams shut against its frame with a rattle. The candles at Nerani's back dance in the wake of its movement, setting the shadows on the wall into a swirling frenzy. She can hear footfalls against the polished floor of the foyer. Carefully, she rolls over onto her knees. Her pearl gown pulls against the ground. It pools around her body, the bustle gathering up in folds beneath her arms.

As silently as she can, she peers over the top of the low railing behind which she sits. She feels quiet curiosity nudging within her. No one has paid the cathedral a visit all day—not since it was cleared for the king earlier that morning.

She is surprised by what she sees. General Byron, dressed in the plainclothes of a Chancian commoner, is making his deliberate way through the foyer. He is alone. His dark eyes study the looming statues of the saints. His hands are clasped at his back. It is strange to see him like this, out of the standard gold uniform of the Golden Guard. She almost does not recognize him.

He is far enough away that she is certain he cannot see her. She is clothed in shadow, hidden beyond the glare of the whispering candles. She rises slowly from the ground. The fabric of her gown falls away from her with a murmur. Obscured by the gloom, she walks along with him as he makes his way down the long line of pews. His brow, creased beneath his short-cropped hair, gives him the appearance of being deep in thought. The square line of his cleanly-shaven jaw is locked. She wonders what has brought him back to the cathedral.

She reflects back on their conversation earlier that morning. She should not have allowed herself to get so close to the king and his men. She should have been hidden away in the bell tower with Roberts and Emerala. They had been alerted to the king's approach—had stayed well away. Yet she had lingered in the foyer in spite of her nerves. She could not help it, so curious had she been. She wanted to gaze upon his face—to lay eyes upon the king that hated her so.

The conversation with General Byron had been a mistake. She has no idea where she found her defiance. She was frightened when he followed her up the steps—had trembled beneath the unforgiving white glare that fell upon her from the window overhead. Beyond the light, the general dissolved into mere shadow—became a golden wraith upon the steps. She could not walk away from him, could not lead him to Emerala and Roberts.

What do you believe in? he asked her. She felt revulsion clench within her stomach like a fist at the question. How dare he think himself superior to her?

Justice.

The look on his face surprised her. For a moment, the mask of composure had fallen away. It was replaced by something stark, something indecipherable. His gaze met hers, then, and she could tell that she had caught him off guard.

He lied to his men; she had heard that, too. She listened from the stairwell as he told them that he ran into a church Elder upon the steps. He made no mention of her at all.

Why? What did he have to gain by protecting her?

He is kneeling now, his eyes downcast as he lowers his head in prayer. He looks so serene among the flickering candles—so vulnerable. His pistol is not at his waist, nor is his sword in its golden scabbard. She wonders what saint he has chosen to pray to. She wonders, too, what it is he prays for—Emerala's capture, perhaps. It is what his king asked his god when he knelt before a saint earlier that morning, Nerani is sure of it.

She creeps closer, allowing herself to emerge from the shadows. His eyes are closed, he will not see her if she inches just a little bit closer. The statue of the saint is turned away from her. She wants to see its immortal stone face—to know what type of god the fearsome general of the Golden Guard chooses to worship.

She is nearly upon him when her cumbersome gown catches upon one of the tall brass candlesticks. It nearly topples over, but she catches it within her hands. Her heart seizes up within her chest. She holds her breath, cursing herself silently. She is no better than Emerala, with her tireless curiosity.

She has managed to only make the slightest of sounds, but it is enough. General Byron's eyes have fallen open. He stares at her through the gloom, his dark eyes glittering.

"Hello," he says. He is still on his knees. His fingers are clasped together upon the low prayer rail before him. The hem of his navy blue jacket brushes against the floor. She remains frozen before him, still holding the long brass stem of the candle. The blackened wick trails grey smoke into the air. Her eyes are open so wide that her skin aches. Red heat flushes into her cheeks.

"I—" she stammers uselessly before falling back into silence. What is there to say? She can see the statue of the saint clearly from where she stands. She does not recognize its lifeless face.

Before her, General Byron is rising to his feet.

"What are you doing here?" she demands

"I came to pray. The religious tend to do that."

She glowers at him, silent.

"You can put the candle down."

"What?"

"The candle." He gestures to the brass stem in her hands. She did not realize how tightly she was gripping it. She holds it between them as though it is a shield. She glares at him, uncertain. A ghost of a smile teases at his lips. There is no trace of malice in his eyes. She places the candle gingerly upon the floor, cringing at the sound it makes.

"If you came to pray, then pray," she says. An eyebrow rises upon his face and one corner of his lip twitches slightly.

"With you standing over me like this? Hardly prayerful, I should think."

He watches her through the shadows, his dark eyes glimmering in the light as he studies her face. She fidgets uncomfortably beneath his gaze, painfully aware of the fusty silence of the dark cathedral that presses down upon them.

"It's rude to stare," she snaps before she can stop herself. Her breathing catches in her throat and she bites down hard upon her tongue. General Byron exhales sharply, the sound caught between a laugh and a sigh.

"Was I staring?"

She presses her lips together and opts to say nothing. *Foolish,* she curses herself silently. *Foolish, foolish, foolish.* Her cheeks sting with color. Before her, General Byron closes the space between them, setting the candles to fluttering in his wake.

"If I were to be honest, I'd have to admit that I came back here tonight hoping to speak with you."

His words shock her into blinking furiously. She says nothing. A thousand questions surge forward in her mind at once, each more unintelligible than the last.

"Why?" she demands.

"To finish our conversation." He says it as though it should have been obvious to her.

"It was hardly a conversation worth finishing," she murmurs darkly. She wonders what it is that causes her to feel so brave now, when she had positively floundered before him in the street the day that they met. Perhaps it is the knowledge that he can do her no harm—not here, under the scrutinizing eyes of the saints. She thinks that maybe there is something to be said for religion after all.

Before her, the smile has faded from his face. He purses his lips, turning away from her. For a long moment, he stares up into the face of the looming, marble statue before them. His hands clasp together within the small of his back.

"Do you recognize this saint?" Nerani hears him ask.

"No," she mutters, glaring over the top of his head at the lifeless eyes of the stoic holy being.

"No, I didn't think you would. This is Saint Michael, the patron saint of Fortitude." He pauses, glancing over his shoulder at Nerani. "My father used to pray to him when I was a child. He would kneel in this exact spot and ask for courage—for perseverance in the face of adversity."

Nerani's eyes narrow as her brows dip low upon her face. He turns his back upon the saint, facing her in full. His gaze is clouded with disquiet.

"Do you think me unjust?" he asks. A muscle in his jaw twitches visibly.

"What?"

"Earlier today, you said you believe in justice," he remarks coolly, proffering a small shrug. "Your implication was not misunderstood. You think I am an unjust man, is that so?"

"I won't respond to that question," Nerani says, frowning lightly. She takes a step back from him in the shadows, feeling her heartbeat quickening in her chest. She has the sudden, acute sense that she has walked into a trap.

"Why not?" General Byron inquires. He unclasps his hands from his back as he mirrors her movements, drawing closer still across the echoing stone.

"Because—" Nerani starts, keeping her blue gaze trained upon his face. "Because to speak out against Rowland Stoward and his men is treason."

General Byron dithers upon the floor, his foot frozen in mid-step as he studies her through narrowed eyes. He is close enough to her now that she can see her own reflection dancing in his eyes.

"If you've returned to try and see Emerala again, you can look on your own," Nerani remarks. She takes another step back and gasps as she collides into a towering column of stone. "I'm hardly her keeper. In fact, I haven't the slightest idea where in the cathedral she is at the moment."

"No?" General Byron muses, disinterested. He takes another step closer, his eyes narrowing in contemplation as he studies her at this new proximity. He exhales softly, his breath sending stray wisps of hair dancing against her burning cheeks. She is backed against the cold stone, unable to turn away. Her breathing grows shallow as she shirks back from him, uncomfortable at his closeness. The tip of his nose brushes lightly against hers.

"Tell me truly what you think of me," he orders quietly.

"It doesn't matter what I think." Her voice quavers in her throat and she curses herself silently.

"It matters to me."

"Why?"

His eyes flicker back and forth across her face. "Tell me," he orders again.

"No."

His brown eyes flash with impatience. "Why? Because you think it would be treason to do so? I can't lay a hand on you in this place, and you know it. You can speak freely." His brows knit together and he adds, "I wish you would."

His closeness is unnerving her—unraveling her. She thinks of the warmth of his hand in the street, and of the way he had looked at her upon the steps of the cathedral. Her heart is in her throat. Her stomach has plummeted to her feet. She can feel his eyes lingering upon her lips. His pulse flutters in the hollow of his throat. She turns her head to the side and says nothing of what she is thinking. Her thoughts are not to be shared—not with him, not with anyone. Not ever.

Sensing her growing discomfort, he draws back from her only slightly.

"You never told me your name."

"I know." The grey stone of the column is cool against her back. She glowers up at him through guarded blue eyes.

"We're hardly strangers any longer," he observes. "Isn't that the gypsy custom—to keep your true name a secret from outsiders until you've become more familiar?"

It is, but she has no desire to share such precious information with the General of the Golden Guard. He has never been a stranger to her—not since his public promotion to general three harvests previously. He has always been a palpable and fearsome blemish upon the horizon—someone to be feared. He is the reason to look over her shoulder—to second-guess her every move. He is a looming, golden presence too dangerous to ignore.

It is important that she remembers that, rather than turning doe-eyed and incoherent beneath the weight of his shadow. Gathering herself to her full height, she looks him square in the eye.

"A stolen conversation in a stairwell scarcely makes us acquaintances," she says pithily. She hopes that he can detect the underlying aversion that laces her words.

His brown eyes bore into her as he surveys her across the flickering, golden candlelight. "What does it make us?"

The heavy manner in which he asks the question is unnerving. *Nothing at all,* she thinks darkly. Not for the first time, she wishes she remained safely tucked away in the shadows. She would have lost nothing by leaving him quite alone. He would have been finished with his prayer by now, and would be gone.

"It makes us enemies. As we always have been."

The air of a smile fades upon his lips. For a fleeting instant, she thinks she sees hurt in his gaze. "Perhaps." His shoulders rise as he inhales deeply. The candles around them convulse—snap in terse, jerking movements. Beneath her flesh, her nerves do the same.

"Two Cairans have been taken into custody of the king," he says, his fists returning to the small of his back. She freezes, caught off guard by the sudden bluntness of his delivery.

"Who?" Her heartbeat quickens. Her fingers clench into fists at her sides.

He shakes his head. "I don't know. They won't give their names."

Good, she thinks. "What have they done wrong?"

General Byron swallows. She can see his pulse fluttering in the hollow of his throat. For once, his dark eyes do not meet hers. He blinks slowly, his gaze studying the clipped flutter of a candle about to burn out.

"Nothing," he confesses at last. "His Majesty wishes to propose a deal."

"With me?" Nerani asks, confused.

"No. With Emerala the Rogue." His gaze latches onto hers. She watches as his mouth drops into a frown. His skin crinkles in the space between his eyes. "He plans to execute them for your gypsy king's failure to turn over a fugitive."

"Execute them?" she repeats, aghast. She ignores his mention of Topan. "They're innocent people."

"They're leverage. Their lives will be spared if Emerala turns herself in."

"And if she doesn't?" Nerani demands. *And she won't.*

He hesitates before responding. "Then they will hang. And when they are gone, his Majesty will find more to arrest. He doesn't enjoy being crossed, and your cousin has done just that. He'll rest at nothing until he has her in his charge."

Nerani can feel white-hot rage boiling beneath her skin. She thinks back to their conversation this morning. He is a man of the law, he swore, a keeper of the peace.

Killer of innocents.

"How is this justice, general?" she seethes, her temper flaring within her in spite of her restraint. This is why he sought her out—this is why he returned to the cathedral. He planned to negotiate with her for Emerala's life.

He is a fool, she thinks, *to believe that he had a chance.*

The mask of composure has settled back upon his features. His face is as stony and as lifeless as the statues that watch them from the echoing darkness.

"It isn't," he admits quietly. His voice is void of emotion. His admission surprises her. For a moment, she is stunned into silence. Somewhere high above their heads, the resonant bells chime the late hour. She can hear the rain pounding relentlessly against the stone turrets. Her heart pounds just as quickly.

Before, General Byron is backing away. "I need to be on my way," he says, speaking as mildly as though she is an old friend that he stopped to greet upon the streets. "Pass the news along to your cousin."

"I'm not your messenger," she snaps.

"Indeed. Nor are you my friend—you've made that clear enough."

He is mocking her, she is sure of it. She resists the urge to spit at his feet. "Get out," she whispers. He turns away from her, obliging. She watches his back as his figure recedes into the darkness of the empty cathedral.

How can he profess to be so honorable, she wonders, *when he leads his life without any honor at all?*

She had doubted his iniquity earlier that morning—just for a moment— as they stood upon the steps in the colorless morning light. He had seemed so earnest—so eager. She had spent the greater part of her day wondering if perhaps his name preceded him—if maybe he truly believed he was keeping the peace, adhering to the law of his intangible lord and god.

Now she knows better. He was baiting her—trying to gain her trust, her confidence. Her name. She bristles at the thought—quails at the memory of his lingering eyes upon her lips.

She thinks of the innocent Cairans that await their execution. She is sure that he did not so much as bat an eye as he threw them into a cold, dark cell— as he condemned them to an unjust death. He knows nothing of justice, or what it means. He is as twisted inside as the king.

Nerani needs to find her cousins—needs tell them what has transpired. Roberts will know what to do. He will go and speak with Topan. They will find a way to fix this mess.

CHAPTER 19

Emerala the Rogue

EMERALA STANDS AS still as stone in the shadows of the catacombs. The air is dense with moisture. It sticks to her skin like a cloak. Outside, it is raining. She can hear the distant pattering of falling water against granite—a streaming assault from the heavens. She imagines silver soldiers—faceless, cold—plummeting down towards the saturated earth; pirouetting in the whistling westward wind.

It is far off—the rain—somewhere high above her head, beyond the grey granite parapets. She is buried much too deep in the earth. She is in a grave of stone—of whispering candles and watchful saints. Of reeking smoke and unanswered prayers.

She is dead already. Rowland Stoward has declared his sentence; has buried her alive.

One idle fingertip traces a line along her neck. She can hear the whistle of the guillotine—can feel the burn of a noose pulling at her flesh. Which is the fate that awaits the Cairans who go to their death in her place?

There is no way of knowing. Rowland Stoward chooses his methods of execution as he chooses his doublets. His mind whirls and spins like the silver raindrops that dance in the wind. It matters not what form he chooses—the Cairans will die. It will be unjust. It will be public. Crowds will gather to stomp and scream and faint. It will not matter to them whether or not the convicted are guilty of their crime—if there was ever any crime at all.

The room about Emerala is as silent as she. The conversation died out long ago, the occupants of the room exhausted from shouting. It is senseless fighting, really. They all want the same thing. She stares at Nerani. The skin about her cousin's bright blue eyes is red and swollen. Her gaze is fixated at the floor. She has not uttered a word once, not since she came bursting forth into the bell tower hours ago, her mouth agape and her chest heaving.

Besides her sits Topan. His hands are folded within his lap. His eyes are closed. The light from the torch upon the wall sweeps back and forth across his silent figure. The flames dance in Rob's wake as he paces restlessly through the king's quarters. His unruly curls stand on end. His dark green gaze is wild.

"I'll go," Emerala says. She has said it already. She knows that it will be met with as much resistance, even now. But something must be done. They are getting nothing accomplished by sitting in silence below the earth. The hours are slipping away from them far too quickly.

Topan's eyes snap open. He does not look at her, but instead at Rob. Her brother has ceased his pacing. He stares into the dancing flame of the torch as though her voice emanated from deep within the flickering blue nucleus of the fire.

"No." Rob's voice is hoarse from shouting. He turns to face her. "Absolutely not."

"Rob, I can't allow innocent people to die in my place."

"So you would prefer to die instead."

She falters. "That's not what I said."

"If you turn yourself in, you *will* be killed." His words are cold. Matter-of-fact—as though he thinks she does not quite understand the weight of the situation.

She blinks slowly and pictures flames licking at her flesh. Sometimes, when Rowland is truly feeling the full weight of justice, he chooses the pyre. It is a slow death—a painful one, reserved for the most terrible of criminals. Traitors. Gypsies who cut down the corpses of wanted men. She understands the situation more than he can imagine.

"Topan says that his Listeners will try to get me out once I'm in custody," she reminds him. Out of the corner of her eye she sees Topan shift his weight upon his seat. Nerani is still staring pointedly at the floor.

"Try," Rob echoes. He shakes his head. "That's not good enough."

"Those captives have done nothing wrong." She can feel herself becoming incensed. How can he be so stubborn? Her temper is rising beneath her skin. The hair on her arms stands upon end as she bristles hotly beneath his glare.

"Neither have you," he points out.

"Rob—"

He cuts her off. "This discussion is over."

"It isn't over until we've found a solution."

"Well, find one that doesn't involve your subsequent execution."

"Roberts." Topan's soft voice is sedating in the gloom of the damp catacombs. Soothing. "You've had this fight before. We're going in circles." His fingers break apart as he rises from the faded red divan upon which he has been seated. His sudden motion wakes Nerani out of her trance. She looks up from the floor, wide-eyed, staring around the room as though emerging from a dream. Her full lips are pulled into a tight line.

Before the king, Rob is fighting to keep his reserve. "We could move on if Emerala would give up her absurd notions of martyrdom."

"She wishes to trade her own life for the lives of those in custody. You must admit—it is honorable."

"It's mad."

Emerala frowns. She can feel her temper snapping within her like a cord that has been pulled too tight. The whole of her body feels as though it is on fire. Perhaps the pyre will be her death of choice after all.

"I'm going for a walk," she announces. Three pairs of eyes study her through the shadows. "Since my opinions are unwanted, perhaps you'll all reach a conclusion without me."

She turns upon her heels before anyone can protest, storming from the room without another word. She knows Rob will not follow her. He does not need to. Topan has ordered Listeners to place themselves at every entrance. At first, she thought it was merely to keep watch in case any guardians should try and come back into the cathedral unnoticed. Now she knows better.

They are there to keep her inside.

For the first time, she truly feels imprisoned.

Her mind races as she storms through the shadows. Her bare feet slap against the cool marble floors. Who is Rob to tell her what she can and cannot do with her life?

It is mine to throw away.

Earlier he had suggested that he was willing to let two Cairans die in order to keep her safe. Had he not been listening to Nerani? The general said that Rowland was planning to kill as many innocent men and woman as he needed in order to force Emerala to turn herself in.

She hesitates in a shadowed corridor. The floor is cold beneath her feet. Inhaling deeply through her nose, she tries in vain to quell her breathing. Her temper begins to abate. Frustration seeps through her pores, taking the place of her anger. It swells beneath her skin like the rising tide. Her gaze catches upon her reflection in a soiled mirror that has been mounted upon the wall.

Her own green eyes stare back at her from her dark, olive complexion. Her cheekbones are tinged with red. She pulls idly at a stray curl as she studies herself in silence.

Fool, she thinks.

She should have left Harrane's body alone. No one has benefitted from her actions. Not her, not the Cairans in custody. *Certainly,* she thinks, *not Harrane the Hostile.* Her fingers tease at her violet girdle where she has kept the dagger concealed since receiving it all those days ago. She can feel the outline of it through the coarse fabric—can feel the cool blade pressing against her flesh. Her heartbeat settles at the texture beneath her fingertips. Her breathing grows even. It brings her some solace to know that it is there, should she need it.

She thinks of the golden-eyed pirate in the shadows and how he had pressed the hilt into her unsuspecting hand. Did he know, then, the extent of the trouble she would stumble into?

She nearly laughs at the thought. There is simply no way he could have foreseen her actions in the square—no way he could have guessed just how stupid of a girl she could be. A sigh escapes from between her lips. She lets her hand drop down to her side.

"What do I do?" she asks her reflection. No response is given. The green-eyed girl on the other side of the glass stares back at her, unblinking. Her thin lower lip trembles.

"Talking to ourselves, are we?"

The voice that greets her in the darkness frightens her heart into pounding. She whirls around, drawing the dagger from her girdle. The light of the candles catches in the skeletal blade—its silvery reflection is thrown upon the shadowed stone walls.

She stares into the darkness and watches as it stares back.

"Who's there?" she demands. The voice—male—had been strangely familiar. "Show yourself."

"Put the dagger down first, I can't afford to be stabbed," the disembodied voice spits back at her. "I'm sure you understand."

She can see the black silhouette of a man moving among the great stone columns in the dark. Reluctantly, she lowers her hand. The candlelight falls away from the blade.

"Come into the light where I can see you properly."

She hears the sound of boots against stone as the man draws closer. As he moves into the reach of the flickering flames she recognizes his face. It is Captain Alexander Mathew, the pirate that gave her aid in the square. His hair falls out from beneath his tricorn hat, sweeping over bright hazel eyes. A crooked grin is plastered upon his face.

"What are you doing here?" Her heartbeat begins to normalize within her chest.

Alexander shrugs. "You told me that if I wanted to see you I would know where to find you."

Emerala blinks at him.

"Well," he says, sighing exuberantly. His chest rises and falling beneath his worn leather jerkin. The top buttons of his undershirt are undone and she can see the dark outline of a skull inked across his chest. His bright gaze scans the stifling darkness. "Here you are, just where I left you."

She places the dagger tentatively into her girdle. Her eyes never leave the smirking pirate before her. "I can't exactly go anywhere, can I?"

"I suppose not. You've managed to stir up a pretty large heap of trouble for yourself, or so I hear."

"Did you think that I spent my days hidden away in gloomy cathedrals for my own amusement?"

At this, Alexander laughs. "To tell the truth, I assumed you'd have broken free from here days ago. You don't seem the type to follow rules."

"I can't very well go anywhere with a price on my head," she mutters. Her expression darkens at the reminder. She wonders if Rob has managed to calm himself down in her absence. Whatever his mood, she is certain he will not change his mind.

"Ah, yes." The grin upon Alexander's face widens. She scowls at him. Why is it that he seems delighted by the news of her warrant?

"What about you?" She is eager to divert attention away from her and onto something else. "I'm sure the Golden Guard was searching for you as well after you helped me escape."

"They were," he agrees. "They are."

"Then why are you still in Chancey? Why wouldn't you lift anchor and leave?"

He winks at her. "It takes more than a handful of angry men with swords to frighten my crew and I away."

She scoffs. "If I had a ship and a crew at my disposal I would have been worlds away from here before the sun rose the next day."

"Interesting," Alexander muses. He purses his lips, his eyes studying her from beneath his cap.

"What?"

"You would leave Chancey?"

"In a heartbeat." The answer falls from her lips immediately. She recalls the endless summers—recalls standing waist deep in the waves and waiting for a ship that never came. She has spent her entire life dreaming of escape.

"What about your family? You would leave them behind?"

She thinks of Rob, and of all the fighting they have been doing. He would be better off without her around.

"I would." Her pulse quivers against the underside of her flesh as she watches the pirate move closer to her.

"Then you have a ship at your disposal," he says. He grins wickedly, his cheeks dimpling as he adds, "And a crew. Mine."

"What are you suggesting?"

"You don't have to hide anymore. We can raise anchor tomorrow—sail away from Chancey. Your king has no hold on the sea. His golden navy can only pursue you so far."

She is about to agree, but something within her pulls at her heart. She thinks of the two innocent Cairans waiting to be executed in her place. If she leaves, they will be killed. Who knows how many others will follow? She thinks of Nerani and of Orianna the Raven. If they are caught—what then? Can she live with the notion that she might have been responsible for the deaths of her family and friends?

"Wait." Her heart sinks. "I can't just leave on a whim."

"Why not?"

"There are consequences for my actions in the square—consequences that innocent people will face if I disappear."

"Aha." He grins, looking thoroughly unperturbed by such a complication. "Yes, I heard. Two Cairans are to be executed in your place."

Emerala is taken aback by his response. Nerani came to them immediately after speaking with General Byron. Topan's Listeners confirmed that they were the first to hear of the news. Even gossip hungry Chancians were not yet aware of the looming execution.

"How do you know?"

"I have eyes and ears everywhere," he says, speaking as though this information should have been obvious to her. "I thought that detail might cause a spot of bother for us. Luckily for you, I always come prepared with a backup plan."

She watches him, wary. His arrogance irks her—how can anyone be so jovial in the face of very real danger? Her life is at stake, as well as the lives of innocent Cairans, and he is making conversation with her as though they are discussing the weather. She supposes it does not matter to him whether or not the Cairans live or die. After all, he has no reason to care for any of them. Thinking back, she is not even sure what prompted him to give her aid that day in the square.

A sudden, nagging suspicion tugs at her. "Why are you trying to help me?"

"Do I need a reason?"

She crosses her arms over her chest. "Yes."

He thinks about this for a moment before replying, "Boredom."

She stares at him, incredulous. "You're helping me because you're bored?"

"I am." His eyes glimmer sharply. "Now, would you like to hear my plan?"

She sighs, assenting. "Fine." She is sure that whatever the plan is, Rob will not agree to it. Especially not if it is coming from a pirate. There is nothing that Rob hates more. Before her, the pirate is watching her with a permanent smirk curling his lips.

"First," he begins, "you turn yourself in."

"Believe it or not, I already came up with that on my own."

"Excellent. Then we're starting off on the same page." Alexander laughs quietly, clasping his palms together. "All of the executions in Chancey take place in the square, is that correct?"

"Yes." Emerala flinches at the thought. The sound of the dropping guillotine whistles again through her mind.

"That's not very close to the palace. You'll have to be transported there."

"True," she assents. "Although what difference does that make?"

"The difference is that it gives me and my crew a much larger window of time to retrieve you from the guardians."

Emerala fights the urge to roll her eyes. "It's an exciting plan, but I'm afraid it's easier said than done. The Golden Guard is a team of highly trained royal soldiers. You don't simply retrieve prisoners from within their custody."

"And?" The pirate's hazel eyes blaze with challenge.

Emerala's gaze darkens. "And they're incredibly skillful fighters. It takes more than imagination and dry wit to break their lines of defense."

"You're absolutely right," Alexander agrees enthusiastically. "It takes pirates. Luckily for you, I have a whole ship full of them."

"You can't just swoop in and carry me away unscathed."

"I can. I have before."

She sighs. "Fine."

His smile widens impossibly. The shadow of his tricorn hat obscures the wicked glimmer in his hazel eyes. "Fine?"

"I'll give it a try," Emerala concedes. "But only because I am completely out of ideas."

"Exceptional," he whispers, rubbing his fingers together.

"You'll have to sell your idea to my brother, though," she says. "And I have a feeling the fact that you're a pirate is not going to sit very well with him."

"He doesn't like pirates?" Alexander asks, feigning surprise.

Emerala flashes him a grimace. "Most people don't."

She gestures for him to follow her, leading him back into the darkness of the cathedral. The mirror upon the wall fades back into black as their reflections edge out of the framed rim of the glass. She wonders what has possessed her, that she would take the advice of a pirate so easily. Rob will be livid, she is certain of it. In fact, if she were not convinced that Topan would be willing to receive the captain in his quarters, she would never have assented to hear out his plan in the first place.

As desperate as she is feeling, she knows that the Cairan king is more so. It is his people that are being threatened. She is nothing to him, she knows. He could easily choose to hand her over to Rowland Stoward and be done with it. No more of his people will be killed—just her. In fact, she wonders how many times the thought has passed unbidden through his mind. It is his respect for Rob, she imagines, that stays his hand.

She glances over her shoulder at the pirate as she walks. He is studying her silently through the gloom, the ever present grin still teasing at the corners of his lips.

So confident, she marvels. She has never met anyone who is quite so sure of himself. If anyone can free her from Rowland's clutches, perhaps it is he.

But why? He was in the wrong place at the wrong time the day she cut down Harrane's body in the square. It would have been hard for him to sneak away without being noticed once she had drawn attention to him. After he brought her safely to the cathedral, she had assumed that she would never lay eyes on him again.

She finds it strange that he would seek her out and offer his aid. She cannot fathom how helping her can possibly benefit him or his crew.

She cannot afford to question his motives—not now.

They need a solution, and it is quite possible that Alexander Mathew has just offered her the only one that will work.

CHAPTER 20

Captain Alexander Mathew

"FOLD?"

"Not a chance in the Dark Below. You?"

Alexander Mathew does not trust Evander the Hawk as far as he can throw him. If he did, he is certain that he would have been dead long before now.

"Aye, you'd like that wouldn't you, Cap'n?"

"Doesn't matter to me either way."

Two golden eyes crinkle in the darkness. "Got that much faith in your hand, do you?"

Alexander settles deeper into his chair and studies the crumpled cards in his fist. Four of a kind. Across the table of splintering wood, the Hawk sits tangled in a cloud of smoke. One stray tendril seeps out from his nostrils and rises into the air above his head. He reminds Alexander of a coiled dragon lying in wait—ready to strike. Alexander raps the corner of his hand twice against the table, leaning back. The spine of his chair creaks beneath his weight as he regards the Hawk through careful eyes. The pirate's face is smooth and undisturbed. A twinkling pile of coppers sits between them.

If he is bluffing, he is doing an exceptional job.

"Tell me why we need Emerala the Rogue." The words escape Alexander's lips before he can call them back. There is more at stake here, he realizes, than a handful of coppers. The lives of his crew, the life of the enchanting green-eyed gypsy, the sanctity of his quest—all of these hang in the balance, teetering precariously on the blade of a knife as Alexander waits to see if he will win or lose against the steel force of Rowland Stoward's Golden Guard.

He is acting on the word of a pirate—acting on the word of a man who would sooner see him dead than call him captain. And yet the golden eyed pirate knows considerably more than him. Decades spent in the company of Alexander's late father has led Evander the Hawk to hold within his hand the key to many valuable secrets—secrets that Samuel Mathew took to his watery grave.

Across the table, the Hawk taps his pipe against his knee. His tongue presses against an incisor as he regards Alexander through careful eyes.

"I already told you why," he mutters, pulling his cards close to his chest. The corner drags audibly across the wood.

"Tell me again."

The Hawk snorts lightly. "Is that an order, Cap'n?"

"It is."

"Your father spoke of her often, before he died," the Hawk says at last, repeating his words from the previous night.

"He never mentioned her to me."

"He trusted me." The Hawk's voice does not betray his temper, but Alexander has known him long enough to see the twist of betrayal in the pirate's golden eyes. The Hawk wanted to be captain once Samuel Mathew died—he would have been captain, in fact, had the pirate lord's long lost son not appeared on the ship months before the man caught ill.

The appearance of Alexander Mathew onboard the Rebellion had rendered everything Evander the Hawk had worked for null and void. His years of devotion to the fearsome lord of the seas paled in comparison to the bond of father and son—the legitimacy of an heir.

Alexander is not fool enough to miss the flicker of hate in Evander's eyes when he is reminded of his stolen fate.

"When my father mentioned Emerala the Rogue, what did he say?"

The Hawk replaces his pipe between his lips, drawing in a deep breath. He exhales expertly, sending a dissipating ring of smoke across the table. It frames Alexander's face, breaking over him in shards of acrid grey.

"Damned if I remember," the Hawk mutters.

"You remember nothing?"

"That's what I said, isn't it, Cap'n?"

"How can you have any certainty that the girl is worth something to us if you can't remember why my father spoke of her?"

The Hawk shrugs. "Too late now, isn't it?" he muses, flicking at a stray copper on the table between them. "You've already offered the Rogue your *expertise*." He grins at that, as if he's made a wonderful joke. Alexander scowls, leaning forward across the table and setting his cards facedown upon the splintering wood.

"Do you know what the crew told me when I arrived onboard the Rebellion?"

"Can't say that I do, Cap'n."

Alexander wets his lip, a humorless smile teasing in one corner. "They told me not to turn my back on you."

Alexander recalls, even now, listening as his father's men regaled him with stories over stale bread and flat ale. They illustrated for him a desperate, floundering boy, with eyes as gold as a hawk's, stowing away on board the ship one spring. He had begged to be given some sort of work—had promised he would be useful. The crew had been good and ready to send him over the plank and let the sharks take care of what little meat he had upon his bones. Samuel took pity on the boy. He allowed him to stay on board, swabbing the deck and emptying the latrine to stay alive.

He were as hard a worker as we'd ever seen, the men told him, *but ruthless. Ruthless.* They told him dark stories of the things Evander did in order to rise in the ranks onboard. Stories of lies and of gambling—of daggers in the dark. It was not the way that Alexander had been raised back on dry land in the Agran Circle. But this was piracy, and there were no rules.

Across the table, the Hawk appears unfazed. His golden eyes lock onto Alexander's face. "It's wise advice."

"Is it?"

"Only a fool turns his back on a pirate. The only bigger fool is a captain who turns his back on his crew."

"So you're telling me I shouldn't trust you?"

The Hawk flashes him a furtive smile. "Is that what you'd like to hear?"

"I'd like to hear why my father wanted Emerala the Rogue."

"Never said he wanted her, did I? I said she was important."

"To my father?"

"To us." The Hawk's smile widens. He leans back in his chair so that the front two legs lift off of the ground. One lanky arm swings over the back of his chair. "Old Sam knew her father, you know? Eliot Roberts, I think was his name."

Of course not, Alexander wants to snap. *How could I have possibly known*? He bites his tongue and waits for the Hawk to continue speaking. When the golden-eyed pirate remains silent, Alexander bristles and relents, desperate to push for more information.

"I asked my father to come back home with me," he explains. "Back when I first came onboard."

He has the Hawk's attention. He can see a distant glimmer of intrigue in the golden gaze. He continues, the secondhand sting of tobacco swirling in his throat.

"I didn't want this life—never had boyhood dreams of being a pirate. I wasn't a runaway or a captive. But I lived on the streets all my life, begging for food for my mother. I spent every day and night looking for work, praying to the Great One for shelter. The island of Senada isn't kind to the fatherless babes of pirates, and I was no exception."

At the other side of the table, the Hawk is silent still. Alexander flicks at his cap, dragging a pinky against his scalp. His hair is matted with sweat where the band has rested against his head for the majority of the day. He tries not to think of his mother waist deep in the surf, screaming at him to get away—calling him Samuel. He tries not to remember the fear he felt each day at the blacksmith's shop or the baker's kitchen as he worried whether or not she had managed to drown herself in a riptide.

"When I came onboard the Rebellion, I meant to kill Samuel Mathew," he says. The words sound cold, even to him. The Hawk does not flinch. He does not blink. He only sits frozen in his chair, shrouded in smoke and shadow.

"I'd sworn to myself I'd get revenge on the man who left my mother a broken woman—swore I'd kill him and take him home for her to mourn."

"Why didn't you?" The Hawk's voice is detached.

Alexander lets out a humorless laugh. He does not tell the Hawk about that final, damning tip he had received from Senada's newly arrived diplomat.

He does not tell him about how he traded his childish need for revenge for his mother's protection—how the wealthy newcomer wanted the map Samuel hunted, and how he had promised Alexander he would care for his ailing mother for the rest of her days if Alexander only saw his father's mission through to the end.

He peers at the Hawk through the smoke. *You're not the only one with secrets, mate*, he thinks. Instead of the truth, he answers the Hawk's question with another question.

"What does the name Ha'Suri mean to you?"

This time, he sees a flicker of ripple across the Hawk's face, disturbing the glassy silence of his expression.

"Where did you hear that?"

"From my father," Alexander explains. "He whispered it to me on his deathbed."

"What exactly did he say?" There is a discernible tremor in the Hawk's voice. The name has frightened him—or, perhaps, he is frightened that Alexander has heard it. It is one of his precious keys—one of the aces hidden in his sleeves.

"I'll tell you," Alexander says, biting back a smile. "When you tell me why I need Emerala the Rogue."

Anger passes through the Hawk's eyes and is gone. "I've told you everything I know."

"I don't believe that for a second, mate."

A long, bitter silence unfolds between them. It is broken only by the whispering rush of the sea beyond the bowels of the ship. It is the Hawk who speaks first, rapping his knuckles loudly against the table.

"This hand has gone on long enough, aye? Let's let the cards speak for themselves."

He tosses his hand down upon the splintering wood. A straight flush—a winning hand. One eyebrow disappears into his unkempt black hair as he gestures for Alexander to do the same. Scowling, Alexander lays his four of a kind gingerly upon the surface.

One step behind.

He is always just one step behind those scheming golden eyes.

He watches, annoyed, as the Hawk eagerly scoops the pile of coppers into his lap. The clatter of coins is loud against the darkened expanse.

Alexander does not trust Evander the Hawk, that much is true, but they both want the same thing, and they will, each of them, do whatever it takes to get there. If the Hawk says he needs Emerala the Rogue, then Alexander will be damned if he leaves the island without her.

Outside the ship, it is a windless day. The creaking groan of the rig is as quiet as a whisper against the cool darkness of his quarters. Over the reeking smoke, he can smell the sea—crisp and clear and green. It always smells that way after the rain, he notes—like a color.

He thinks about his conversation with Emerala the Rogue the previous day, and of the blue-eyed Cairan woman who had burst into tears at the thought of saying goodbye.

Emerala, she whispered, her voice breaking. *Don't you understand what he's suggesting? You'll be leaving here for good. You won't see us again.*

But Emerala had been unfazed at the prospect of saying goodbye.

Alexander wonders what Emerala is doing now—wonders if she has already left the cathedral to make her way back to the square. The execution of the Cairans will be taking place at high noon. Alexander saw the two empty nooses hanging in the square that morning, the golden knots carefully secured.

Ignoring the smug look on the Hawk's face, he turns his attention back to the lanky pirate.

"You'll stay away from the execution today."

"Aye, Cap'n."

He can hear the curling sneer in the pirate's voice. Swallowing his annoyance, he rises from his chair. "We can't afford to be associated with the girl. If any of the guardians are on the lookout for us the day of her execution, our plan will be ruined."

"Aye, Cap'n," the Hawk repeats. "You know me, I'm not about to ruin my chance to spill golden blood."

And what about my blood? Alexander wonders. *Will you spill that, the moment you're given the chance?*

Shrill, screeching screams reach them from deep below deck. The sound sends a chill down Alexander's spine. Prized pets—the necessity of every pirate lord of the Westerlies. That was what his father had called the shrieking parrots the first time he brought Alexander below deck to see them fluttering about their cage.

"Feathered demons," Alexander grumbles.

"Rats with wings, aye?" the Hawk agrees. He gives his coin pouch a shake, his eyes glimmering at sound of bulging coppers. Since Samuel Mathew's death, the birds have been silent—despondent—mourning the loss of their master. Alexander made sure that they were kept fed and their cages were clean, but otherwise he forgot about them entirely.

Until this morning.

He and the crew had awoken to seven screeching birds at dawn. Nothing anyone said or did would calm them down. Samuel Mathew had fondly called the largest of the parrots Old Salt. It was he who instigated the angry ruckus that morning, loudly proclaiming one shrill phrase over and over.

Gold blood bleeds red!

Alexander bites back a smile. "Gold blood bleeds red," he murmurs aloud. His fingers tease at the pistol in his belt—dance against the sword in his scabbard. Across the table, the Hawk grins.

"Aye, we'll see, won't we?"

CHAPTER 21

General James Byron

THE MARCH TO the square is long and cumbersome, slowed considerably by the eager crowd of onlookers that gather beneath the storefront awnings to catch sight of the prisoners. James Byron rides at the head of the black, barred prisoner's carriage, listening to the rhythmic patter of hooves against stone underfoot.

"Keep them back," he calls to a foot soldier, gesturing with one gloved hand to a particularly rowdy group of bystanders that surge forward to get a better view. The guardian moves to obey, shouting orders as he brandished his gun in a show of force. The bystanders fall back at once, their eyes glazing over with disappointment as the heavily barred carriage clatters past.

Byron adjusts his weight upon his saddle, tightening the reins. Beneath him, his decorated mount lets out an unhappy whinny, tossing its head. The whites of the horse's eyes flash beneath its golden blinders as the great, black stallion catches sight of the pressing crowd. Leaning down, Byron pats the creature lightly on the neck. The earthen musk of the horse tickles his nose, drowning out the smell of urine and rot that exudes from the tight, claustrophobic alleyways to his left and right.

Sitting upright, he expels a small, tired groan. His bones are stiff with exhaustion. His eyes burn in their sockets. Last night had been another restless night, fraught with dreams that led him to wake sweating in a wild fervor, hopelessly tangled in his sticking sheets. The contents of his breakfast, taken hurriedly in his quarters before the dawn, are unsettled in his stomach. Each step taken by his mount jostles his innards, threatening to upend his diet all over the street.

Last night, he dreamt of the blue-eyed woman. He dreamt of her burning— dreamt of the sound of her screams rending the night in two. Each time, he found himself trying to reach her, to help her, and each time he was met with unbridled hate.

You've done this, she told him, the fire peeling away her skin. *You, and you alone.*

He dreamt, too, of his father, old and grey and smiling at him from a dinghy out at sea.

The Great One blessed us with a bountiful harvest this morning, James. Run and tell your mother that we will eat well tonight.

He is unfocused today—rattled. This morning as he reported to Rowland to inform him that Emerala the Rogue had not yet shown her face, he found himself missing the presence of Prince Frederick more profoundly than ever before. What would his old friend say, he wondered, if he were still with them? The eldest prince had always been a hopeless flirt and an unreasonable risk-taker. It was Byron who talked him out of trouble—Byron whose good sense edged the prince back from every ledge.

Should've kissed her when you had the chance, James, Frederick would have laughed. *Don't be a total prat, that's what you wanted, wasn't it?*

She wouldn't have me, Byron finds himself reasoning silently. *I've sentenced her cousin to death.*

Is that what he wanted? Is that why he allowed himself to get so close—to let down his guard against his better judgment? Her crucifixion of his character has stuck with him—plagued him—in the days since he first pulled her to him on the crooked steps and demanded to know her thoughts. He does not understand where this driving need for her approval was born. He has never been the type of man to care what anyone else thinks of him, certainly not a Cairan born woman.

No—that can't be what he wanted. It isn't.

And yet last night, he had also dreamed of his lips finding hers amid the dancing candlelight—dreamt of the warmth of her melting away beneath him. That time, when he woke, it was to find himself sighing his release into the darkness, wishing for sleep to return more fervently than before.

His thoughts are a jumble of incoherencies, strung together with exhaustion. A permanent groove has burrowed its way between his brows. He is talking to ghosts, dreaming of ghosts, thinking of ghosts.

It is a waste of his time.

Hoof beats upon the cobblestone rip him back into the present. Glancing over his shoulder, he sees Corporal Anderson riding up to the front of the column. Byron's stallion whinnies at the approach, startled by the arrival of another rider.

"Well?" Anderson draws his mare in close. His eyes stare straight ahead as he glances out across the idling crowd of watchful Chancians. Byron knows what it is he's asking—knows what he wants to hear. He feels a flicker of annoyance pass through him.

"It's taken care of."

"You made sure the message got back to the cathedral?"

"I did."

"Good." He can hear the sneer in Anderson's voice. The sound of it causes Byron to bristle angrily, his already coiled temper threatening to snap.

"And Corporal?" He reaches out and takes hold of Anderson's golden reins. Pulling hard at the bit, he wrenches the mare in close. The beast's ears flatten against her head in agitation as she draws alongside Byron's stallion. Byron lowers his voice to a dangerous hiss. "Question my authority like that again, and I will destroy you, do you understand"

He does not wait for Anderson to respond. Instead, he raises one gloved hand and slaps the mare hard upon the rump. She takes off with an angry snort, trotting off through the columns of marching guardians. Byron is certain that Anderson will not stay silent about his treatment.

Good, he thinks. *Let him go and cry to his lord father.*

Rowland Stoward likes to surround himself with people, but only because he enjoys the sound of his own voice. He must imagine that other people do as well. The men of his court are pompous, well dressed puppets. Silent placeholders. Disposable. Anderson's father will have no pull in the court.

Byron pulls his stallion up short as they round the corner, arriving at the square. Already, the crowd is growing. The occupants are restless as the sun climbs higher into the sky. Dismounting, Byron hands his horse to a waiting private and gestures for a nearby squadron of guardians to lead the carriage around to the back of the executioner's platform.

"Ready the prisoners," he orders. His words sound as though they are coming from someone other than him. He turns his back on the carriage, shutting out the creaking groan of the wheels as the two innocent Cairans are carted away. Scanning the faces of the crowd before him, Byron searches for a pair of vibrant green eyes—a head of wild, dark hair.

It is a pointless search. He does not think that Emerala the Rogue will come.

He recalls the cold hatred in the blue-eyed Cairan's gaze as he spoke to her in the silent cathedral. Her anger had been answer enough. The Cairan people would not hand over the Rogue to the crown—at least not yet. The Cairan king, if there truly is one, will call Rowland Stoward's bluff.

Upon the dais, a guardian is reading off a list of the captive's crimes before they are led out upon the platform. They are lies, all of them, falsified for the benefit of the listening Chancians. The crowd below bellows obscenities towards the waiting captives, clamoring incoherently above one another as they surge forward upon the cobblestones.

Byron itches beneath the heavy golden fabric of his uniform. The sun is hot against his shoulders. He fights the urge to fidget. If only the Chancians knew the truth—if only they knew how innocent the prisoners truly were of any crime—perhaps they would not be so bloodthirsty then.

How is this justice?

He can hear the Cairan woman's voice in his head as clearly as though she is standing right next to him.

This is not justice, he thinks. *This is murder.*

He knows what his father would say were he still alive. Byron imagines him standing in the crowd, that familiar, disapproving frown etched upon his face. For a second, he thinks he truly does see him lingering upon the outskirts of the mass. His breathing catches in his throat. The moment passes and he sees that it is just a white-haired old man, stomping his feet in anticipation.

Behind him, the prisoners are being led onto the platform. The shouting rises in volume as they are drawn to a standstill before their respective nooses. From where he stands, Byron can hear the woman sobbing.

The executioner's voice extends through the square like thunder. "These Cairans, for their crimes against the crown, are hereby sentenced upon this day to be hung by the neck until dead." Byron stands as still as stone and listens to the proclamation, staring forward at nothing.

The steady drumbeat falls into reverberating silence. Three, brassy blasts emanate from a trumpet at Byron's back. The crowd quiets as if on cue. A hundred necks crane forward to get a better view. Children, their caps tied tight upon their heads to keep out the sun, rise upon their toes. It is sport, for them. It is relief from the monotony of the island.

Byron does not need to turn around in order to see what they are seeing. He can hear the whispered ripples of awe panning out across the throng of people as though someone has dropped a pebble into the sleeping sea.

Rowland Stoward, his imperial Majesty, has emerged onto the highest, gilded dais that sits behind the executioner's platform. Several guardians flank him—no doubt he is nearly completely concealed from view. But he is there all the same, taking a seat within his great gilded tent—holding up his heavily ringed fingers for attention.

The audience before him is rapt.

Rowland Stoward almost never attends the executions. Under normal circumstances, he is content to wait in his court, surrounded by pompous lords and powdered ladies. He later listens to the gruesome reports delivered by the dutiful Golden Guard. It is the secondhand memory of the event that satisfies him—the description of the crowds screaming and of the suffering criminal, dying for his sins.

He does not like to be any closer to death than he needs to be. He is frightened by mortality. In fact, Byron muses, he is only present today because he is convinced Emerala the Rogue will appear.

"Cairans," Rowland barks. His honeyed voice sounds out of place among the commoners that fill the square—spill into the alleyways like ink. "Any last words?"

Byron can hear the smile in Rowland's voice. This is nothing but a game to him, as is almost everything. The lives of two Cairans mean nothing at all.

"Please," stammers the Cairan man, "we are innocent of any crime! You must believe me."

"That's what they all say, isn't it?" Rowland sings. The crowd laughs as though he has told a great joke. Byron imagines those black, beady eyes, riddled with increasing impatience, scanning the crowd for the green-eyed girl that has eluded him.

How long will he wait?

Not long.

"HANG THEM," he commands after scarcely a moment has passed. His voice cracks, letting off a discordant squeak that Bryon has come to associate with the snapping of his royal temper. The Cairan woman moans as the nooses are fastened about their necks. The crowd is silent.

"STOP!" The woman's voice that echoes through the expanse is shrill—desperate to be heard in time. A hundred heads turn every which way, trying to locate the speaker. Byron turns to look at Rowland. The great king has held up one finger to the executioner—wait. A wolfish grin is creeping across his face.

"Who spoke?" he asks. "Let her come forward."

The woman's voice is clearer now, casting out across the silenced crowd that gathers in the square. "Emerala the Rogue."

The crowd parts in confusion, glancing around at one another as though the explanation for this unusual display might be found written upon the faces of their neighbors. Only one woman, her green eyes gleaming with defiance, stares directly at the king. Byron watches as Emerala the Rogue makes her slow way towards the platform. Her black curls are wild. Her ill-fitting gown is askew—one bare shoulder exposed in the sunlight. There is no trace of fear upon her face.

"How kind of you to accept my invitation," Rowland says, nearly purring with delight. His voice emanates from a distance, and Byron realizes that Rowland has retreated even further into his tent. He is frightened of her, Byron marvels—scared of this wisp of a woman, barely out of childhood. What can she do to him here, surrounded as he is by the golden elite?

"I must say," Rowland continues, addressing her from behind the impenetrable safety of his Golden Guard. "I was beginning to be worried you would not make it in time."

Several people in the crowd have begun to murmur amongst themselves. They expected a hanging at noon. Overhead, the sun is beginning to fall away from the sky. It creeps across the swath of saturated blue, dropping slowly back towards the sea.

The Rogue has yet to respond to Rowland's goading. She continues through the crowd in silence. Her bare feet are soiled beneath the hem of her gown. They press against the uneven grey stone, her toes creasing. She does not speak until she reaches Byron.

"Hello," she says, her green eyes finding his. Her voice is even.

Byron grimaces back at her. "I didn't think you would come."

"And allow innocent people to die in my place?" she asks, incredulous. "I'm not you."

"General," barks Rowland. "What are you waiting for? Arrest her. Bring her to me."

A clamor rises in the watching crowd—a unanimous question washes over them like a wave. Careless of the hundred unblinking eyes glued to his every move, Byron moves to grab hold of the Rogue. He pulls her close to him. One unruly curl tickles the end of his nose.

"Don't attempt any of your usual tricks," he mutters into her ear. "Not here."

"I wouldn't dream of it."

As he leads her back towards the gilded tent his gaze catches on a pair of familiar blue eyes at the front of the crowd. His stomach lurches and he nearly falters a step. It is Emerala's cousin, dressed in the gown of a common woman of Chancey. A black fascinator is pulled low over her face to try and hide her eyes. In her trembling hands she wrings a soiled white handkerchief.

I'm sorry, he wants to say, but the words would be useless—unheard. His stomach churns uneasily, the contents growing again unsettled beneath the revulsion in her steely eyes. He forces himself to pry his gaze away from the young woman's face as he leads Emerala the Rogue into the Rowland's tent. Rowland beams up at the gypsy from his ornate, golden chair, his black eyes twinkling with mirth as he takes in her ragged countenance.

"Emerala the Rogue," Rowland muses. "We meet at last. This is the girl who has caused so much trouble? Look at her, scrawny little thing. She's nothing."

The Rogue is silent and stony before him. Byron can feel her trembling beneath his grasp, but he is certain that it is a product of her rage and nothing else.

"Bring her closer," Rowland commands. He looks foolish, sitting upon his makeshift throne and surrounded by guardians. Their ceremonial swords are drawn. They shimmer in the sunlight that slips in sideways through the gauzy fabric. The golden men close in upon the king as she is dragged closer. Her bare feet scuff audibly against the ground.

What can she do? Byron finds himself wondering again. She is but one girl, unarmed and alone.

He draws to a standstill before the throne, his grip tightening upon the Rogue's arm. In the heavy silence of the tent, he hears the king let out a sharp intake of breath. The sound is pained—troubled. It is not the sound of victory. It is, instead, redolent of heartbreak. Looking up, Byron is surprised to see the great grin fading fast from Rowland's face. Those black beady eyes are studying the gypsy before him in growing trepidation.

"I know you," he remarks.

The Rogue is silent before him. Her gaze is fierce.

"I know your face," Rowland murmurs.

"You don't," the Rogue assures him icily. "I've never laid eyes on you before."

"Your eyes. Yes, yes—I've looked into your eyes." Rowland's words trail off into silence. He is left muttering to himself amid the stifling quiet of the tent. He looks to Byron like a man drowning—suffocating beneath the sea of gold shoulders that rise and fall in a calm collective.

"Who would have thought that after all these years—" he trails off again, frowning up at Emerala the Rogue as though she is a ghost.

Years? Byron is caught off-guard by the king's odd choice of words. He recognizes the distant look upon the king's face. It is the same, sleepless gaze that sometimes asks him for the late queen Victoria in the night.

My wife, send her here. She has delayed too long.

A sharp dagger of realization twists deep within Byron's gut. He is elsewhere, the king, and Byron does not know what to say to bring him back.

After several more silent moments, Rowland seems to realize he has stumbled. Those black eyes dart around the expanse—backtracking, calculating. He recoils beneath the sideways glances of his golden men. Three bulging fingers, red skin ballooning out from beneath jeweled bands, tap against the gilded armrest of his chair. His throat clears. He shakes his head, clearing away whatever cobwebs have formed there. The smile is back upon his face as though it never wavered. Like a shadow passing over the earth, whipped on by the wind, the moment is gone.

"I suppose you think you're clever, don't you? Waiting until the last minute like that?" Rowland asks the Rogue. His voice has regained its normal sense of regency. Byron adjusts his feet beneath him, making a solid effort not to make eye contact with any of his men. He can feel their questioning gazes glued to his face, following his lead.

Rowland's mind is slipping, he thinks. *And now they've seen.*

He will have to speak to them later on—tell them that they are not to mention his odd comments again. Not to one another and not to anyone in the courts.

Before the throne, the Rogue has not provided the king with an answer, only spat upon the ground at his feet. She is a fearless woman. But brainless. Rash. Byron fights the sudden urge to shake her. In front of them, Rowland only laughs, holding his hands over his great big belly. The guardians act as though they have not seen. Their eyes are lifeless. Their shoulders are rigid.

"Did you think it was smart, girl? Hiding out in the cathedral?" He sneers up at her. "You see, that is my god who resides within those stone walls, and it is me to whom the Great One gives aid."

"Your god did not deliver me to you. I came here myself."

"Is that so?"

"You have me in your custody. Let my people go free."

Byron is surprised at the Rogue's boldness in addressing the king. One does not simply command Rowland Stoward. It is disrespect—it is treason.

He supposes that perhaps she feels she has nothing to lose. She will be executed no matter what she says.

Upon his gold-plated seat, Rowland strokes his chin, making a great show of considering the Rogue's demands. After a moment, he leans forward upon his chair. Byron can hear the gilded wood creaking beneath his weight. "You are hardly in a position to make demands, gypsy, don't you agree?"

"That was the deal," she snaps back at him.

Rowland chuckles softly. "Yes, well, you see, I am afraid I cannot keep to it."

His words leave Byron staggered. Beneath his grasp, he feels Emerala stiffen.

"My good Chancians have come to see a hanging, and they believe that the two Cairans before them are terrible criminals. It would be in poor taste to simply allow them to go free."

"You promised," the Rogue whispers, robbed of her bravado. Rowland laughs at that. The sound leaks out from between his lips as though he is being tickled.

"My promises are gold," he assures her. "To everyone but a treacherous Cairan brat."

Snapping his fingers, he draws the attention of the waiting executioner on the platform below.

"Hang them." His voice rings out through the square. It is followed by the frenzied shouts of the impatient crowd, rising to culmination. Boots stamp upon the cobblestone. The executioner pulls the gilded lever that operates the trapdoor beneath the feet of the doomed Cairans. Byron hears the Rogue cry out in horror as the captives drop through the floor. The prisoners struggle uselessly against the golden nooses, their bodies flapping like fish upon a hook.

Byron does not see any of this. His eyes are turned, instead, towards the crowd—searching, he realizes, for the blue-eyed Cairan at the front of the throng. She is gone—lost amid the rioting and shrieking mass. He does not know what he expected to see once he found her. She could not hold any more hate in those steel blue eyes.

"General," snaps Rowland.

"Yes, your Majesty?"

"Take her to the dungeons before her people can try any of their tricks."

Byron nods obediently. He gestures for another guardian to grab hold of her other arm. As they lead her away he catches sight of the two pairs of bare feet hanging limp below the platform. It is a windless day. They are still.

Byron has seen many dead bodies in his lifetime and never flinched. But these—he cannot force himself to look at them a moment longer. Between her captors, Emerala the Rogue has found her voice. Over the tumultuous sound of the shouting crowd she screams obscenities at the king. Her voice is swallowed in the noise. Byron does not attempt to silence her. Why should he? He can hear his father's words upon her tongue. He can feel the scathing eyes of the blue-eyed Cairan scorching his skin.

Deep within his spirit, something snaps.

CHAPTER 22

Roberts the Valiant

ROBERTS THE VALIANT stands in the diminishing afternoon and thinks about Death. In his youth, he often heard the Mames describe Death as a woman. She was bent and aged, with a twinkle in her eye. When a man was old and near to passing she appeared at his bedside. She was compassionate—Death—kindly and warm. She held the hands of the deceased in her withered fingers and whispered words of comfort into their ears. When it was time to leave this earth, she led them back to the sea.

He blinks into the setting sun and thinks that if the stories are true, she must not come for those who are ripped so abruptly from the world. She comes bearing peace and comfort. She cocoons the dying in serenity. That's what the stories say.

Roberts has seen a great many deaths—too many deaths. They have been violent and bloody. They have come too early and been too abrupt. The victims never leave in peace. They are not still. They struggle and they cry, their fingers clawing at the remnants of the living. He has seen Death, and it is not a woman. It is not some kindly, old caretaker come to ferry the children home. Death is cold and hard. He bears a sword and he uses it with ruthless malice. He is cruel and impatient.

Death is golden. Death is all around him.

Roberts sighs, running his fingers through his unruly black curls. The day is coming to an end with a vapid lull. The heavy red sun lingers tremulously upon the horizon, reluctant to extinguish its balmy rays beneath the ocean. At his back, the city of Chancey sits quietly in the dwindling light. The lifeless grey walls are bathed in an unearthly glow. The uneven rooftops throw scattered shadows into the golden midst. From a distance, it appears as though the whole city is aflame.

He takes an idle step upon the muddy path on which he walks. He does not remember leaving the city—heading out into the open fields and farm-land of the countryside. His thoughts have been all consuming. His mind fights to be blank.

He thinks of the two pairs of bare feet hanging beneath the platform. He will never forget the way they looked, hanging lifeless and still. The struggle had gone out of them—the sinews fell lax—and they were quiet. It was a windless day. They did not move again.

He wishes he could remember their names. Topan told him, he is sure of it, but he had hardly been listening. He has been far too distracted—far too troubled. His sister's decision to turn herself over had struck in him a chord that he could not shake. Anything Topan might have told him went in one ear and out the other.

Anyway, he had been certain he would come to know their names well enough once they were set free. They should have been set free. That was the deal.

Hello, he would say, *I'm Roberts the Valiant. You're here because my sister exchanged her life for yours. Now I have to watch her die.*

It was the most selfless thing she had ever done.

Unwise. But selfless.

The Cairans are dead. The plan—Emerala's great, foolproof plan—has failed. The Cairans are dead and Emerala will be executed.

Roberts attended the hanging that day against the wishes of his king. Topan had forced both him and Nerani to swear that they would stay far away.

You'll want to intervene, he said. *But you cannot. You have to let her go. Do you understand me?*

Yes. I'll stay away.

Roberts waited until he had seen Nerani safely back to their quarters at the outskirts of Chancey and then he headed to the square. He did not go anywhere near Emerala. In fact, he did not even see her until she stepped onto the platform before the crowd. He made sure to stay far in the back, well out of sight. He watched, dread weighting his heart like an anchor, as General Byron took hold of his sister and dragged her before the tyrant king.

By the time the bodies dropped there was nothing Roberts could do. He was too far away—he would never make it in time. He would never be able to snatch her back, not surrounded by guardians as she was.

He stands in silence upon the pathway, his hands shoved deep inside his pockets. The clouds overhead drag crimson slants of light across the grass. The air seems so much clearer here—out beyond the walls of the city. Up ahead he can see the blackening outline of the tangled forest. He fills his chest with air. Exhales. Far across the great, green expanse the unfurling leaves flutter on the wind.

He recalls the bitter words he shouted at Topan later that afternoon.

What have you solved? he demanded, fighting back angry tears. *Two of our people are dead and now that monster has my sister!*

Calmly, always too calmly, Topan reminded him of the preposterous plan.

Damn the plan! Roberts cursed, his fist coming into contact with the cool surface of the stone wall. *And damn the pirate that suggested it! Do you think that captain cares a lick about our people?*

No. Topan's indigo gaze was steady. *But he cares about Emerala.*

Roberts had nearly exploded with rage at that.

Rowland won't stop. When the pirates don't follow through and my sister is killed he still won't stop. He'll continue killing our people.

At that, Topan simply nodded. *Maybe so.*

It was very shortly afterwards that Tophurn entered to not so subtly hint that perhaps Roberts take a walk.

So here he stands, staring into the shaded wood and waiting idly by for his sister to be killed. He wonders how much time will pass before the announcement is made. He imagines Rowland Stoward will not wait very long. The large crowd of Chancians present at the hanging witnessed Emerala's arrest. They will want answers. Once they have them, they will want another execution. They are hungry for another show, and Rowland will be all too eager to provide them with one.

Roberts's father gave him one request—one simple, final request. *When I am gone, you must be the man of the family.*

What has Roberts done but allow them to be slaughtered one by one? He lay sobbing, his cheek pressed deep in a pool of blood, as his mother was murdered. And now he sits idly by, his tail between his legs, waiting for his sister to be killed.

He is aware of the stranger on the path behind him long before the man becomes visible. Over the distant echo of waves churning against rocks he can hear the squelching footfalls in the mud.

"Valiant?"

He turns at the sound of his title. It is Captain Mathew. The sun is at his back. The sharp black shadow thrown by his tricorn hat obscures the features upon his face but there is no mistaking that pretentious lean—those oversized golden buttons upon the long red jacket.

"What are you doing out here?" Roberts demands. He scarcely works to try and disguise his dislike for the young pirate.

"Your gypsy king mentioned you had gone out for a walk to try and clear your head."

"And you thought you'd find me here, of all places?" Roberts asks, gesturing towards the scattered copses of trees about them.

The captain shrugs. He squints towards the Great Forest. The treetops are giving off an audible sigh. "This is where I would go."

Roberts does not provide him with an immediate response. He scuffs the big toe of his foot into a wayward patch of damp green grass at his feet. He can feel resentment for the pirate building up around his heart like plaque. He has nothing to lose, this thief. He can sail away whenever he pleases. Emerala's fate will never weigh on him as heavily as it weighs upon Roberts.

Her brother.

Her protector.

"I understand, you know." The pirate has taken a few steps closer to him in the silence. The first gleam of twilight is bright upon his sun kissed face. One eye is squeezed tight against the glow. The flesh upon his cheek breaks out into a dozen black splinters.

"What do you understand?" Roberts snaps. "What?"

"I understand that impossible need to protect what you love the most. I understand the feeling that you would go to the ends of the sea to keep her alive—keep her happy."

Roberts shakes his head. His black curls are falling down into his eyes. "I don't think you do understand," he remarks disdainfully. "I don't think you have any idea. You're nothing but a pirate. You don't love anything but the sea. You have no family—no loyalties."

The captain stares back at him—unblinking. After a moment, he smiles. "You may be right."

"I am right," Roberts snaps. "And now, because I listened to you, innocent Cairans are dead."

"They would have died anyway."

Roberts can feel his anger twisting in his gut like a knife. How can he be so impassive and still expect anyone to believe he gives a damn? He spreads his feet further apart upon the ground—feels the mud squish between his boots. The evening dew is saturating the earth. He can smell the rich loam underneath his feet, smell the salt of the sea upon the air. His flesh prickles with the chill of night as the orange sunlight overhead begins fading to violet.

"And Emerala?" There is a tremor in Rob's hand as he speaks. "She'll die too?"

Is that how it is going to be? Is this some sick game of yours?

"No," the pirate says. His hazel eyes twinkle merrily in the twilight. His shoulders are taut with excitement—like a young boy that has caught his first fish. "Rowland Stoward sent out a herald not two hours past. Emerala is to be executed tomorrow at dusk."

He delivers the hearsay as though it is something positive—something to be celebrated. Roberts feels his gaze darkening. His fingers clench into fists at his sides. "And this is good news?"

"Well, yes. It means we'll have darkness on our side. Although unfortunate, our arrangement is hardly foiled by the death of the two gypsies today. Everything will go as planned. Your sister will not die tomorrow."

"I was never in agreement with this plan. It isn't possible."

"Everything is possible," the pirate disagrees.

"Rowland is more powerful than a handful of pirates. What if you fail?"

"I won't." The pirate's tone exudes confidence. In the dusk his silhouette fades to black—contorts in the gloom. His buoyancy does nothing for Roberts. Only a fool is that sure of himself.

But if he somehow manages to succeed—

"I'll never see her again," Roberts says, confirming what he has already been told.

We have to let her go, Nerani said to him the night before. *If that is the only way she is going to live, we have to let her go. She never wanted to be here anyway. You know that.*

Before him, the pirate is quiet. "Not for a while, at least. It's for her own good."

"What about you?"

The pirate appears intrigued by the question. "What do you mean?"

"How does this benefit you? What do you get out of helping my sister? You haven't asked for compensation. Am I to believe you're doing this out of good will?"

The pirate laughs at this, his cheeks dimpling. It is a small sound, barely audible. He stares down at the toe of his boots before glancing sideways up at Roberts. "Would you believe that I don't quite know why I'm doing this?"

Roberts thinks about this. "No."

"I thought not." The pirate smiles and tugs at the golden scruff upon his chin. "Well, if you wanted an honest response, that's the only one I can give you."

"It's a terrible response," Roberts says pithily.

"I agree."

Silence hangs in the air between the men. Roberts does not know what else to say. He supposes he has no other choice than to trust the pirate. What else is there to do? If he does not give him his support—if they do nothing at all—Emerala will most certainly be executed.

At least, then, they are trying to save her. At least, then, they are doing something. Still, he cannot shake the looming feeling of trepidation that has taken root within his gut.

"We should be getting back, mate." The pirate's voice sounds out of place over the steady rise of crickets chirping in the high grass.

"Most likely," Roberts agrees numbly.

"Tomorrow, then?"

He hesitates. The grass is slick with moisture beneath his boots. "I thought we were expected to stay out of your way." The words do not escape his lips without some trace of hostility.

The captain shrugs. "It would be better if you weren't there, but I hardly think I can keep you away."

He's right, Roberts thinks. *There's no chance I'll entrust my sister's fate to pirates.*

If they are truly going to go through with this, then Roberts will make sure that he is there to guarantee that they do the job correctly. He purses his lips, holding back any argument that threatens to leak out from between his clenched teeth. The pirate has already turned his back to him—has already begun making his way back towards the grey walls of the city.

Slowly, letting his feet drag through the sleeping earth, Roberts follows. He glances out at the sea. The moon is a flat, circular disk of silver. It is low in the sky, dancing idly upon the oily black surface of the ocean. He thinks again of Death, and of the stories he heard as a child.

He thinks of a woman, old and grey, bending down and kissing a sleeping Emerala upon the forehead. He pictures those gnarled white fingers taking Emerala's hand—leading her into the sea.

He thinks of Saynti, the Cairan queen executed for her heritage, and of how the Mames say to pray to her is to pray to a goddess.

The wind is blowing through his hair, tugging relentlessly at his black curls. Salt stings his lower lip.

Not yet, Saynti, he thinks. *Don't take her from me yet.*

Away in the trees he thinks he sees the shadow of a woman, her slender form watching in silence. Waiting. But he blinks and there is nothing there. It is only the night, playing tricks upon his eyes.

Seranai the Fair draws back behind the thick copse of trees in which she is concealed. Roberts is staring at her—directly at her—and yet she is sure there is no way he can make her out in the blackness. She is rendered invisible by the shadows of the leaning tree trunks—a shapeless wraith in the dark.

She exhales through her nose. Her grey eyes, silver in the moonlight that trickles down between the fluttering leaves overhead, follow Roberts and the captain as they make their silent way back to the walls of the city.

Everything is going exactly as planned. She does not know what the Hawk said to his captain in order to convince him to take Emerala on board, but it matters not. In a matter of days—hours, even, Emerala the Rogue will be out of her life forever. She grins, her teeth grinding against one another as she stares at the fading outlines of the two men on the horizon.

It is a dangerous undertaking, trying to rescue the young woman from the grasp of the king. She cannot imagine how the captain plans to succeed. She supposes it matters not. The outcome makes little difference to her.

If Emerala is rescued, she will sail away from Chancey, never to return.

If the pirates cannot get to her in time—if she is executed at dusk—well, that in itself is a good enough solution for Seranai.

Emerala will be dead, and Roberts the Valiant will be hers.

The sun has extinguished its last light beneath the swollen silver sea. From off in the distance she can hear the lonesome howl of some feral beast of the forest. It stretches up towards the black sky, speckled with flecks of gleaming silver stars.

She only need be patient for one more day.

One more day, and the sniveling nuisance of a girl will be gone.

CHAPTER 23

Emerala the Rogue

THE CELL IS black and cold. Emerala sits upon the grimy floor and hugs her knees to her chest. Her green gown billows out around her, dragging through the urine soaked hay at her feet. Dank air compresses against her exposed skin. She sniffles. Her grip tightens around her legs. Fingernails dig through the fabric of her gown, bite into flesh.

She has never felt so foolish. She should have known—should have seen through Rowland Stoward's ruse. His deal was as rotted and as false as his heart. Try as she will, she cannot rid herself of the image of that wolfish, hungry grin, smiling down at her even as he called for the deaths of her people.

She thinks of Rob and wonders if he feels victorious. His doubts have once again proven to be correct. He knew the king would never follow through.

Do you truly believe he will honor a promise made to you? A Cairan? You are nothing to him.

It is beginning to seem as though Rob is always right. She thought he was foolish for doubting, then. Now, his words ring with incredible foresight. She shudders in the chill and adjusts her weight upon the hard floor beneath her. Her backside aches. Her bones are stiff. How long has she been sitting upon the floor in silence, frozen and alone?

Tomorrow this nightmare will be over, one way or another. She blanches at the thought of death. Her insides feel as though they are coated in ice. Her throat aches from hours of suppressed tears. She must allow herself to have faith in Alexander Mathew—faith in his crew. Just because the two Cairans are dead does not mean she is doomed to suffer the same fate.

She tries to remind herself that the *Rebellion* is captained by a pirate lord—tries to reassure herself that Alexander and his crew are far from typical men. If they are capable of besting the wild seas, they can handle anything. They have seen the world. Rowland's golden elite has never sailed beyond the horizon.

There is more than just a chance. She has to let herself believe that.

There are footfalls upon the walkway beyond her cell. An orange tinge of light smolders in her peripherals, setting the rounded stone corner of the corridor ablaze with dancing light. She cocks her head to listen.

The footfalls grow louder—heavy boots upon damp stone. There is the squelching sound of splashing water and a sigh. A shaded figure appears beyond her cell. A lantern is thrust into her face. She stares into the darkness beyond the orange haze, blinking like mad. She can see a golden clad figure standing erect beyond the rusting bars. His face is cast in shadow, but the light of the swinging lantern catches in his white-blonde hair. He looks familiar—she has run into him before. He is an official—a corporal, by the insignia upon his sleeve. She cannot recall his name.

There is a moment of breathless silence before he speaks.

"You should rise, Cairan, in the presence of your superior."

She blinks faster, feigning deafness.

"Have you no respect?" His tone is even—cool. His question is rhetorical. Emerala ignores him. Instead she lies back, lowering her bare shoulders onto the reeking floor. A shiver goes up her spine as the dank water of a puddle laps against her flesh—tickles her shoulder blades. Her green gaze roves to the ceiling. She watches the darkness battle with the light.

"Fine," he says. "Lie there in the grime. You are no more than animal anyhow. Untamed, foul thing."

Emerala sighs. Her breath tastes stale upon her tongue. "Have you come here to hurl insults at me all day? Or do you have something important to say?"

Her voice is hoarse from lack of use. Beyond the reach of the corporal's lantern she can hear the breathy laughter of another prisoner. The voice is mad—choked with the dust of someone who has been abandoned in the darkness, left to wait for death. Forgotten by men. A chill creeps through her skin. She fights to keep her expression blank.

"See," begins the guardian. "I thought you would be grateful for a bit of conversation. I know how sharp that tongue of yours can be. Silence hardly suits you."

"What does it matter? I've nothing to keep it sharp for." A dull ache has begun to throb behind her sockets. The light is hurting her eyes. Or perhaps it is the smell of urine.

The corporal chuckles. It is a forced sort of sound—dry and lifeless. "I'll get right to the point, then."

"Please do." She can taste the brassy twinge of blood upon her tongue. She did not even notice how roughly she had been chewing her lip. The guardian takes a step closer to the bars of her cell. His long black shadow stretches and contorts, creeping up the wall until it looms over her like some nefarious demon.

"I know your people, Cairan. And I know you. His Majesty is delighted to have you within his grasp, but I know better."

He waits—an intentional pause. The deep, dark shadows beneath his brows explore her supine figure upon the floor.

"Do you?" Emerala asks, after a moment has gone by.

"I do. You would never have handed yourself over without an escape plan. You're much more cunning than that."

"I'm flattered that you think so," she says flatly.

"You have something planned." It is not a question.

"You're right," she retorts. "I intend to use old magic to turn you all into the pigs you are while I make my dramatic escape."

That same, crazed laugh leaks out from the darkness. It is closer this time. In the distance she can hear the rattle of rusted bars. Someone hisses softly, and the echo of the sound slithers across the shadows. Her stomach turns.

"You can make light of this all you want, gypsy. But I promise you this—if you or your people so much as attempt an escape, I will condemn all of you."

Emerala considers this. She sits up, letting her wild, black ringlets fall about her face. "Who made you king?" she asks, defiance riddling her words.

She can see the black slit of his lips widen into a grin as light and dark fight for space upon his stony features. "I am an extension of his Grace, and in the streets of Chancey my word is law. Think very carefully about your next move, Emerala the Rogue."

And then he is leaving. She listens to the sound of his footfalls receding on the cool stone. Emerala rises to her feet—presses her cheeks between the bars. The golden aura of light is drawing away from her skin, leeching the warmth from her flesh. She watches the circle of orange grow smaller and fade to black. She is left blinking at nothing. Residual fragments of white light drag across her retinas. She rubs at her temples. Exhales through her nose.

The man in the shadows is chuckling softly, rattling his chains.

"Emerala the Rogue…" he whispers into the darkness. He speaks with the tongue of a dead man, beckoning to her in the gloom.

"Who made you king?" The words come out in a barely audible hiss. The sound is smothered by the impenetrable shadows.

Swallowing a whimper, Emerala presses her hands hard against her bodice. Beneath the curving whalebone, she can feel the outline of her dagger. General Byron had found it upon her as he searched her for weapons earlier that afternoon. She had felt his fingers slow over the bulge beneath the trailing lace stays—had felt his eyes upon her face. And then his fingers moved away, searching onward. He said nothing. He made no point to remove the weapon from her person.

She sighs, running her finger along the outline of the narrow blade. Its presence, however useless, provides her with some, small flicker of comfort.

Saynti, she thinks, sending up a prayer to the blessed dead, *please let the captain succeed.*

CHAPTER 24

Captain Alexander Mathew

THE NONDESCRIPT COLORS of dusk are settling in the air, casting the buildings around Alexander in indistinguishable shadow. He blinks into the sleepy grey silence, a bead of sweat tracing the hard outline of his jaw. Beneath his red jacket, his white undershirt is sticking to his skin. When did the spring become so damned hot? He cannot remember. He leans against the faded red brick of the building at his back. The pressed stone is clinging to the residual heat of the afternoon sun. It scorches his flesh through his clothes.

Across the way he hears a whistle—sharp. Two golden eyes are watching him from a dark alleyway cluttered with reeking trash. The Hawk holds one long finger to his lips. *Silence.* His free hand cups his ear. *Listen.*

Over the distant rumble of the sea, Alexander can hear the muffled cacophony of Chancians in the square. They all went to the center of the city an hour ago, each eager to get a good view of the execution.

A traitor to her country—that was what the heralds cried only the day before. Emerala the Rogue was woman guilty of sneaking pirates into the midst of Chancey—of using witchcraft to harbor them within her home. It is a laughable charge, truly, and yet it is just enough for the bloodthirsty Chancians, and it is a stroke of luck for Alexander. No one will be surprised when Emerala the Rogue is whisked away by pirates, not after the countless rumors that she has spent the spring cavorting with fearsome brigands.

He thinks on this, smirking into the growing gloom. Across the street the Hawk is staring pointedly at him, still cupping his ear. It is not the rabble in the square that he hears. His golden eyes narrow. He jabs a finger into the street. Alexander leans forward, listening intently.

After a moment, he hears it—the slow creak of uneven wheels upon cobblestone. It is accompanied by the clatter of hooves. There is a whinny, sharp.

Here she comes.

Alexander glances around the darkened street. It is empty. Silent.

Exactly how it should appear. His men have disappeared into the doorways and windows and walls, blending into the shadows carried in upon the silver moon. They await his signal, their blood rushing, fingering their daggers.

We'll fight them with our blades, he ordered them earlier that afternoon. *It's too dangerous to use our pistols. We don't want to attract any more attention than we need.*

The men had been all too eager for the chance to slit golden throats. They hungered for the agility and grace of hand-to-hand combat. He knows they will obey his order. He also knows that the guardians will most likely follow the same tactic. They, too, will be reluctant to attract any attention. If word gets out that the guardians have lost control to pirates the city will be thrown into pandemonium.

He breathes deep. His cheeks fill with air. *Here we go.*

"She's coming," whispers a voice in his ear. The Valiant. Alexander nods, bringing his finger to his lip. The Cairan glares at him from underneath a wild mop of curls. Beneath his free arm he holds an angry looking black cat. The animal is thin with matted fur. One ear is ripped, nearly missing, perhaps pulled off by some stray dog. Its green eyes gleam like discs in the silver moonlight. They watch him with a dislike that is identical to the Cairan that clings to its midsection.

"This had better go as planned," the Valiant murmurs.

"It will if you keep quiet," Alexander hisses back. He eyes the crooked blade in the Cairan's shaking fist. He wonders if it is fear from which the young man shakes, or if it is anger. He hopes it is the latter. He hopes the Valiant will live up to his namesake.

Down the street, the first of the guardians have come around the corner. They march on foot, their eyes scanning the shadows. Their hands are tight upon the hilts that protrude from their leather scabbards. A sound emanates from the dark, trash filled alley. A younger guardian, green with inexperience, jumps at the sound. Alexander rolls his eyes. The Hawk can never pass up the chance to have a bit of fun. He is like a tiger with its prey, playing with his food before he eats it.

An older guardian slaps the young soldier hard on the back. "What, are you frightened of the dark? Keep yourself together, Private." One gold strip bands his upper arm. Alexander does not know what this signifies, but he assumes the man is of a higher ranking position.

The carriage rounds the corner as well, dragged along by two black horses. Their gold reins gleam beneath the silver moon. They toss their heads, nostrils flared. Their ears are flat against their scalps. The whites of their eyes match the froth that seeps out around their bits. They sense the imminent danger, even if the guardians cannot.

"Get control of those animals," the older guardian orders. His voice is sharp. His eyes peer into the darkness. There is the crack of a whip snapping against the air and one of the horses lets out an agitated whinny.

The barred black carriage is nearly eye level with Alexander. It clatters slowly by, the wheels rising and falling with jarring rhythm upon the uneven grey stone. The two horses are just before him. The smell of sweat and earth tickles his nose. He feels the Valiant tense at his side and he knows what the man is thinking.

Emerala is inside.

The Valiant's voice reaches his ear in a hiss. "Now?"

"Now."

He watches as the Valiant sets down the cat and gives it a light kick on the rear. Spitting in irritation, the scrawny black cat darts out beneath the legs of the horses. Already on edge, the two animals let out frightened shrieks. They rear up upon their hind legs, kicking at the darkness with wild black hooves. The carriage swerves wildly, nearly missing a cluster of alarmed guardians.

"Keep control! KEEP CONTROL," the older guardian snaps repeatedly. The man at the front of the carriage tugs on the reins, trying in vain to soothe the frightened animals. Several of the guardians have drawn their pistols. They peer into the settling dusk, searching for the invisible aggravator.

There is a hiss, followed by a bitter meow. The cat darts out of the way of the flailing hooves and races, back arched, into the safety of an alleyway.

"You fools. Put away your weapons," spits the guardian in charge. "It was only a cat."

There is the sign.

Within seconds the whole of Alexander's crew has descended upon the horde of guardians, their daggers and cutlasses gleaming as silver as the moon. They slip out of the shadows from every direction, dropping down from rooftops and climbing up from sewer drains. Alexander sees the first of the guardians go down, their ankles slashed open by daggers from below. A few of his men surface, grinning and reeking of piss, their blades dripping crimson.

The night air is overtaken by the sound of clashing swords. They fight in eerie silence, each side trying to prevent the waiting Chancians in the square from hearing the battle. In the midst of it all, his laughter the only accompaniment to the reverberating song of swords, is the Hawk. His face is splattered with blood. His eyes are bright beneath his brows.

Gold blood bleeds red, Alexander thinks wryly.

His gaze turns to the carriage. He gestures for the Valiant to follow him. Two guardians are upon them as soon as they slip into the streaming silver moonlight. Alexander brings his sword up just in time, sparring the swing of a singing blade. His arm quivers with the shock of it. His pulse quickens beneath his flesh. He shoves the guardian backwards, matching him thrust for thrust. Each time the blades connect he feels something spark within him. His heart is pounding against his chest. He fights the urge to cry out in exultation. He realizes that the wild joy upon his face is contrasted by the fear in the eyes of the young guardian across from him. Within a moment, he knows he has him. He kicks the blade from the slumping boy's hand at the same time as he bring his cutlass down flat across his scalp.

He does not kill him, but only knocks him unconscious. He does not have the will to kill the boy—it had barely even been a fight.

At his side, the Valiant is doing his part. His swordplay is weak—clearly he has not had much opportunity for practice. And yet the Cairan is strong. The muscles of his arm tense as he snaps the neck of his opponent, his hands gripping the skull of the newly deceased guardian. The body goes limp in his grasp. He thrusts it aside, retrieving his crooked sword from the ground where it fell.

They reach the door of the carriage. No one else is around. The battle has moved further down the street.

Too easy, Alexander thinks. But he does not have the time for doubt. His men are doing their job well, that is all. They are skilled fighters, and fearless. The guardians thrive upon the fear of their enemies for victory. They depend upon it. They are nothing without it, only dogs with their tails between their legs.

He gestures for the Valiant to join him by the carriage. Sheathing his cutlass, he watches as the Cairan does the same. It takes two of them to pry open the door, so tight are the black hinges. As soon as they do so, Alexander's senses are assaulted by the sharp smell of decay. He pulls his undershirt up over his nose.

"Damn them," curses the Valiant. His face is contorted in disgust. It is dark within the carriage, but there is enough moonlight trickling in the open door for them to make out what lies within. Two Cairans, newly killed— ropes still secured about the raw flesh of their necks—lay side by side upon the cold, black floor. Pinned to the bodice of the woman is a piece of parchment. Alexander reaches in and rips it off of her corpse. The slanted writing is done in a lazy hand. The pen blotted several times, rendering the ink almost illegible.

For your troubles.

"Damn them!" the Valiant curses again, louder this time. Alexander crumples the parchment into a ball. His skin feels as though it is on fire. They knew. The bastards. This was all for show.

Where is she?

The battle is still raging all around them, and yet the tide is quickly changing. More guardians have arrived in droves. They beat Alexander's men back, driving them towards the sea. At the back of all of them, his dark gaze scanning the skirmish from the top of a rearing mare, is the notorious Corporal Anderson. He is frowning, chewing his lip in consternation. In one gloved hand he steadies his steed by her golden reins. In the other, he grips a grey, lifeless head. Alexander stares at the scalp through the silvery gloom. Mouth agape and face splattered in blood, and still it is recognizable. It is one of his crew. His blood boils.

"Retreat!" Alexander shouts. His crew has already begun to race back into the shadows before the word crosses his lips.

"ARE YOU MAD?" the Valiant roars, grabbing at Alexander's shirtfront. He wrenches him towards his nose, glaring at him through bitter, green eyes. "They still have her. They still have my sister."

Alexander grimaces, prying the Valiant's fingers from his collar. "Not here, they don't."

Anderson is as still as stone at the far end of the street. The head dangles from his fist. Their eyes meet. He does not smile. The dark lines upon his face are grim.

"Kill them," he commands his men. "Kill them all."

CHAPTER 25

General James Byron

JAMES BYRON HEARS the ringing clash of steel long before he reaches the ambush. His blood thickens in his veins and he lets out a low curse, drawing up his reins. Beneath him, his stallion draws to a clattering stop. The beast tosses his head, the whites of his eyes rolling. Dismounting hard, he holds up a fist for the soldiers behind him.

"Halt!"

The column of guardians that march behind the prisoner's carriage falls still. The steady cadence of boots echoes through the alleyways, petering off into eerie silence. In the sudden quiet, the shivering ring of sword against sword becomes louder still.

"Anderson was right," he growls beneath his breath. "Damn him to the Dark Below, he was right."

The corporal had insisted upon sending out two carriages—one false wagon to go ahead, and a true prisoner's cart to follow. When Byron denied him his request, Anderson went to the king.

She's a wicked woman, your Majesty, he explained. *She has dark powers working for her. I would not let anything go to chance.*

Corporal Anderson is hardly a religious man. He attends mass and he knows the prayers, but he is a man of logic—of rational thought and cold, hard war tactic. He does not believe in the Evil. If he does, he feels no fear of it. Yet he knew exactly how to play into Rowland's hand. He left the great man quaking in his throne, crossing himself in fear.

Do whatever you need to do, Rowland told him. *The witch must be executed tonight.*

Standing at the head of the carriage, Byron lets out a stream of curses under his breath. He scans the darkness up ahead, his mind churning. It doesn't take long for the frantic clatter of boots against cobblestone to reach his ears. Someone is coming.

He draws his pistol, ignoring the worried snort of his steed. From the shadowed street up ahead, he can just make out a flash of gold as a breathless guardian rounds a corner. He is running as fast as his feet will carry him, the wind catching in his billowing golden cloak. The side of his face is spattered with blood.

"General Byron, sir," pants the man, drawing to a stop only a few feet away. Byron recognizes him at once.

"Private Abel. What news?"

"We're under attack," Abel manages through gasps. "Our men are dropping like flies."

Rage broils within Byron, hot and heavy. "How?" he snaps. "They're civilians. Finishing them off should be simple for soldiers of his Majesty."

Abel fidgets nervously beneath Byron's glare, one hand pawing at the fast drying blood in his eye. "With all due respect, sir, it isn't the Cairans."

Immediately, Byron realizes what has gone wrong. He does not need to ask, although he does so anyway, his voice as cold and as stiff as ice.

"Who is it?"

"Pirates. They're coming out of the ground and dropping like flies. We can't take them alone."

Byron grits his teeth, the muscles in his jaw twitching. A spasm of pain has begun to throb behind his eyes. He glowers at the private before him with contempt, feeling unusually angry—feeling the rage within his chest climbing inexplicably higher. The sight of Private Abel wiping furiously at his blood spattered face only serves to ignite his wrath still further.

"Are you frightened of a little blood, private?"

Abel pauses midway through reaching into his uniform for a handkerchief, his pallid face turning crimson beneath his superior officers stare. He opens his mouth to speak, but Byron speaks first, unwilling to hear whatever it is the private might stammer out at him.

"There's no reason to be frightened of men. That's all those pirates are—men. Nothing more. Your fear is a disgrace to the uniform you wear."

Abel nods, his face reddening impossibly further. The fast drying blood disappears against his skin. Holding up a hand, Byron lets out a sharp whistle. Moving on cue, the guardians behind the carriage pick up their march.

"Head out," he calls, watching them maneuver past him and down the street. "Swords at the ready! Keep your eyes open, men! These brutes don't fight fair and they don't fight clean. Use whatever means necessary to put down their numbers and clear the streets."

His voice carries out across the night without so much as an echo, swallowed immediately by the pounding of boots against stone. He watches them until they disappear around the corner, listening still to the distant ring of steel—the screams of the dying.

Only when they have gone does he turn his attention back to the private before him. The soldier is watching the column of guardians retreat around the corner up ahead, the discoloration in his face finally beginning to normalize.

"Private Abel," Byron barks. The young soldier jumps, turning to face him.

"Yes?"

His better judgment crying out for him to stay behind and do the job himself, Byron orders, "Stay back. Guard the gypsy. Perhaps a woman will not frighten you as much as a man."

"Y-yes, sir."

Byron glowers down at the private for a moment more before glancing over his shoulder at the prisoner's carriage. The towering, barred structure is silent and still in the dark. From behind the bars, he can just make out two, glimmering emerald eyes watching him. He locks his jaw, his teeth grinding hard against one another, and heads off down the street after his men.

The road ahead is empty and dark—the marching cadence of the soldiers has turned to the discordant rhythm of battle. He walks slowly, his head pounding as he leads his stallion through the narrow roadway. In spite of the battle raging ahead, he feels no pressing urge to rush—feels no drive to run to the defense of the dying.

Why, he asks himself, *did I leave that useless sod to guard the carriage alone?*

He is about to turn back when a figure barrels out of the darkness and slams into him full force. He grunts, absorbing the blow as fists rain down upon his chest. Releasing the reins, he snatches at the flailing shadow before him, taking hold of the narrow, pallid wrists and holding the figure at arm's reach. Two furious blue eyes stare out at him from a pale, pinched face, and he immediately recognizes the Cairan woman from the cathedral. His heartbeat quickens needlessly, sending his blood rushing through his veins.

"Great After," he curses. "I could have killed you."

She ignores him. Her voice is a hoarse cry of desperation. "Where is Emerala?"

He swallows thickly, still grasping her wrists within his fists. She is inches away from him, her braided hair cascading around her face in curling locks of brown. A heavy cloak of midnight black enshrouds her narrow figure, rendering her darker than a shadow in the street.

"It isn't safe for you out here."

"As if you care," she hisses. "What have you done with my cousin?"

"Nothing," he swears. "I haven't touched her."

"You swore to me—you swore that if she handed herself over, those prisoners would go free." She spits at his feet. "You're nothing but a liar."

His anger threatens to explode within him. The pain behind his eyes is unrelenting. Quick as a flash, he grips her chin between his fingers, jerking her gaze up towards his face. She struggles against his grasp, her shallow breathing audible in her throat. Her bosoms heave beneath her tightly laced bodice.

"I never lied to you," he nearly snarls. "I'm not the one in charge. I follow orders, nothing more."

"Does blindly following orders absolve you of all responsibility, then?"

Her words are cold. He thrusts her away from him, watching as the stormy blue of her gown billows out around her narrow frame.

"Where is Emerala?" she demands a second time.

"Why do you hate me?" he asks, surprising even himself with the question. Her eyes narrow dangerously. He continues, adding, "I've done nothing to you—nothing to hurt you, nothing to bring you any sort of harm."

Her chin rises in quiet defiance. "Are you truly so dense that you believe your actions have not caused me harm?"

He chews the inside of his lip, watching the color rise in her cheeks. "I can't have you despise me. I can't have you look upon me the way you look at me."

"Why?"

"Why what?"

"Why does it matter to you whether I hate you or not?"

Byron is silent for a long moment, studying the curve of her lips—lingering upon the rise and fall of her chest. In the distance, the ringing of steel beckons him to battle. His blood sings beneath his skin. With his instincts calling out for him to stop, imploring him to behave with dignity, he pulls her roughly to him, drawing the warm curves of her into the frame of his body. His lips crush against hers, seeking her out desperately beneath the watery moonlight that trickles over them. He feels her gasp against his lips, feels her mouth parting at his touch. Their breathing, shallow and clipped, mingles upon his tongue.

She pulls away first, pressing hard against his chest with her balled up fists. For a long moment they stand nose to nose in silence, her eyes flickering wildly across his face. And comes the slap, stinging and sharp across the side of his face.

"Why would you do that?" she snaps, breathless. Her voice is hoarse. He swallows thickly, starkly aware of the taste of her still lingering on his tongue. His chest rises and falls erratically beneath his doublet. His brows furrow as a deeper wanting stirs within him.

"Your cousin in another carriage," he admits quietly, not answering her question. He is not entirely certain he *has* an answer to her question. "If you go back the way I came, you'll come upon her in minutes."

The woman falters a step, her expression growing cautious. He can see the wheels in her head turning as she processes the meaning of his words. "You knew about the ambush?"

"No. The second carriage was a precaution, nothing more."

He thinks, suddenly, of his parting words to Private Abel. *Perhaps a woman will not frighten you nearly as much as a man.*

The words are out of his mouth before he can call them back. "She's being guarded, but only by one private. He's a novice—easily spooked."

The high color is leeching out of the woman's cheeks. She does not take her eyes off of his face, not even to blink.

"Is this a trick?" she whispers. Her words disperse into the night like smoke.

"No."

"Why are you helping me?"

He hesitates before replying, his eyes lingering too long on the curves of her face. The answer that pops unbidden into his mind is too treacherous to utter aloud. He feels his insides stirring at the sight of her chest rising and falling beneath the trickle of moonlight—feels the prickle of his skin beneath her cool, blue gaze—and he knows, instantly, that he will say whatever it is he needs to say.

"Justice," he murmurs, echoing her own response.

She says nothing in reply. Her nose wrinkles slightly as she studies him in the growing dark. Overhead, the silver moon climbs higher in the sky, casting them both in a wash of insipid light.

"You should go," he says. "If I come back with my men and you're still there, I'll have to arrest you as well."

He turns away from her before she can say anything more, pulling himself with ease into his saddle. His stallion lets out a whiffle of air beneath his weight, tugging restlessly at the reins. Glancing down, he sees that the blue-eyed woman has not moved from where she stands, clutching at her cloak and studying him through eyes that have narrowed into curious slits. Her lips are parted slightly, her breathing unsteady still.

"Thank you, James Byron," she whispers.

He grimaces back at her. "Get out of here," he orders. "Hurry."

He turns his horse to go, clicking his heels to urge the stallion into a trot. Over the sound of clattering hooves, he thinks he hears the woman call out, but he loses her words against the rising clash of steel.

CHAPTER 26

Emerala the Rogue

THE CARRIAGE IS still. Outside, the night has gone silent. Emerala sits motionless, her stony face gleaming beneath the circle of silver moonlight that trickles in from a narrow opening in the roof.

What is going on?

She draws herself off of the cold floor and onto her knees. As quietly as she can, she peers out of the barred window of her prisoner's carriage. In the grey street she can see but one guardian, his golden back to her as he surveys the night. His sword is drawn. Even from here she can see it trembling in his hand.

She sits back hard upon the cool surface of the carriage. The heavy fabric of her gown fans out about her waist like water. She fingers the shaded ripples, frowning into the olive swath of cloth. Everything had been going exactly as planned. What happened?

Just before dusk she was escorted out to the carriage, just as Alexander Mathew had promised she would be. The light of the setting sun ripped across the sky in varying shades of gold and orange. The sight of it scorched her retinas, so accustomed had she become to sitting in the utter blackness of her cell. Blinking away stinging tears, she allowed herself to be shoved unceremoniously into the carriage.

The door was slammed shut. She heard the snap of a whip and the whinny of a horse and off they went. The pace was slow, measured. The rutted journey across the uneven cobblestone street soon caused her to feel sick to her stomach.

Alexander will be here soon, she thought. She tried to quell her jitters. She sat back against the cool black wall of her cage and shut her eyes.

Before she knew it, the carriage had drawn to a stop.

HALT! The voice was unmistakably that of General Byron. The cadenced sound of boots against stone was immediately silenced.

They're here, she remembers thinking at once. Her nerves were replaced by the heat of anticipation, dispersing like spreading flames just beneath her skin. She took a deep breath, fingering the concealed dagger beneath her bodice. It was only a matter of time, and she would be free.

The silence lasted for too long. She waited, listening. Nothing happened. Finally she heard General Byron shout in aggravation.

Anderson was right, he snapped. His voice came from immediately outside the carriage. Hooves pulled at the ground. *Damn him, he was right.*

And then: *General Byron?* A frantic voice—young. Alarmed.

What? General Byron snapped. Hooves clattered against stone.

We're under attack. Our men are dropping like flies.

How? The general's voice was low and dangerous. *They're civilians. Finishing them should be simple for soldiers of the king.*

With all due respect, sir, it isn't the Cairans.

Then who is it?

Pirates. They're coming out of the ground and dropping from the skies. We can't take them alone.

It wasn't long before Emerala heard a whistle, sharp. The sound of boots upon the street began again, faster this time. The clatter of hooves picked up to a brisk trot—skidded to a stop.

Private, barked General Byron.

Yes, sir?

Stay back. Guard the gypsy. Perhaps a woman will not frighten you nearly as much as a man.

Emerala does not fully understand what has happened, but she understands this: the plan has failed. For whatever reason, Alexander and his men have attacked the wrong place. She groans quietly, the sick feeling creeping back into her gut. She cannot stay here, idle and waiting for her death. She must do something. If no one is going to come for her she will need to be her own savior. What does she have to lose?

She lowers herself onto her knees. Cautiously, desperate not to make a sound, she crawls across the floor of the carriage. Her olive gown drags against the smooth, black surface like a whisper. Reaching up for the door, she gives it a tug. It does not budge. She attempts to slide it open from several different angles, to no avail. The effort leaves her panting and annoyed. The door is barred shut from the outside.

Outside of the carriage, the guardian is still standing with his back to her, staring out into the darkness. She rises to her feet, her legs shaking. Her arm is just slender enough to squeeze between two of the bars. Carefully, very carefully, she reaches downward towards the barricade. Her fingers just barely brush the stained wood.

"Hello?"

The sound of the guardian's voice causes her insides to go cold. She snatches her arm back through the bars, slamming her elbow against the steel in the process. He does not turn around at the sound of her muffled cry. He has not even noticed her. She nurses her throbbing joint, peering out into the darkness at his gleaming golden back.

"Who's there? Reveal yourself!" His voice quakes as he speaks. Emerala fights the urge to roll her eyes. This is who they left behind to guard her? *Coward.*

An eerie noise emanates out from the shaded alleyway before him. The guardian is backing, slowly, drawing closer to the carriage. Another noise spills out of the dark, this time to his left. He jumps, startled, and holds his sword before him.

"Reveal yourself," he orders again.

There is movement in the shaded alleyway into which he stares. Thick, violet smoke twists out of the shadows, snaking around the private's ankles. The vague outline of a woman is visible in the dark.

"Who are you?" the private asks.

"Do you believe in the old magics?" hisses a voice. Emerala starts, her eyes widening in recognition. The voice belongs to Orianna. The private bumps into the carriage—jumps.

"M-magic?"

221

"Dead magic. Gypsy magic." That same, eerie noise is still seeping out from the shadows. Someone laughs in the darkness. "Curses—the kind that will make you beg for your god."

Emerala is staring directly into the back of the private's neck. He is close enough to see the beads of sweat that gather beneath the golden collar of his cloak. In an instant, she sees her chance. Her fingers are steady as she pulls the dagger out from her bodice. She glances down at the iridescent hilt in her fist, studying her wild, green-eyed reflection in the shimmering blade.

Without another moment of hesitation, she thrusts the dagger through the opening of the bars, driving the blade down hard between the soldier's shoulder blade and neck. The guardian cries out, dropping to his knees. His sword clatters to the ground. Deep, crimson blood blossoms across the gold cloth of his uniform. He grips at the iridescent hilt with his fist. Red seeps through his fingers.

Across the clearing, Orianna emerges from the darkness. She pries the sword from the soldier's fingers and brandishes it against his neck. Her twilight colored gown melts into the night. She looks eerie beneath the hoary light of the moon.

"Stay right where you are," she commands. With her free hand, she gestures toward the shadows. A second figure appears in the moonlight, her blue eyes wide with worry, and Emerala recognizes Nerani at once. Her cousin's lips are set in a grim line as she takes in the bloody private.

"I thought pirates were coming to save me, not you," Emerala remarks as Nerani pulls loose the barricaded door. It swings open with a screech. She steps down, her bare feet scraping against the cobbled stones.

"So did we," Orianna says with a shrug. "We were watching from the shadows when it all went wrong." She flashes an implicative glance at Nerani. Nerani scowls and avoids her gaze, staring instead at the private.

"We need to leave," Nerani says. "Now."

"What do we do about him?" Orianna asks.

"Leave him," Nerani says confidently. "He won't pursue us."

Emerala hangs back, uncertain. "What about Captain Mathew?"

The look Nerani gives her is as hard as steel. "The plan failed, Emerala. The pirates are being driven back to the sea. You need to come with us now."

Emerala shakes her head. She thinks of the silver haired corporal and of his threats in the dark. "If I do, this will condemn everyone."

"It might," Nerani agrees. "But Topan has a plan. You must come." Without waiting for her consent, Nerani takes her hand and tugs her roughly away from the still gasping guardian at their feet. In the distance, Emerala can hear the sound of hooves upon cobblestone. Horses, coming this way. The guardians are returning.

"Emerala, let's move," Orianna urges. Emerala digs in her heels, glancing back over her shoulder. Her dagger is still protruding from the neck of the wounded guardian. She glances at the iridescent hilt, gleaming in the moonlight. She thinks of the pirates, lifting anchor—sailing out into the wild sea without her. She thinks of death, and of dying at the stake before all of Chancey. It was to be a burning—she had seen the guardians stacking the bales of hay as she was led to the carriage earlier that afternoon. She would be sentenced to die as a witch.

For now, she is alive. The night air is tickling her lungs and her flesh. Her feet are hot against the stone underfoot. There is not a minute more to waste. She runs.

A cry from the shadows causes her blood to run cold.

"THERE," a guardian bellows. "She's getting away!"

Emerala does not dare to look over her shoulder as she races from the clearing. Her heart pounds against her chest. Her feet slap against the cobblestone.

"Faster," she hears Orianna hiss from the darkness besides her.

She runs as fast as she can. She can hear the guardians on their heels, the drum-like cadence of their boots pervading the night air all around her. What will they do if they are caught? They cannot fight. They have no weapons.

They'll be killed, all of them.

She can hear Nerani gasping for breath besides her as they turn another corner. Where will they run? Where will they find sanctuary now? Her throat burns.

"HALT," a voice bellows.

She does.

"What are you doing?" Nerani shouts, her voice hoarse. "We have to run, Emerala!"

Emerala ignores her, turning to face the guardians. The three golden men draw to a standstill before her, drawing their swords. Their chests rise and fall with exertion beneath their uniforms. One of them has blood—not his—spattered across his face.

"You can have me," Emerala says. "Just let them go."

"Emerala, are you mad?" hisses Nerani. Two of the guardians rush forward, grabbing her roughly by the arms. They thrust her hard upon the stones. She bites her lip to keep from crying out—to keep from giving them the satisfaction.

Her green eyes meet her cousin's across the shadows. Orianna has disappeared into the darkness.

"Nerani, get out of here," she snaps. "Don't be a fool."

Nerani shakes her head, a sob rising to her throat.

"Run, Nerani, GO," she screams, feeling spittle fly from her lips. She hears the sound of bare feet fading into silence upon stone and relief rushes into her chest.

Behind her, she can hear the singing of the third guardian's blade.

"I'm sure the king will want you to take me alive," she says, her voice quavering.

"You're in no position to negotiate, scum."

It has begun to rain. Rivulets of water run down her face. Thunder rumbles sleepily in the distance.

"Do it, then," she whispers.

There is a sharp pain at the side of her head and the world goes silent.

CHAPTER 27

General James Byron

JAMES BRYON STANDS erect before the throne. He is alone. The room is silent. Empty. He can hear his breathing sweeping against the polished floor at his feet. The great, gilded chair looks even larger without its usual inhabitant. It glitters with a gaudy iridescence, the embossed golden pattern pocketed by black shadows where the light does not quite reach. Overhead, fat cherubs pluck at harp strings and prune their full, white feathers. They stare down from their puffed, pink clouds with menacing, black eyes—poking out from behind bloated red cheeks.

The room is eerie in silence, he thinks, with portraits of music spanning the breadth of the vaulted ceiling—the whole of the Great After frozen in time. He, himself, is probably going to the Dark Below, if there is such a place. He does not know if he minds so much, not if the Great After is truly full of round, impish angels like the ones above his head. He stares into his boots and frowns.

Rowland Stoward is attending mass, although it is not the time of day for the religious ritual. He called for the Elder shortly after hearing the news that pirates were pillaging his shores—after hearing that Emerala the Rogue had escaped. He gathered his courtiers and stormed off to his quarters.

Rowland is afraid, as he always is. He believes in the power of incense and prayer. He believes that his god, wherever he may be, will offer him holy protection from the darkness of Cairans. Surely, Byron muses, the king must believe it is the Evil that allowed her to escape his grasp.

If that is so—if it is the fault of the Evil that the Rogue is free—well, then James Byron is certainly well on his way below. He clears his throat. The sound echoes like a snarl through the empty expanse.

It was not that James did not expect some sort of uprising. He did—but he thought it would come from the Cairans. He was not blind. He understood how suspicious it was that the Rogue should hand herself to the crown so easily. He knew, too, how enraged the Cairans would be by the murder of two innocent Cairans.

He knew, and he was not concerned. His men could handle a clumsy rescue attempt from her people. They would be driven by rage—the Cairans—and if there is one thing he has learned in his line of duty it is that angry men make easy prey. They are disorganized and sloppy—like fish on the hook, flopping aimlessly in an attempt to get free. Fighting off Cairans would have been easy. Quiet. Fast. The guardians and their prisoner would have only been held up by moments. The execution would go on.

It would have, of course, had Emerala the Rogue not escaped from her carriage.

It would have, had James Byron not faltered in his duty and betrayed his crown.

One golden door at the far side of the king's court is squealing open. A narrow, nervous face peeks in through the crack.

"General Byron?"

He swallows. His throat is dry. "Yes?"

"His Majesty will be along momentarily, if you will kindly wait a few moments more."

"Of course. Thank you."

The door slams shut. It is as loud as exploding gunpowder. Its echo ricochets through the room and slamming into James's golden chest. A sheen of sweat has formed across his upper lip.

"You damned fool," he whispers. His voice spills out into the emptiness, resonating back at him in a derisive echo. What was he thinking? Why had he told the Cairan woman where to find her cousin? Why had he left the carriage carelessly guarded by a lone private, newly initiated and unused to his duties? Private Abel had not been killed, but Byron is certain the boy will wish he were dead by the time Rowland Stoward is through with him.

Unlike Abel, James Byron is not to be punished. In fact, Rowland sent him his royal regards earlier that morning. Byron is to be commended for joining the attack against the pirates and driving them back to the sea. He is not to be blamed for the Rogue's disappearance. That, it would appear, is the fault of the Cairan witches who freed Emerala the Rogue with their black, forbidden magic.

Byron bites back a groan.

If only Rowland knew that Emerala's escape had been entirely his fault.

Thank you, James Byron.

The sound of his name—his real name—on the Cairan woman's tongue had nearly caused him to turn his stallion around. He does not understand how the blue-eyed gypsy has managed to undo him so entirely, that he would betray his king—his lord, liege and lifelong idol—so completely. He does not know what he was thinking, damned fool, as he pulled her to him beneath the moonlight and pressed his lips to hers. His cheek had stung for a near hour afterwards, the stubbled skin burning from the strength of her slap.

She had asked him if blindly following orders absolved him of responsibility.

Does he do that, he wonders? Does he blindly follow orders?

He has always looked up to Rowland—has always admired the great king and his legion of golden soldiers since he was a young boy, still chasing after his mother in the royal kitchens. He remembers numerous arguments with the disillusioned Prince Frederick— remembers the disagreements growing more and more heated in the days leading up to that last, fateful goodbye.

Rowland Stoward refers to the day as the death of his eldest son. He mourns the young man along with the deceased.

Byron knows better. He was there the day the prince threw down his crown and left.

Why do you worship him, James? Frederick had demanded of him once. His auburn hair glistened with slivers of gold beneath the sunlight as they walked in the great stone garden. Byron can recall bristling at the question.

I don't worship him.

You do, Frederick protested. *You treat my father as if he's some sort of untouchable deity. He's not a god, James. He's barely even a man.*

Byron's eyes had darted nervously around the garden; suddenly worried that someone would overhead. *You shouldn't say things like that,* he snapped.

You see? Frederick said, shoving him lightly. *This is what I mean.*

Byron scowls up at the painted cherubs overhead. He thinks, suddenly, of his father. He thinks of a lesson the old man gave him as a boy as they huddled in a rocking rowboat and waited for the morning sun to burn the grey clouds off of the sea. The cliffs of Chancey drew a stark black line through the haze.

The Great One put his fingerprint on all of us at birth, but so did the Evil. It is because of this that we are sometimes incapable of defining right from wrong. It is easy, as men, to let hate warp our opinions and render them ugly. You listen closely to your heart, James, because that's where the Great One put his fingerprint.

In me? James's frozen fingers gripped at the net full of flopping silver fish.

In everyone, his father said. *But not everyone knows when or how to listen.*

How will I know?

You'll know, boy.

At his sides, James Byron's fingers clench into fists at his side. He can feel his heart pounding against his ribcage—fluttering in the split intervals with painful alacrity. He feels alive—more alive, perhaps, than he has felt his entire life.

He thinks of Rowland, kneeling before an empty altar, choking on incense, and believes for the first time that the king's prayers are unheard. He thinks of that great bearskin cloak, the bulging shadow of a beast, and imagines the dark fingerprint of the Evil scorched upon his crown.

He thinks of his father, laid to rest in his rowboat, sent out to sea to make his journey to the Great Above. The sea was still and clear as glass, he was told. He had not been there to see.

He thinks of the blue-eyed Cairan, and how perfectly her body had fit into his—thinks of the taste of her, still on his tongue even now. The sound of his name upon her lips had been so sweet. It dawns upon him that he would have given her anything—would have done anything—to stop her from looking at him with so much hate in her eyes.

James's heart fills with resolve, his mind with anger, and slowly, the ache in his gut begins to subside.

CHAPTER 28

Roberts the Valiant

IT'S OVER.

Roberts sinks to his knees. It's over. He presses the palm of his hand against his heart, breathing hard. He cannot feel his heart beating beneath his chest, not anymore.

"No." The word croaks out of him, already broken. His knees scrape against the stone. Death has hounded him like a dog all throughout his life. He has seen its face time and time again, always watching, always waiting. Lingering in the shadows, its bony grip closed about its sword—its eyes cold and hard.

Not this time, he thinks. *Not Emerala. Not my sister.*

He feels a hand upon his back. He shakes it off, his shoulders heaving in a silent, breathless sob. Somewhere nearby, he can hear the quiet wails of grief that fall from Orianna's lips.

They killed her, she said when they met back at the cathedral. She was drenched in rainwater, her black locks sticking to her ebony skin. *She's dead.* Besides her, Nerani stood as silent and as still as stone, staring into the shadows through unblinking blue eyes.

The words meant nothing to Roberts, not right away. He felt nothing. He understood nothing. Death was so common to him—an old friend. The sound of its name did not faze him anymore.

Not my sister, he thinks again. *How could you take her?*

He shouts hoarsely, the sound spilling away from him in a mournful echo. His fingers ball into a fist and he slams them hard against the floor.

"Rob," he hears Orianna cry, her voice thick with tears. He ignores her.

Somewhere on the far side of the room, he hears Topan murmuring softly. He glances up, confused that someone, anyone, can find a voice.

Before him sit Nerani and Orianna. Orianna's jeweled eyes are muddled with tears as she continues to sob without abandon. One dark line divides her forehead in two, splitting down the bridge of her nose. Nerani, in stark contrast, looks as though she has seen a ghost. Her skin is drained of color—her eyes are wide. She clutches her fingers together in her lap and sits as if dead.

"The order has been given." Tophurn's voice in the doorway startles him. Across the room, Roberts hears Orianna hiccough softly

"Yes?" Topan sounds like a man awaking from a dream. His figure is shapeless beyond the dark shadows. "So it has begun."

It is not phrased as a question, but Tophurn gives an answer nonetheless. "It has."

"And?"

A pause. "It is exactly as you feared."

"What?" Roberts demands. His fingers clench and unclench at his sides. Sweat pools in the lines upon his palm. There is a curious prickling beneath his skin. At the other side of the room, Nerani stares intently into her lap. "What?" he asks again, more urgently this time.

"The usurper has decided to blame today's spectacle upon the Cairans," Topan explains quietly. "He's pointed towards us as responsible for the murder of guardians."

Roberts is numb to his words. His stomach churns uneasily within him. His fist is bloody against the stone, the knuckles ripped open. He thinks of how easily the guardian had fallen after he snapped his neck—thinks of the blood of the others that spilled across the cobblestones like ink, pooling within the grout. He does not regret it, not for a moment. He would kill a thousand more if it would bring his sister back.

"The people of Chancey are sheep," Tophurn snarls. "Easily led. They will believe that we are to blame because that is what is easiest to believe. To lay blame upon the pirates would be to acknowledge that our shores are not as safe from foreign attack as they are led to think."

"The usurper can't have that kind of fear running rampant among his people." Topan says. "He will begin to lose control."

Not my sister, Roberts thinks again. He thinks of the last conversation they had—of how they had shouted at one another across the cool shadows of the dusty cathedral. Everything he had ever done—everything—had been to protect her.

He is the boy hiding beneath the couch.

He is the boy vomiting in the powder room.

He is the boy with the dead sister.

He is not a man.

"Roberts, are you listening?"

Everyone in the room has turned their eyes upon him. He raises his emerald gaze towards Topan and says nothing.

"Gather yourself," says the Cairan king. "Take a moment to grieve, but take care not to wait too long. There is no time, my friend. I need you to go, now, with Tophurn. Knock on all the doors. Tell our people to hide. Instruct them to lock their windows and doors—to stay put within their homes. They are not to move until you come again to retrieve them."

Retrieve them?

"Retrieve them for what?" he asks, his voice hoarse. "Where are they going?"

But he already knows. He suspected the moment he first set foot in Topan's quarters—the moment he saw the unfurled maps, the trails marked with red ink. His suspicions were confirmed the day they visited Mame Noveli and heard her archaic tale. He thinks of the way the smoke had choked off the breath in his throat, had plunged him deep into memory. He heard, once, that amber was the stone of reincarnation—that to burn it was to invoke the ghosts of memories, dead and buried.

He had landed in a dream to find himself thrashing upon the steps of the palace, his bloody hands on his throat as he gazed up into the face of the traitor Lord Stoward, the first king of the usurper's line.

Look at me while you kill me, coward, he had snarled in the voice of Lionus Wolham. *It's the least you can do.*

Now, Roberts looks to Nerani—his only remaining family. She is staring back at him, her hands entwined in her lap. Like a summer storm blowing over the island, the tears have dried up and gone. Her face is as pinched and as white as the day had gathered her within his arms and told her that her mother and father had died.

He wonders if Emerala's killer looked her in the eye as he cut her throat, or if he simply gutted her from behind.

His stomach churns and he is nearly sick.

At the front of the room, Topan watches him through careful indigo eyes.

"We leave for the Forbidden City within the fortnight," he says. His voice sounds as though it is coming from a thousand miles away. "The time has come to disappear."

CHAPTER 29

Captain Alexander Mathew

THE SEA IS as deep and as black as the sky, its surface laced with slivers of blue. Only a faint twinge of violet lingers upon the eastern horizon. Alexander stands at the helm, staring at the fading strip of black upon the water, its jagged borders encompassed by the golden rays of the sleepy sun that hides behind it. His fingers grip the splintering wood railing before him.

Overhead, the black sails swell with the eastern wind. It is a good day to be at sea. The *Rebellion* will be carried far by the currents.

The farther, the better, he thinks and scowls. Before the sun sets in the west he will no longer have to look behind him and see the forsaken island of Chancey, and for that he is glad.

It should have been easy. Slit a few throats, snatch Emerala, and lift anchor. He did not anticipate that the guardians would be one step ahead of him. He hates being made to look like a fool, and that was exactly what they did.

He could have stayed and fought—the guardians may have increased their numbers but they did not increase their skill. Even outnumbered Alexander was certain that he and his men could have taken the lot.

But what for?

He did not know where Emerala was being detained. Even if he and his crew drove back the onslaught of soldiers, they would still need to find Emerala and make for the sea. It was not worth the risk—not when he had no idea why he needed her.

BACK, he had shouted, brandishing his cutlass over his head. *Back to the sea!*

His men listened easily enough. They had their fun. The space between the cobbled stones was pooling with the deep crimson of spilled blood. Only the Hawk lingered in the alleyway, his golden eyes surveying the carnage around him with euphoria.

Got her? he shouted to Alexander. He shook his head—*No.*

She's not in there?

He shrugged. Several guardians were racing at them, swords drawn. He waited long enough to see the Hawk remove his pistol from its holster before he turned and ran. The sounds of gunshots were stark against the humid night.

The Valiant was nowhere to be found.

The rising sun is scalding his eyes. Alexander looks away from the smoldering golden circle of light, staring down instead into the cool blue surface of the ocean.

He does not have time for regrets. The plan did not work. How many times did his father try and fail? Too many times to count. He has the map—that in itself is a success. He will find a way to interpret the strange runes upon the parchment, of that he is certain.

He hears footsteps behind him. He does not need to turn around to know who it is.

"She's asleep," the Hawk grumbles, lighting a pipe. Grey smoke rises and dissipates on the air, snatched to sea by the stinging wind.

"You shouldn't have done that," Alexander says. "You shouldn't have killed those soldiers. Did you leave your mark?" He thinks of the two copper coins upon the eyes—the Hawk's eerie trademark. His signature, he called it, once.

"Aye, I did."

"They'll know it was you that killed them."

"Nay," the Hawk disagrees, "I'm not that notorious." He moves to stand besides Alexander at the helm. Alexander glances at him at of the corner of his eyes and sees that a lopsided grin stretches across his lips. He pulls the pipe out from between his teeth and sighs, expelling smoke.

"Even so," Alexander says, and frowns. The Hawk turns to face him, replacing the pipe between his teeth with a grimace. One eye falls shut against the radiant sun.

"Look," the golden-eyed pirate proffers. "I'm not scared of a clean cut soldier. Those boys would sooner have browned themselves than taken a sword to my neck." he considers this and laughs. "They did, I bet."

Alexander wets his lip, staring out to sea. His tricorn hat dips low over his eyes, shading the unrelenting brilliance that hangs above the horizon. "Why do we need her?" he asks the whispering waves. "Why do we need Emerala the Rogue?"

"How many times do I have to tell you? I don't have a clue," the Hawk replies. He gives an indiscernible shrug. His golden eyes squint closed in the growing morning glare and crow's feet splinter across his face.

"I think you do," Alexander disagrees immediately.

"Aye?"

"Yes, I think you're lying."

There is a long pause. Alexander can taste the pungent sting of the smoke upon his tongue. Besides him, the Hawk is studying the dirty beds of his nails.

"Well if I knew, I'd tell you wouldn't I?"

"I don't think you would," Alexander remarks, glancing up from the sea.

The Hawk looks back at him at that, one eye still squeezed shut. His pipe dangles uselessly out of one corner of his mouth, trailing smoke. He surveys Alexander in silence for a moment before letting a low laugh eke out from his chest. "Well we've got her," he says. "One way or another."

Alexander purses his lips—considering the Hawk's words as a frown settles in across his face.

"So, what now?" he asks.

The Hawk grabs hold of his pipe and pries it from between his lips. "Not a clue. You're cap'n, Cap'n." It is not said without a trace of derision.

Alexander presses his cap down farther upon his head, holding it steady against the buffeting breeze. "We need to find out what my father would have done once he had the map in his possession."

The Hawk is silent. His fingers trace lines upon the railing as he squints up into the blue sky overhead. After a moment, he walks away without another word. Alexander watches him go, feeling resentment rise within him.

He knows without a doubt that the golden-eyed pirate is withholding infor-mation—important information. He sighs and tugs at the rim of his cap. The sun is scorching his skin beneath his jacket. Summer has arrived.

He will turn the ship towards the Westerlies. Maybe a stint upon the mainland will do his crew some good—do him some good. He needs space to clear his head and figure out his next move.

He glances back out toward the eastern horizon. The island of Chancey is already nothing more than a blot upon the sea. A grim smile settles across his jaw. He thinks of the Cairan girl sleeping in his quarters—thinks of her tangle of black hair and eyes like the sea. He thinks of how his men had crossed themselves when she came on board.

An omen, they said, spitting. *Bad things are coming.*

Omen or not, he thinks, the Rogue is here to stay. They will sail onward.

CHAPTER 30

Emerala the Rogue

EMERALA'S EYES FLUTTER open and she finds herself staring up into a low ceiling of exposed wooden beams. Her body feels light—weightless. It rises and falls in time with the sluggish beat of her heart beneath her chest. She exhales lightly, blinking as a prickle of sunlight sweeps across her face and disappears. Her head throbs and she hears an unremitting rush of murmuring waves deep within her skull.

She presses her palm to her pulsing forehead, staring down her nose at her supine figure. She is on a cot—not her own—in a room that she has never seen before. At the end of the bed, she can see her toes peeking out from beneath her olive gown. They blur and sharpen and blur again as her eyes struggle to regain focus.

Where am I?

It takes her a moment to become conscious of the pair black boots that rest upon the cot by her waist. Her fluttering gaze travels away from the boots, drifting across black breeches and a black jacket and coming to rest upon the sleeping face of a man. The lanky figure leans back in a spindled, wooden chair, his arms crossed over his chest. His sleeves are pushed up to his elbows and she can see the black outline of a bird soaring across his forearm. His tricorn hat is pulled low over his eyes, obscuring the upper half of his face. His lips are parted and his breathing slips out from his mouth in a low snore.

Emerala feels discomfited by the man's proximity to her. Her heartbeat quickens in her chest as she does a quick study of the room around her. Sunlight sweeps in through several, soiled windowpanes to her left. Flickering, golden motes shiver in the shafts of radiance, casting the entirety of the expanse in a fuzzy, ethereal glow. Emerala narrows her eyes and wills her gaze to focus. A brass chandelier hangs from the middle of the ceiling, its curling, black wicks unlit. It creaks back and forth in a pendulum motion, moving in perfect time with the chronic rise and fall of Emerala's body. A low, wooden desk sits at the forefront of the room, covered in curling bits of parchment. Over her shoulder is a heavy door. Stippled sunlight spills through a latticed panel in the wood.

Emerala drags her knees up to her chest, careful to avoid the boots of the sleeping man. She swings her legs over the side of the cot, pressing the soles of her feet silently against the dappled wooden floor underfoot. The lanky man gives off a loud snort and she freezes, her backside suspended several inches off the cot. He smacks his lips, slumping down farther against the creaking chair. Emerala lets out an inaudible sigh, blowing black ringlets of hair out of her eyes.

Emerala rises onto her toes, cringing as the wooden floorboards creak beneath her steps. She inches slowly towards the door up ahead, reaching her fingers out for the brass knob. There is the jarring sound of the chair clattering upon the floor and she jumps as a figure slips between her and the exit.

Emerala finds herself staring up into the pointed, golden eyes of the pirate from the square. He grins down at her, shadowed laugh lines bordering his lips. Wild, black hair sweeps across his brow beneath the rim of his hat.

"You," Emerala remarks. She clutches at her aching head and wayward curls poke upwards through her fingers. She tries to remember what the pirate had called himself. He had given her a Cairan name, she remembers. Her emerald eyes settle upon the soaring outline of the bird upon his forearm and it comes rushing back to her.

"Thought you'd sneak out, did you?" the Hawk asks, his grin widening impossibly. He leans down towards her and she can feel his breath tickling her skin.

"I—" she starts and stops, glancing around at the radiant room. The floor drops away beneath her and she feels her stomach plummeting towards the floorboards. She stumbles forward ungracefully, her arms flailing. The Hawk catches her by her underarms, dragging her back upright. She finds herself nose to nose with him beneath the cool shadow of the corner. A wicked gleam flickers across his golden gaze and he laughs.

"You don't have your sea legs yet, aye?" he asks, his eyes crinkling.

Confusion knits across her brow. Her head is pounding at the back of her eye sockets.

"What?"

"You see, Rogue," the Hawk says, leaning back against the door. "People like you and me, we're not meant to be bound to the land. The sea, it's like—well it's like a siren call. We can't ignore it. It's in my blood." He reaches his hand towards her and she feels a finger brush lightly against her clavicle—linger above her heart. "It's in your blood."

She draws away from him, her eyes narrowing dangerously. "Where am I?" she demands.

"You're right where you want to be," the Hawk insists. "You're right where you need to be."

His piercing eyes slide away from her and drift towards the windows. She follows his gaze, feeling her breath catching in her throat as she sees what lies beyond the thick-paned glass.

It is the sea. Crisp and clear and blue, it yawns away beneath her as far as the eye can see. Her heartbeat quickens and she returns her gaze to the pirate before her.

"Welcome," he says, doffing his cap and giving her a jaunty bow, "To the *Rebellion*."

Turn the page for a sneak peek into Book II of Rogue Elegance Due out in Summer 2017!

BOOK II

The Rogue and the Elegant

SOMETIMES, AGAINST THE pervading darkness of the night, Seranai the Fair finds herself struggling to keep her demons at bay.

She leans back against the warm brick wall of Mamere Lenora's whorehouse and listens to the barely subdued sounds of lovemaking that filter down through the soiled windows overhead. The night is dark, to be sure. Black as pitch, even. The moon is at the end of its cycle, ready to rebirth in a silvery travail, dragging its empty, white light upon the cobbled stones of Chancey.

She, too, feels as hollow as the moon's empty echo. She tilts her chin upward, her pallid skin glowing in the orange light that flickers out from a second story window. She is a woman in limbo—frozen in time as she awaits her next move. She frowns, the lines around her mouth deepening as the corners of her lips pull downward. Somewhere up above, she hears a faint clattering noise. A light fizzles out, pitting one section of the street before her in increasing shadow. There is a giggle, hushed, then silence. Somewhere off in the darkness, a stray cat yowls.

When will it be time?

She recalls again the Hawk's last, ominous caveat, delivered to her among the peeling wallpaper of the brothel during that first meeting.

There may be blood shed, before the end, he warned her, his golden eyes glittering in the candlelight. *There will be casualties.*

Her fingernails drive themselves hard into the palms of her hands at the memory, and she fights to keep her thoughts from drifting further back— from calling into memory the wet copper reek of pooling blood, from her father's lips opening and closing like a fish as he lay dying on the slab of stone

243

before her. She thinks, instead, of Nerani the Elegant. Is she the type of casualty the Hawk was thinking of the first day he and Seranai met?

Likely not.

Seranai fiddles with a stray lock of her hair, so blonde as to almost be completely white. An unseen force tugs the corners of her lips upwards.

Selling out Nerani to the guardians had been easy enough. It was easy enough, yes, and yet something unsettling rests in the pit of her stomach. She had watched with barely concealed glee as the guardians threw a hapless Nerani down upon her knees, binding her hands at the small of her back before dragging her off down the cobbled streets. Relief flooded her as they turned out of sight and the sounds of their boots faded to silence. Nerani had not begged. She had not screamed. She had only waited, her sky blue eyes pooling with tears as she was arrested for her crimes.

Seranai should feel wonderful, but she does not. The demons that plague her in the dark follow her now all throughout the day, tugging at her mind and tormenting her senses. Something is amiss.

Nerani the Elegant should have been burned at the stake.

She should have been hung by the neck until dead.

She should have been, and yet not even a notice of public execution has been distributed among the citizens of Chancey. No herald has streaked through the street upon his horse, trumpeting the announcement of her demise.

What are they waiting for?

She arches her back, ignoring the fabric that adheres itself to her skin in the sticking heat leftover from the unforgiving day. The darkness that settles over Chancey presses against the earth like a blanket, making the stale air hang heavy. It does not bring with it the usual cool relief of night.

She can feel James Byron's presence in the dark street before she sees him. His arrival, as quiet and as sudden as the rain, sends a small shiver down the nape of her neck.

"Hello," she says, opening her eyes at the sound of his footfalls on the stone. He always did have a distinct way of walking, she notes, his footsteps firm and self-assured—a meticulous swagger. His presence on the steps before her is suffocating. She pulls at the high, lace collar of her dress and frowns.

"Good evening," James says, inclining his head in her direction.

"What brings you here?" An uneasy flutter sweeps against her insides. She recalls the warning he had left her after his last visit. Is that why he is here, now? The night feels suddenly cold, in spite of the humidity. There is no wind, but she shivers all the same.

"Come to make good on your threats, have you?" Her voice is constrained. Quiet. He looks startled by her question. His brown eyes momentarily lose their impenetrable exterior. It is then that she notices how unkempt he appears. His is donned in his everyman clothes, his gold standard replaced with grey homespun cloth and black breeches. His face is unshaven. He looks as though he has not slept.

"You look awful," she remarks. Some of her initial fear falls away from her as she takes him in. He does not seem to register her remark.

"I need a favor," he says. His brown eyes meet her. She is shocked to find his usually cold gaze entreating.

"A favor?" she repeats, unable to keep the disgust out of her voice. She is not quite certain she has heard him correctly.

"Yes."

Not likely, she thinks scornfully. And yet her curiosity ebbs at her, willing her to hear him out and see just what it is he needs from her.

"Just what could the formidable General Byron possibly need from me? A quick fix, perhaps? We are at a whorehouse."

The derision in her voice does not go unnoticed by James. He winces visibly, and for a moment she can see beneath the cracked veneer in his decorum. It hurts him to be standing here before her—hurts him to need anything from her. He closes the space between them, taking the steps two at a time until he reaches the stoop where she stands, partially concealed in shadow. His eyes flicker back and forth as he makes sure they are quite alone.

"This is serious, Seranai."

Hearing her name on his tongue evokes, as always, those sudden, unwanted feelings. She pushes them away, growing angrier with herself. *Quiet, you demons,* she thinks.

"I am as serious as I've ever been. The nerve of you, James—coming here on your hands and knees—begging me for help after all of this time."

His shoulders crumple slightly under the weight of her words. She fights the urge to smile. She is stomping relentlessly on his cherished pride, and it brings her more joy than she thought possible. He stares at the floor between them, watching it as though expecting it to open up and swallow him whole. After a few moments of silent consideration he glances back up at her. His dark eyes have once again hardened to steel.

"I'm afraid I won't beg on my hands and knees. But you *will* help me."

"I will?" she asks, a challenge lacing her words. She is not afraid of him— not here, when so much as a scream from her will call to the windows all of the inhabitants of the house and her patrons. One scream from her, and the unblemished record of James will be forever sullied. He cannot afford such a mistake. He cannot lay a hand on her here. Her own grey eyes narrow into slits in the darkness, matching him in their indifference.

"You will." His echo holds, within it, a sense of finality.

"We will see, I suppose. What is the favor?"

He swallows, leaning in. "You have contacts of some sort, don't you?" He phrases it as a question, but he does not wait for an answer. "You have a way to get inside the Forbidden City, should you need to?"

"I already told you, the city—"

"Don't," he snaps, cutting her off. His fingers shake at his sides and he closes them into fists. "Don't lie to me. I know it exists."

She purses her lips. Considers.

"I don't know what you could possibly mean by contacts. You more than anyone know that I don't affiliate with my people."

He frowns. "I also know that you would never enter into any situation without first having an escape plan. If you wanted to get into the city, you could."

She contemplates this. *Clever,* she thinks. But then he always was smart.

"Right?" he demands, after a few moments of uncomfortable silence have elapsed between them. His voice cracks slightly and she starts, surprised at his unraveling conduct. She wonders how long it has been since he last slept.

"Right," she assents. "Let's say that I do have contacts. What is it you need?"

His tongue darts out over his lower lip. "There was a woman arrested here a fortnight past. You may have known her. She is a Cairan, herself."

Seranai feels her blood run cold. Her knees slam together beneath her petticoat. "Yes," she says, and her voice comes out in a squeak. The demons within her are writhing in the pit of her stomach—wailing like banshees deep within her head. She struggles to gather herself. "I know of her. You will be speaking, I assume, of Nerani the Elegant."

James pauses at the sound of her name, an unusual splash of color rising along the line of his cheekbones. She takes silent note of this and continues.

"What of her?"

James glances around carefully, his brown eyes studying the shadows as though he expects someone to surge forward out of the darkness at any given moment.

"I need you to arrange for you and… Nerani…to return to the Forbidden City."

Unable to help herself, Seranai's lips fall open. She gapes at him in silence, incapable of grasping what she has just heard. There is a distinct buzzing in her ears and she fights the urge to shake her head clear.

"But," she begins and falters. She swallows hard, tasting something bitter on her tongue. Her veins run cold beneath her flesh. "She was arrested."

James looks momentarily anguished. His gaze is as dark as the dreaded Dark Below. "I know. I'll be bringing her here."

"What? When?"

"Tomorrow night," he states simply, his gaze holding hers.

"You—" She starts and stops again. White-hot anger surges through her skin, the heat curling in her fingertips. "You can't," she says at last. "You wouldn't. What you're talking about doing—that's treason."

She hisses the last word through clenched teeth, her fists resting upon the wide whalebone netting of her hips. His gaze turns murderous. In a flash, his hands enclose around her throat. She cries out, her skull cracking against the warm brick as he shoves her backwards. Deep red and white spots fan out across her vision. His face is inches away from hers, all traces of decorum gone. In its place she sees only quiet rage.

"You will not mention that word again in my presence, do you understand?" His voice is so low that it is almost inaudible. She lets out a guttural cry, gasping for breath as his hands loosen slightly upon her throat. Her grey eyes widen with realization as his shoulders rise and fall erratically.

"You're in love with her," she states blankly.

There is a footfall upon the creaking wooden staircase just inside the front door.

"Seranai?" someone calls out. It is Mamere Lenora. Two hands slide away from her neck, leaving behind a dull throbbing as air rushes down her throat and into her lungs. She can feel him slinking back into the shadows.

"Tell her you're fine," James whispers. He is in control of his voice once again. The words that reach her ears in the darkness are weighted with an unspoken threat: *Or I'll kill you.*

She does not doubt that he will. Not anymore.

The front door squeals open and Mamere Lenora pokes her heavily painted face out into the darkness. "Great After, it's hotter out here than it is inside." She tilts her head in Seranai's direction. Her eyes are red and puffy from crying, which, Seranai notes with a heightened level of disgust, she has been doing every day since that cursed Nerani's arrest.

"Are you well, darling? I thought I heard a commotion."

Seranai waves her away with an idle hand, acutely aware of her bosoms rising and falling within her tightly laced corset. Her demons claw relentlessly at her insides, raking her gut and tearing at her lungs. "I'm quite alright, Mamere."

"Are you certain? You look as though you've been frightened half to death."

"I had a scare, that's all. A stray cat popped out of the shadows just now."

It is a poor attempt at a lie, but Mamere nods knowingly, as though a wayward cat would be quite enough to strike fear into the heart of anyone. "I understand. We've all been on edge since Nerani's arrest—I can only imagine how *you* must be feeling, poor dear. To see one of your own snatched up like that. Just terrible, it is. Why don't you come on inside? It isn't good to be out here in the open where guardians might be snooping about."

If you only knew, Seranai thinks scathingly. She shakes her head, all the same. "I'll be in in just a few moments," she says, trying to smile. "Don't worry yourself about me."

"Of course, dear." Mamere flashes her a warm smile before disappearing back into the house. The door clicks shut behind her and James reappears. His boots are silent on the wooden stoop. His face is as grey and as still as stone. He does not blink.

"I'll be bringing Nerani to you tomorrow at sunset. You *will* be waiting here for us. You *will* make the arrangements for your safe return back to the Forbidden City."

"And if I refuse?"

"I'll make sure it's you that hangs in her place."

He does not wait for her to respond. He takes his leave in silence, his shoulders squared against the pressing heat of the night. Without the gold of his uniform, it takes him only moments to disappear entirely into the darkness of the crooked alleyways. Seranai stares into the street, feeling revulsion pooling within her stomach like bile.

The demons within her have settled into silence. An eerie calm passes over her.

So the fearsome General James Byron has fallen for a Cairan. The great, infallible guardian finally has a weakness.

A thin smile curls the corners of her lips. She glances up at the new moon and sees only dark, formidable sky.

She will make arrangements to return to the Forbidden City, if that is what he requires of her. Perhaps it is time, after all, to introduce herself to Roberts the Valiant. Returning Nerani to her cousin will certainly sweeten the deal. And there is not much time remaining until the Hawk's promised return.

And then, she thinks, ignoring the sharp throbbing of her head. *And then.*

James Byron has just given her a bit of rope, and she will see to it that when the time comes, it is she who ties the noose.

About the Author

KA Dowling is an award-winning writer living just outside of Boston, Massachusetts. She has been writing stories as long as she can remember, and has been daydreaming about fantastical worlds and imaginary heroines for even longer than that.

Dowling lives with her husband and their smelly Boston Terrier, King Henry, both of whom graciously put up with her late night writing spells and her exasperating propensity to leave a trail of distracted clutter in her wake. Her favorite animal is the Tyrannosaurus Rex and she has wanted to be a sea-faring pirate for much of her adult life. This story is her way of living vicariously through her fictional characters.

She's thrilled that you've picked up her book, and she hopes you enjoyed every last word. To read more of what Dowling has written, check out her website at www.kadowling.com.

61323353R00163

Made in the USA
Middletown, DE
10 January 2018